And Again?

A Stand-Alone Sequel to

My Time Again – A Time Travel Novel

Ian Cummins

List of Chapters

1	The Story So Far	5
2	A Routine Medical Appointment	7
3	Lunch at My Club?	17
4	Project Petra	25
5	Anna's Story	29
6	Not Again?	35
7	Anna Does London	44
8	Brands Hatch	55
9	First Report	63
10	Gathering Intelligence	68
11	The Tallest Church Spire in the UK	73
12	The Princess and the P.D.	76
13	Here We Go Again	83
14	It's Not Unusual	94
15	A Couple (of) Lunches	103
16	Keeping Secrets	110
17	Important Dates	115
18	Lockdown	124
19	False Dawns	131
20	Tales of Old London	137
21	Reinvigoration	145
22	The City with the Highest Rim of the Plate	151
23	Preparations	156
24	Third Time Lucky	162
25	Old Maid	167
26	A New Chapter	172
27	Moonlighting	177
28	A Great Day for a Walk	182
29	Repeating Something I've Not Done Before	188
30	A Rookie as MVP	194
31	The Hunt for a Red in November	201
32	Star-Crossed Lovers	206
33	Loose Ends	214
34	Changing Planes	220
	List of Characters	227
	Acknowledgements	229

1 The Story So Far

A summary of the book 'My Time Again', to which this book is a stand-alone sequel.

On October 7th, 2022, on the eve of his 70th birthday, Graham Henderson attended a meeting with his financial adviser at an office in City Road, London. During the meeting, he reminisced about his eighteenth birthday, recalling how it had probably been his worst birthday ever.

The following morning, Graham woke to find himself transported back to that very day, fifty-two years ago, with all his memory intact.

Once the shock had worn off, he lived out his life for the second time. His memory of events and trends yet to come made his life much more financially comfortable but he found it very difficult to form any lasting personal relationships. His only successful relationship was with Carol, a fellow time traveller.

It emerged that her journey had commenced exactly ten years earlier than Graham's when she had visited the very same office block as Graham had. However, her meeting had been with a lawyer to finalise the termination of her unhappy marriage. During that meeting, she had reminisced about her wedding day, and it was to that day she had been transported back the following morning.

Whereas Graham's transition had been smooth, his apparent loss of short-term memory posing very few problems as he had arrived in his first week of university life, Carol's transition had been traumatic. Her apparent loss of memory and absolute refusal to proceed with what she knew would be a disastrous marriage caused her to spend some time in a recovery facility. Later events caused her more psychological problems, and after a few happy years as Graham's partner, she spent the last years of her life in an institution before dying on the very date on which her time travel had begun.

In the rerun of his life, Graham discovered that while he could successfully make small changes to his and other people's lives, attempting to avert major disasters was not easy. His three attempts in this area all failed – the best he achieved was some mitigation or delay of the outcome.

During this second life, he met John Bishop, a British Secret Service employee. They first met when they were both involved with the Middle East, and they shared information for their mutual profit. Later, Graham re-established contact with John and told him his time-travel secret to get his help with alleviating the effects of the Covid pandemic in the UK.

Graham learned that John's work had led him to manage the security of an experiment being run by Professor Karbajanovic, who was researching methods of transmitting information directly into the human brain. The work was conducted at Moorfields Hospital in London, and the initial objective was to restore sight to patients who had lost the use of their optic nerves. The government, however, saw other possible uses for his work and set up an experiment to transmit data from the hospital lab to an office across the road where the hospital was located – City Road, London.

The experiment had initially been conducted in 2012 and had disastrous results. The technicians in the receiving room all died in their sleep the night after the test. Work was suspended until the government called for a rerun – with the recipients being two known Russian double agents. The experiment aimed to influence Russian thinking during the heightened tension of 2022 and was scheduled to run on the tenth anniversary of the original test.

It was obvious to Graham that the time travel he and Carol had both experienced must be linked to this experiment, so he persuaded John to arrange a meeting with the professor, during which Graham told his story.

Nothing could prevent the experiment from going ahead, and Graham decided that he would prefer to return to his original life, where he had considerably less wealth but enjoyed the company and the affection of his children and grandchildren. So, on the proposed day of the experiment being rerun, he arranged a meeting with the same financial advisers where his journey had begun. At the meeting, he gave a false account of himself – stating his financial position (as close as he could remember it) as it was in his original life.

The next morning, he awoke to find himself back where it had all begun, his wealth gone but his family restored. He decided that the professor needed to know about the effects of his experiment, and, aware of the security surrounding the professor's department, secreted a letter to him in the hospital's internal mail system requesting a meeting.

It is at this point that we return to the story.

2 A Routine Medical Appointment
October 2022

Graham opened the last of the six envelopes that had been delivered to his home that morning. One was a late 70th birthday card, two were standard letters that he had read and consigned to the recycling pile, and the remaining two, statements for his bank account and his credit card, had been set aside to be cross-checked and filed.

He would not normally have even read the first two letters since it was obvious that they were junk mail. But he was taking care to read everything these days just in case it contained any clues that would help him restore his short-term memory and resume as close to a normal life as he could. This last letter, however, had to be read twice, and it then necessitated a pause for thought.

His short-term memory problems were not the normal ones experienced in old age. They were not even memory problems in the strictest sense of the definition. Just the results of time travelling. Events from the previous week were only visible in his memory through the telescope of his fifty years away on his time travel adventure, and this was causing him occasional problems.

The twice-read letter was from the office of Professor Karbajanovic at Moorfields Eye Hospital and invited him to attend a follow-up appointment after his recent surgery. The reason for his pause for thought was quite simple – he had not had any eye surgery. Not with Professor Karbajanovic, not at Moorfields Eye Hospital, nor with any other surgeon and at any other hospital. Even with his limited short-term memory, he was certain of that.

But Graham knew this was not an administrative oversight. He took the letter, with his two pieces of filing and his unfinished breakfast cup of coffee, into his home office, where he opened his laptop and checked his calendar. He was reasonably sure that he had nothing in there for Friday, the date he had been requested to attend for the appointment, but as the years advanced, and with his fifty-year absence, he found it prudent to double-check.

The page in the calendar was empty so he entered the appointment for 4:30 p.m. as requested in the letter. The request at the foot of the letter read:

PLEASE BRING THIS LETTER WITH YOU
AS PROOF OF YOUR APPOINTMENT.
PRESENT IT AT THE HOSPITAL MAIN RECEPTION DESK
15 MINUTES BEFORE THE TIME OF YOUR APPOINTMENT.

He took a plastic folder from his desk drawer and placed the appointment letter into it. He returned to his laptop and searched for the letter that he had written a few days previously and printed a copy. Before placing it in the folder, he read it one more time. Beneath his home address and the date, it read:

Professor

On Friday, October 7th you conducted an experiment in remote communication from your hospital laboratory to a building on the opposite side of City Road.

I was in an office on the 6th floor of that building at the time of the experiment and was affected by it.

I also know that you conducted a similar experiment exactly ten years previously and I know what resulted from that experiment and why there was a ten-year gap between the experiments.

The reason I know this information will assist you in understanding the effects of your communication – it will also confirm some of your suspicions concerning the parallels between your method and the method used by entities that are often referred to as paranormal.

I would like to discuss this with you, and I fully understand the importance of secrecy. Might I suggest that you access my medical records and invite me for a follow-up appointment to ensure we meet in private? Alternatively, we could meet at your club in Tavistock Square or at any venue and in any other way you request.

I look forward to hearing from you.

Graham Henderson

He was surprised at how quickly the professor had responded. When he had handed the letter to the hospital receptionist a week earlier, he had wondered whether he would even receive a reply at all. The circumstances of the experiment he had referred to and the secrecy surrounding the whole programme that the Professor was engaged in had necessitated him being rather vague in his note.

His reference to 'paranormal communication' was irrelevant to the message he wanted to convey, but he was referring to part of the conversation they had had on that different plane of time. He knew this topic was of interest to the Professor, and this tactic of using information that makes someone say, 'How the hell did he know that?' was one he used to help convey the truth of his message. It was a tactic he would use again.

He was not sure that this was enough to get a response. Even with the ruse he had undertaken to deliver the letter, he was unsure if it would even reach its intended recipient. And then it was questionable whether the professor would take the risk of replying. But the fact that he had replied, and replied so quickly, intrigued Graham, and he looked forward with considerable interest to their meeting.

-

When he presented himself at the hospital's reception desk, the intrigue had grown, and, in the cavernous reception area, he began to feel a trifle nervous. He had added a third piece of paper to his plastic folder, on which he had noted the key points he needed to convey when they met. He had treated the event just as he would an important client presentation in earlier years when his job entailed installing computer-based project management systems. Failing to prepare meant preparing to fail, he remembered.

On his piece of paper, he had listed the key points that he felt the professor would want to know, and on the previous day, he had rehearsed his presentation to make sure he could string them together coherently. Graham calmed his nerves by reminding himself that he had all the advantages. He knew more than his audience. He had nothing to lose, no matter what the meeting outcome was. And, smiling to himself as he thought about it, he had the advantage that he had met the professor, but the professor had not met him. That was just one of the logical conundrums of time travel that they would tackle together, he hoped.

The receptionist looked at his letter, immediately picked up a phone, and keyed in an extension number.

"The professor's 4:30 appointment is here," she said, and then, after a brief pause, "Yes, I'll send him up."

Turning to Graham, she instructed him to take the lift furthest away from the reception desk. "It will take you directly to the fifth floor," she said and returned his appointment letter to him.

As he exited the lift, he was met by a middle-aged woman, whom he noted was 'in civvies', which put her in the minority of the people he had seen so far, the vast majority of whom were in white coats.

"This way," was all she said, and proceeded to place her security card into a slot that allowed a set of doors to open. Graham was no expert in these matters but had been admitted through security gates while visiting many establishments in his career. This looked like a very serious set-up, he thought. His companion said nothing, simply leading him down the corridor.

As he had done on countless customer visits during his long career, he tried to take in the atmosphere of his surroundings and the feedback he was receiving from the demeanour of people he encountered.

His escort was probably tired at the end of a long week, he thought, but her complete lack of interaction was still on the unfriendly end of the scale. Every fibre of her body seemed to portray an unwillingness to perform the task of showing him to his appointment. Surely, she should be assuming that Graham had recently had eye surgery and might need reassurance and a friendly face. If that had been so, he would have needed to seek warmth and understanding elsewhere.

She showed him into the last office on the corridor. A small room that was obviously the professor's lair. It contained nondescript National Health furnishings: an overfilled bookcase, a visitor's chair, and a desk with only a computer screen and keyboard, a ruled paper notepad, an expensive pen, and a two-tier block of black plastic filing trays on its surface. Graham noticed that the top tray contained a buff-coloured file with his name on it.

An old-fashioned coat rack was in the corner, with the obligatory white lab coat, dark raincoat, umbrella, and, somewhat incongruously, a man's trilby hat hung on it. The only decoration in the room was a framed picture hanging on the wall to Graham's left. It was a street scene from an East European city, but it was impossible to tell if it was a watercolour or an extremely faded oil painting.

The professor got up from the large chair behind the desk and extended his hand in a friendly greeting. He was tall and thin and appeared uncomfortable and awkward in every movement. He was wearing a three-piece suit made of material that looked far too heavy for a warm late autumn day like today. He seemed to take a long time to reach his full height of over six feet.

"Thank you, Margaret," he said to his taciturn colleague. "If we overrun, feel free to leave. You don't need to wait for me," he said with a smile but did not receive one in return.

"Thank you, professor," she replied. "I will see you again on Monday, then," and closed the door.

Graham and the professor shook hands, and after checking that Margaret had closed the door, the professor spoke with a voice that betrayed a slight accent.

"Mister Henderson, your note was, to say the least, somewhat intriguing. You obviously have some knowledge of the work we have been doing here, and I am intrigued to discover what information you have for me. And, if you will forgive my cynicism, I wonder what you will want from me in return. But your note was so interesting, and your method of delivering it so astute, that I thought it would be worth giving you half an hour of my time."

"I will do my best not to disappoint you, Professor. I believe that you will find what I have to say interesting, and I want nothing more than to assist you in your work by providing you with information that I could only deliver face-to-face. May I launch into the story?" Graham felt that the formality he was being shown and the tense situation were making him use more formal language than usual but felt it may well be the best way to communicate.

The professor nodded assent, Graham looked briefly at his notes and began.

"I will tell the story as concisely as possible, and it will seem that some points are not relevant, but please trust me; it should all become clear before the end.

On Friday, October 7th I had a meeting with my financial adviser on the 6th floor of the building opposite", he pointed toward the window behind the professor. "At eleven o'clock, I was standing by the window, and Eric, the man I was meeting, asked me a question. He knew that the following day was my seventieth birthday, and he asked me about my previous birthdays. He wanted to know which had been my best birthday, but I was not able to answer this; instead, I told him that my worst birthday had been my eighteenth. I had newly arrived at university and had no friends with whom to celebrate the occasion. His question made me think for a few seconds about my feelings on that day. Having told him about the day, I thought no more about it. We continued our meeting, had lunch together, and I returned home. The only other aspect of that day that is worth noting is that in the evening I felt exceptionally tired and went to bed early.

The next morning, I woke, and it was not my seventieth birthday, it was my eighteenth birthday."

Graham paused to make sure this, the key point of everything he needed to convey, had been fully appreciated before continuing.

"Professor, I subsequently found out (and I will shortly explain how) that at the precise moment that I was looking out of the window and thinking about a specific day in the past, you fired a powerful beam of energy from this building towards the fifth floor of the building opposite. I am here to tell you that a side effect of your energy beam was to make me experience time travel."

Graham knew that this was the most important but also the most preposterous part of his story, and so he decided to restate it.

"I had travelled back in time some fifty years, with my memory intact," he continued. "I remained in the time zone to which I had jumped, and went on to re-live my entire life. I had my time again, as they say."

He paused again to gauge the professor's reaction and to allow him to interrupt if he wanted. The professor made a few notes on his pad and listened attentively.

"Please continue," he said, and Graham checked his notes. He had thought long and hard about how to sequence the facts most logically and went on to his next point.

"I know that our time together is rationed, so I will not go into any detail about how I spent my second life other than how it led me to know what you were doing here. However, I will be happy to discuss any other details you wish with you later.

"Before I had any idea about the cause of my jump, I reached out to see if anyone else had experienced anything like it. I came across just one such person. We met and exchanged information, and I discovered she had been in the same building on the other side of City Road exactly ten years before. She had been meeting her solicitor to arrange details of her divorce, and at the precise moment that you fired your beam, she had been standing by a window on the fourth floor, thinking back to her wedding day. The day after she visited her solicitor, she awoke to find she had been transported back to that wedding day thirty years earlier.

"We discussed our experiences and eventually worked out that we had both been in the building opposite on the day before our jump back in time. It was the only thing we had in common. But we were not able to make any connection to this hospital or yourself until one more piece of evidence dropped into place."

He paused again to give the professor a chance to interrupt, but he continued to make notes and waved a 'carry-on' sign.

"During my second life, I met a man whom I came to know as John Bishop. However, since he was employed by one or another division of the secret services, it is entirely possible that this was not his real name. Apart from Carol, the lady I referred to earlier, he was the only person to whom I told my time travel story. Even though I first met him in that second life during the late nineteen seventies, I did not tell him about my time travel until 2018. The reason was to elicit his help to do whatever was possible to mitigate the effects of the coming pandemic.

"When I told him my story, as soon as I mentioned that Carol and I had both visited the building across the street, he made the connection to you and your experiment. He had worked with you in the early days when you first sought government funding and became involved with the security services."

"John Bishop, you say?" the professor interrupted. "I'm afraid that name means nothing to me."

"As I said, he used more than one name."

"Can you describe him?"

"He was stocky – about average height. Spoke with a very slight Welsh accent. His physique and the scar tissue that gave him prominent eyebrows were the result of his love of playing rugby which lasted from his childhood until well into his forties."

"Could be Martin Knight," the professor said quietly.

"He worked closely with you and set up the office in the building across the street but left after the events surrounding your first experiment," Graham said carefully. He knew he was treading on dangerous ground, recalling events the professor would probably prefer to forget.

"Yes, that's him."

"Hmm. John Bishop and Martin Knight," Graham mused. "I wonder if he was Roy Castle and Mervyn King as well," trying to bring some levity.

The professor looked puzzled.

"Chess joke?" Graham said, and the professor acknowledged mirthlessly.

"So, John (or Martin) told me about your experiment – and the tragic results of that first experiment that had caused him to part company with you and brought your programme to a premature halt. He thought it would be useful for you and me to meet, so he arranged a meeting for all three of us at your club in Tavistock Square. At that meeting, I explained what had happened to Carol and me. You explained your experiment and told me about the connection you believed might exist between your new method of communication and that which occurred during paranormal events."

Graham noticed the professor's expression of puzzlement had become more pronounced, so he interrupted the flow of his narrative.

"Yes, it takes some getting used to. I can speak about a meeting at which you were present, but you have no recollection of it. I have come to understand that there must be different planes of time. That's the only way I can make sense of it. You and I met on a different plane of time. I have been on both planes and can recall events from both. I have memories of two different histories. but you, like just about everyone else in the world, have only a memory of one version of history. I'd be delighted to discuss this whole concept with you, but I believe we may have time pressure," Graham continued, making a theatrical gesture of consulting his wristwatch.

"Yes, yes, please continue," the professor urged.

Graham was concerned that the professor's expression signified that even his capacity for assimilating new information might be in danger of overload. He had completed the major points planned for his presentation but expected the notes the professor had been taking to produce some questions that might be tricky to answer.

"I have pretty much completed the main points of my story. As I'm sure you can understand, there is a great deal more that could be covered, but I have stuck to the salient points as far as I could. After the meeting in your club, there was no more contact between us.

"I worked with our mutual friend from the Secret Service to achieve some mitigation of the Covid pandemic, and then, when the calendar came around to October 7th, 2022, I decided to take the risk of trying to move back from the plane of time on which I was, to the one in which we both currently find ourselves. I returned to the office on the sixth floor," Graham once again pointed behind the professor, "And focussed my mind on the situation on this plane of time. To put it simply, I concentrated on my grandchildren, of whom I am very fond and whom I had not seen for over fifty years. The following morning, I found that I had succeeded in making the return journey to this plane of time."

He paused again and watched the professor nodding quietly to himself and looking at his notes.

"Do you have any questions?" Graham asked.

"Oh, so many. So many," he answered and exhaled as if he had been holding his breath for several minutes.

"But you are aware that I am being observed by the security services, so I must not let this appointment last too much longer lest it raise suspicion so I will limit myself to one key point. Could I ask you to just expand a little on your thoughts about there being multiple planes of time?"

"I will do my best. But you must understand that I am merely an amateur in this field. An unfortunate bystander, perhaps. But I had the advantage of discussing the subject at length with Carol and have read a few articles on the subject." The professor nodded his understanding.

"In moving back in time, I entered the same world, but my entry back into the world caused a split. Perhaps I could illustrate?"

He took the piece of paper with his meeting notes out of the folder, turned it over, and placed it on the desk. He removed a pen from his pocket and drew a horizontal line across the middle. At the foot of the paper, he wrote three numbers to create an axis. 1970 at the left, 2020 just to the right of centre, and 2050 at the rightmost edge.

"I started here," he said, drawing a dot three-quarters of the way along the line and then a curved line reaching back towards the start of the line. Where it re-joined the line, he drew another dot. He drew a small diagonal line from this second dot and then continued it in parallel to the original line.

"So, I travelled along this parallel line, this separate plane of time. I could draw another loop to show Carol leaving the original timeline before I did, and joining the original line a little after I did. Then there would be a separate junction for her path, which would then meet up with the branch line I was travelling along."

He hoped the railway analogies would help clarify the complex point he was trying to convey. Not for the first time in his life, he noticed how difficult it can be to explain something to someone when you barely understand it yourself.

"On the line that ran parallel to the one I had left, events in history unfolded the same. But it was inevitable that even if I had not tried to change things, the fact that I was rerunning my life meant that events were being changed. Each minor decision I made would have some influence on someone else.

"To give one simple example, I spent no money on cigarettes in my second life, whereas I had been a regular smoker in my first life. This must have had an economic effect somewhere. But there were also more potentially significant changes. For example, I decided to take a different career path. Which meant that on that plane, I never met the woman I married on this plane. Therefore, two children were not born, and neither married nor produced any of my four grandchildren. You understand what I'm saying?"

"I think so," the professor answered slowly.

"I can go into more detail about other actions I took, but overall, I learned that some things could be changed and some could not. Minor changes occurred all the time, but any attempt at a major change seemed doomed to failure.

"To explain this, I can visualise it as a flowing river. If you were to go close to the source of the River Thames, you could divert a certain amount of water, and nothing much would change further downstream. But if you tried to divert too much water, it would find a way of returning to its original course. Do you follow me?"

"So, did you try to change events?"

"Yes. I was able to ensure that a notorious serial killer was caught sooner, and thus a few victims were spared. And the people in a large area of this country had a shorter reign of terror to endure. There seemed to be no comeback on that. But when I tried to prevent the accidental death of an important person, I was only able to postpone the event for a short time."

The professor was nodding – perhaps with understanding, perhaps with mental exhaustion, Graham couldn't tell. Momentarily, the professor seemed to be lost in thought, before speaking again.

"What you have told me raises so many questions, but I fear we must end our session now. We've already exceeded the normal thirty-minute time allocation, and if we take much more time, I can expect someone to start investigating. Mister Henderson, could I prevail upon you to meet again soon? There is so much I would like to know."

"Of course. I'd be pleased to help – if I can."

"I am not sure how to arrange another meeting between us without raising suspicion, but I will find a way."

The professor escorted Graham back to the lift. Aware that there were still others in the offices, he briefly engaged in polite chit-chat for the first time until they shook hands just before the lift doors closed.

He walked back to the tube station looking around him at the road that had had so much influence on his life but was just a normal busy thoroughfare for thousands of other people.

The tube journey was short, and it was only when he sat on the train home that he reviewed the meeting in his mind. He felt that he had delivered the message just as he had wished, and he was pleased that the professor seemed keen to meet again. He had no choice but to wait and see.

Meanwhile, the professor carefully considered what he had heard. The natural first reaction would be to completely dismiss the preposterous story he had just heard. But there were so many reasons to believe it. Starting with the point that his visitor had made in his original letter but which they had not had time to discuss.

He had long thought that the communication protocol between the eye and the brain could explain the thousands of unexplained sightings of ghosts recorded worldwide. Now that he had proved that it was possible to communicate directly to the human brain without a physical connection, might this not be the method that beings without physical form would use to communicate with living humans? He had rarely felt confident enough to expound his theory, but this stranger seemed to know about it.

He also had a seemingly plausible explanation for his strange experience and had no apparent reason to fabricate the story and go out of his way to relate it. But perhaps the biggest reason for believing the story was that the professor wanted it to be true. It may well hold the key to solving an extremely tricky and very important problem he was facing.

3 Lunch at My Club?
November 2022

'It's like the old saying about London buses,' Graham thought. 'You wait ages for one, and then three come together'. His analogy was not very good, but it would do. It was his third trip to the city within the space of a month. He had visited several times in the previous year – lunch with a friend, a couple of sporting events, and a few theatre visits. He would remember them if he thought hard enough. But that was the problem; he had to think very hard about recent events because his short-term memory was still almost non-existent.

This was one of the hangovers from a lengthy period of time-travelling. Events that had occurred a few months ago on this plane of time were remembered by Graham as events that had happened to him fifty-two years ago. He was doing everything he could to rectify this. He knew that he had to think of his period 'away', his second life as he sometimes referred to it, as something that was not *real*. He must consider it as a book he had read, or a movie he had seen. Not real life.

He gazed out the window as the train proceeded through the southern suburbs of London. 'Take it all in' he said to himself. 'Re-familiarise yourself with a journey you have taken often enough. A journey into London from the home you have lived in for over thirty years; forget that you have only lived there for less than a month in the last fifty-two years of your memory.'

His mind turned to the meeting to which he was headed. He assumed he would meet the prof again, even though the invitation had been from Doctor Greenwood – whom he was sure he had never met in either of his lives. The invitation was to have lunch at the professor's club in Tavistock Square. He knew that the prof was a member of this club and that John Bishop, their mutual contact in the secret service had arranged for all three of them to meet there in Graham's second life. He had mentioned this meeting to the prof when they met the previous week, and the prof had hinted that if he wanted to talk again, he might have to execute some subterfuge since he was being watched.

-

His suspicions were confirmed shortly after he gave his name at the club's reception desk. He was shown to a private dining room and was joined there shortly afterwards by the prof.

"I trust you are not disappointed to see that it is me you are meeting, Mister Henderson" the professor began with just a hint of the discomfort he must have felt to have to undertake this deception.

"Neither surprised nor disappointed. And please call me Graham."

"Thank you. Since both my first and last names offer such challenges to pronunciation, most of my friends and acquaintances just call me 'prof', so please do likewise."

Graham smiled and nodded.

"I am permitted to have a leisurely uninterrupted and unsupervised lunch at my club from time to time, but if I were to advertise that I am meeting anyone, then I fear that that person might come under unwanted investigation."

"I understand," Graham said and smiled. He found himself in the unusual situation of putting the prof at ease on his home turf.

A waiter appeared and they busied themselves ordering two lunch courses, and Graham declined the offer of any alcohol to accompany what promised to be a good lunch. He thought it was highly likely that he would need all his wits about him. Once the waiter had left, the prof felt able to move from polite conversation to the reason he had asked for the meeting.

"I would like to thank you for the detailed explanation you gave me at our last meeting and for the effort you have put into making sure I was fully informed about some of the aspects of my work of which I was unaware. But you have left me with several unanswered questions, and I trust you will allow me to ask them?"

"Of course," Graham replied. "I'll do my best to answer."

"There are a couple of issues – one is mostly curiosity, but the other may well lead on to other issues."

Graham gave a 'go ahead and ask' gesture.

"Taking the first, you spoke about a lady named Carol who shared your experience, and I believe, part of your life with you, but I feel you did not complete her part of the story. May I ask what happened to her?"

"Do you mean, what happened to her on that other plane of time, or on this one?" Graham asked.

"Both, I suppose," the prof replied.

"Well, her jump – that's how we always referred to the step back in time – her jump had a much more painful landing than mine. I was extremely lucky that when I landed, my complete lack of short-term memory was a very minor problem. I landed back in my first week at university when absolutely everything about my life was new. My memory was only 'missing' a couple of days of the orientation week, and

I could make up for that quickly enough. As I said, everything was new – so the fact that I didn't recognise anyone and could not remember what had happened the previous day, the previous week, or the previous month was not a problem.

"You see. jumping back and retaining your memory is great in some ways – it enables you to place extremely lucky bets and to make astoundingly wise investment decisions – but it has its disadvantages. You remember the previous week not as the previous week, but as a random week in your life, fifty years ago. You understand?"

The prof nodded his head slowly.

"But for Carol, when she made her jump, this lack of short-term memory was a major problem," Graham continued. "She woke on the morning of her wedding day, surrounded by friends and family. Unable to remember what had been done and said recently by anyone, struggling to recognise familiar faces and utterly disorientated by her surroundings.

"I can tell you that seeing people suddenly become fifty years younger, or, even worse, come back to life several years after they have passed on, is disturbing. I found it very difficult when I returned home and met people a few at a time. I'd prepared myself for the shock, and even then, it was both difficult and unpleasant. For this reason, I kept myself separated from my family for most of the rest of my second life.

"Carol had to deal with it all at once. Not only that, but she also knew that she was about to enter a marriage that was going to be disastrous. The man she was about to wed was not what he purported to be. There was no way she was going to go through with it. So, to cut a long story short, she had something of a breakdown. A short time later, her parents had her sectioned and she spent some time in an institution until she was deemed to be 'cured'. After that, she hid herself away. I suspect she might have become a nun if she had had had any religious leanings. But she did the next best thing and became a teacher in a small private girls' school on the south coast."

"Until you rescued her?" the prof asked, showing that he was taking it all in.

"You could describe it as that," Graham smiled.

"And did she make the jump, as you call it, back to this plane of time?"

"Not in the same way. She was always in a somewhat fragile state, and on the date of her original jump, October 2012, she was in no fit state to attempt anything. On that day on that other plane of time, she died."

Graham paused and sipped from his glass of water.

"I'm sorry to hear that," the prof said. "I can see that not everything about this time travel experience is positive."

"You could say that", Graham replied, his mood having dipped as he thought of Carol and how little joy she must have had in either of her lives.

"And were you able to discover what happened to her back on this plane of time?"

"Yes, it was one of the first few things I did when I made my return jump. But I found out that she lived a few more years, but maybe because of the difficult life she had experienced in her marriage, or maybe just her general frailty, she died five years ago," Graham said.

Thankfully the depressed mood that had developed within the room was dispelled by a knock on the door and the arrival of their first course. They conducted some light conversation as their dishes were placed in front of them and they began to eat. Graham felt he had to let the prof know he was ready to continue, and so said "You have a second question, I believe. One that may lead on to other issues?"

"Yes, this is a deeper issue." He hesitated as he formed the question in his mind.

"I know you must have thought about this, and maybe even discussed it with your friend, but have you any idea how or why this time travel happened?"

Graham placed a large piece of toasted Camembert into his mouth and chewed it slowly, allowing himself time to formulate his answer.

"Sadly, the discussions that Carol and I had were very speculative. It was only much later - after she had died - when John (our 'mutual friend' from the security service) told me about your experiments that he and I were able to consider the subject more carefully."

Another large bite let him think a little more. He felt he needed to establish common ground with the prof before letting him know his speculations.

"As I understand it, you were experimenting quite successfully on a local basis, within the one room, to enable an image seen by one person to be perceived by another person and thus duplicating the function of the optic nerve, is that correct?"

"Yes. We were making good progress in helping those whose optic nerves were damaged to regain their sight. We had built a device capable of achieving this – but it was far too cumbersome to be practical. About the size of a suitcase. We needed outside investment to enable us to miniaturise it to make it feasible for a person to wear or carry it, and that's why we went for government help."

"And they wanted you to transmit the images across larger distances?"

"They saw other uses for the communication protocol, and we had to follow their direction to get the funding."

"And when you sent this signal across the road to the other building, it had some unforeseen and very unfortunate effects?"

The mood in the room dipped for the second time as the prof recalled the events of the first experiment.

"We had to increase the signal strength much more than anticipated, and although no ill effects were seen immediately, unfortunately, all the people who received the signal died in their sleep that night."

A knock on the door preceded the removal of their empty dishes and the arrival of the second course. Graham was glad of the break and a chance to move on to his theories.

"My knowledge of the workings of the human body and the human brain is as poor as any layman. The only way I could get any hint of understanding of how this happened was to think in terms of a subject I know a little more about - computers."

The prof frowned at the introduction of a topic where he felt uncomfortable about his limited knowledge, but Graham acknowledged it and did his best to reassure him.

"Don't worry, nothing too technical. It's just that when a computer is left idle, sometimes it can be pre-programmed to do some types of 'housekeeping' on its own. For example, there's a process called 'defragmentation' where the computer will automatically examine the stored information and reorganise it more efficiently. Then, when the computer is restarted, it can access that information more quickly. Another example of what I'm getting at is that sometimes you receive a message from the computer telling you that you have not used a particular application for a long time. The computer offers to delete it.

"I know that some people have speculated that our brains do something in a similar vein when we sleep. We perceive this as dreams, but it may well be our brains sorting out what information they can keep and what they can discard. And then they reorganise the remaining information in a better way."

"Yes, I have heard this," the prof answered in a way that said, 'but I don't understand where you are going with this.'

Graham continued undaunted. "So, what I was thinking was that when you sent this strong signal, it affected the part of the brain that starts things up again. What they call 'rebooting' in computers. Maybe your signal affects that part of the brain in a way we don't understand. I received that signal at the same moment as my brain was focussed very strongly on a specific date. When my brain did its next reboot, in other words when I woke the following morning, the normal date function was overwritten, and my brain reset itself to the date that had been there when the signal was received. Exactly the same procedure would have happened to Carol.

"Furthermore, the people who received the full-strength signal in your first experiment may well have had the re-boot function of their brains destroyed, which prevented them from waking up."

The prof looked less than one hundred percent convinced.

"It's only a theory. Have you been able to come up with anything better?" Graham asked, genuinely wanting to know and at the same time expecting a negative answer. He received a brief shake of the head, and so continued.

"The only anecdotal evidence I can give to support my theory is that I've found I dream a helluva lot more since I retired a few years ago. I've often wondered if that's because my brain is finding loads of stuff I no longer use. Stuff from my job: technical information, prices, customer details, and so on. Maybe it's deleting it, or just moving it. Telling me it's moving it to one of the back shelves because in the past, I used it every day and now don't seem to need it any more."

Graham was aware he was now rambling. He would welcome an interruption, but there didn't seem to be any sign of one coming.

Eventually, after an awkward pause, the prof asked, "Do you think that this time travel experience could be repeated?"

Graham had spent a lifetime dealing with customers and listening carefully to their questions. Additionally, during his time-travel, he had always been on guard for unusual questions – just in case he said or did something that appeared weird and might lead to an awkward situation. Hence, he felt confident that the professor's question was not being posed idly. He suspected this might be the crucial question that the prof had wanted to ask all along and that what he had been asking so far had merely been leading up to this.

He chewed his next mouthful of sea bass slowly before responding.

"I can only speculate – but I don't see why not. Do you have any reason for wanting to know?" he asked, feeling very confident that there was one.

"Not really," replied the prof and Graham wondered how to deal with the fact that he was being lied to.

They soon finished the main course and Graham refused the offer of a dessert but asked for a cup of coffee. He remained silent, hoping that this would prompt his companion to move on to what he really wanted to ask.

"I suppose it would be useful to know if what happened to you by accident could be achieved deliberately," he pondered aloud. "It might help me solve a problem."

"Can you tell me anything about the problem?" Graham asked, feeling that he might at last be nearing the real reason for his luncheon invitation.

"Can I trust you with a secret?"

"Professor, I travelled in time. For the last fifty years, I have kept hundreds, possibly thousands of secrets. I believe I can be trusted."

"It's just that it's important and a little personal."

The prof showed every sign of being hesitant to reveal something he would prefer not to, but then seemed to summon up his courage and burst forth with his story.

"For the last twenty years, I have had the privilege and the pleasure of having the most wonderful assistant in my job that anyone could ever wish for. Her name is Anna, Anna Mueller. She has been part of my work for so long – a trusted and valuable part – that I am wondering if I will ever be able to continue the work without her." He paused, and Graham guessed that the professor wanted his explanation to be more businesslike and less emotional.

"The day after our most recent experiment – Friday, October 8th – she didn't return to work. It was so unlike her. Not even a message. I was so worried that I went to her apartment that evening to find the problem and discovered that she had completely disappeared."

"Perhaps you had better explain what you mean when you say she has completely disappeared," Graham responded.

"There was no sign of her at the apartment. The furniture and the contents of the kitchen are still there. But there was no food in the refrigerator. I took the liberty of looking in her bedroom. The wardrobe and the drawers were virtually empty."

"And I assume there was no note and that she has not contacted you or the hospital in any way."

The prof gave a very miserable shake of his head.

"Have you notified your watchers?" The question drew a quizzical look. "Our friends in the Secret Service," Graham explained.

"Of course. I knew I had to – not only for my own sake but because there are obviously security implications."

"And have they told you anything?"

The prof gave a look that was easily understood. It said, 'What do you think?' without the need to move his lips.

"But that is part of the mystery to me. I expected them to be concerned. To question me at length, to make some noise. But they haven't. It's as if they don't care, or at least that's how it seems to me. I've asked them a couple of times if they have anything they can tell me. I've tried to phrase it in different ways. But I have received nothing back. The hospital has allocated a replacement staff member to cover Anna's duties – you met her last week."

"Ah yes, the lovely Margaret. Is she a temporary replacement?"

"I certainly hope so. In so many ways." The prof looked about as miserable as a human being could be.

Graham wondered if Anna was being missed solely for her contribution to his work – and strongly suspected that the problem might go deeper than this but said nothing. He had a feeling he knew where the conversation was heading, and, realising that the time the prof was allowed for an unsupervised lunch break might be limited, he decided to ask the obvious question.

"Are you asking me if I think you might be able to go back in time and find out what has happened to her?"

"Of course." The reply was given a little sharply, but it was probably deserved, Graham thought. He had been rather guilty of stating the bleeding obvious.

"You realise that you cannot change things, don't you? No matter what you might do on another plane of time, when you return to this plane of time, she will still be gone," he asked.

"Even if I cannot change it, I must find out what has happened to her. I can deal with it if I know. Without knowing what happened, there's no way of even beginning to know what to do."

The prof seemed lost in thought for a few minutes. He drained his coffee and looked at his watch.

"I think I have probably used up my grace period," he said.

"Is there anything else you think I might be able to do for you?" Graham asked.

"No, you have been very helpful. And most generous with your time, thank you" said the prof, emerging from his misery.

He asked Graham if he would mind leaving the club alone, as the bill had to be settled, and it would be better if the two of them were not seen leaving the building together. Graham understood and bade farewell to his lunchtime companion.

"If I can be of any more help, please let me know," were his parting words, and he descended the few stairs from the club to the street level, wondering if they would ever meet again. He had some good reasons to hope they might but several better reasons to hope they might not. He had a life to get on with and had hoped and anticipated that a meeting (or at most two meetings) with the prof would act as the final chapter of his time travel adventure. He now had a strong feeling that he could not yet consider the matter closed.

4 Project Petra
October 2013

"Come in, John, take a seat and make yourself comfortable."

The Colonel indicated the set of lounge furniture which, along with his oversized antique desk, occupied a considerable portion of his large office. John Bishop settled himself into one of the armchairs.

"Thank you for sparing me some time on this auspicious day. Can I get you something to drink?"

"A cup of coffee would be nice. Thank you, sir," John replied. The Colonel was probably the only person in the building who could summon up a pot of freshly made coffee with a single phone call. He was also the only person John would call 'sir'.

"You know we're very grateful for the way you've allowed us to handle things for the last few months," the Colonel continued, airing the ridiculous possibility that John could have done anything other than do as he had been politely but firmly requested to do.

"You've been spending some time on your retirement home, I assume. Where was it again?"

"Down in South Wales, sir," John replied, knowing full well that the Colonel would have known exactly where his retirement home was and that he had hardly left it for the last twelve months.

"Well. We're now sure that all the dust has settled. The entire incident has been investigated by everyone who wanted to investigate it, and no fault has been found with this department or anyone else. Dreadful business, but one must acknowledge that accidents will happen at the forefront of scientific research. Terrible, nonetheless."

John thought of making some comment about just how terrible a business it had been. Even a time-served operative like himself had been shocked by the sudden and unexplained death of three innocent technicians. After a second's thought, he decided to merely nod and grunt his assent.

"But that's all behind us now," the Colonel continued. He paused as a knock at the door announced the arrival of a tray of coffee and biscuits. When the Colonel's secretary had served the two of them and departed, he carried on. "I just wanted to meet you today and personally thank you. Not just for the way you handled the incident at the time, but the way you've co-operated with the inquiries since, and the way you've kept your head down for us. Can't have been easy – but I hope full pay has helped a little."

"Of course, sir," John dutifully replied, wondering if this was indeed the reason for the meeting or if something else would sneak its way onto the agenda.

"Well, you can rest assured that it has all been satisfactorily closed off, and you can resume your plan to retire. I understand you'll be spending this morning on the boring paperwork and admin stuff and then having a bit of a do this afternoon. I won't be there – you know I like to give you fellows a chance to unwind. But you go with my best wishes and my gratitude. You can return to being plain John Bishop again." The Colonel was finishing his coffee and making it clear that the meeting was now at an end. John was relieved that there had been no surprises. It appeared that his final project, complete with its disastrous ending, was to be permanently closed down.

"Actually, I'll be plain Tom Woodward, sir," John replied as he got up. "That's how they know me in South Wales." The Colonel gave no response. 'Maybe there is something he doesn't know, after all,' Tom thought. 'Or maybe he just doesn't get the joke.'

As predicted, the rest of his morning was spent signing an unbelievable number of documents and returning items belonging to the organisation that had been given to him for his use over the years. From the office, he adjourned to a back room at the local pub where his farewell do took place. Plenty of food, even more drink, and a humorous speech from his immediate boss. The only surprise was the farewell gift from his fellow employees, which John knew was paid for out of their pockets. (The organisation had a policy of not giving anything to ex-employees – just in case.) His colleagues – soon to become his ex-colleagues - had raised over a thousand pounds, an unheard-of amount, and it was given to him in the form of an Amazon voucher.

"Didn't know what to get you, old chap. But we thought you'd now have plenty of time to read those odd books you like – so this should help you buy plenty of them."

After a couple of hours and more than a couple of drinks, John caught the evening train from London Paddington Station to Swansea and hoped that he had finally turned his back on the part of the world in which he had spent his entire working life.

-

At nine o'clock sharp the next day, the Colonel was once again welcoming a visitor to his office and sharing coffee and biscuits.

"David, I wanted to have a chat with you about a new project that I'd like you to take on. Well, actually it's an old project but it is new to you and I'm hoping that you will be able to bring it a new lease of life."

David Allinson, a junior colleague of John's, had served the unofficial two-year apprenticeship since leaving Cambridge University and was delighted to receive the news that he was to be granted responsibility for his first project.

"Which project is that sir?" David asked.

"Well, you will no doubt remember the project that your colleague, John, was working on before his enforced furlough."

"I thought that had all been closed down, sir."

"Yes. I'm glad you thought so – that was what everyone was supposed to believe. But we need to give it a new direction and a new project name to go with it. I'd like you to take a more 'hands-on' approach. We need to encourage the professor to continue his research so that its considerable scientific benefits can be enjoyed. We've passed his findings on to another team, and they've been working on it – but we need the particular skill set that the professor and his team have. After all, the project now has two separate threads."

"Two separate threads, sir?"

"You'll understand when you've read the briefing papers. They'll be in your inbox when you get back to your desk. But I wanted to speak with you first.

This project is a two-headed monster. It was originally of interest to us as a method of communicating over a wavelength that nobody else had discovered, so nobody else could intercept it. But it now seems that the project has another facet. There is a beam that can apparently be transmitted through a closed window from the other side of a busy street and cause those in the receiving room to all die of apparent natural causes within twenty-four hours. I trust you can understand how that might be of interest to us." The Colonel paused for a moment before adding, "And to other parties."

"Your brief is to encourage the professor to recommence his work and to encourage him in every way you can. You will report every aspect of progress to your section head and let us know if there are any barriers. We will do all we can to remove them. Do you understand?"

David replied that he did – even though he was not entirely sure. A thorough reading of the papers and a few hours of thinking would be necessary.

"One additional thing," the Colonel said, bringing dread to David. He hated anything that was expressed as just 'one additional thing'. The sting was always in the tail.

"Now that this is a double-headed project, ensuring that security is watertight is even more important. I want you to re-examine everyone involved in the project and maintain close supervision of this aspect as the project moves forward. If you encounter anything out of the ordinary in this respect, I do not want you to include it in your normal report. You are to bring it directly to me."

David showed his naivety with his final question of the meeting. Still, the Colonel understood that he was dealing with a member of the generation who perhaps asked questions that his generation understood without asking.

"Why's that, sir?"

"I'm expecting that other parties might become interested in this research project and take steps to find out more about it. I need to know who they are and what steps they are taking. Is that clear?"

For the second time in the meeting, David answered yes to something he was not sure he fully understood.

The one thing he did understand was that he had to come up with a project name. It was standard procedure and one of the responsibilities of the project manager. He knew the project began as a method of helping the blind to see, and wondered if he should choose a name in keeping with that aim – it would help disguise the real purpose, which might be useful. However, he found it difficult to come up with a positive-sounding project name associated with blindness. Project White Stick or Project Seeing Eye just did not seem appropriate.

He reverted to the old favourite naming method and played around with some acronyms before he came up with Private Extra Terrestrial Radar Array. Project Petra it would be – and since Petra was also the name of a famous TV dog, it would have that nice cuddly name that some like. Totally appropriate for something capable of secretly killing unfriendly targets.

5 Anna's Story
1967 – 2003

Anna was born in 1967 in Dresden, which at that time was part of the Deutsche Demokratische Republik, which "The West" referred to as the communist state of East Germany, where she enjoyed a happy home life with her family. Her father progressed from the position of lecturer to eventually head the History Department of the Technical University of Dresden, while her mother taught at the Erweiterte Oberschule "Pestalozzi", the school which Anna and her younger sister, Cornelia, attended.

An event in her early childhood was to shape the rest of her life. She and Cornelia were playing in the park, their mother sitting nearby talking to other mothers and enjoying the summer sun when it happened. A group of young boys were acting boisterously on the roundabout – one of them removing his belt and holding it out while the others pushed him faster and faster. Cornelia chose the wrong moment to run past and was caught full in the face by the flailing piece of leather.

Anna would never forget the rest of that day. The screams of pain from Cornelia, the panic of the other children and the mothers, the ride in the ambulance, and the arrival at Dresden Medical Academy.

It was quite the most enormous building she had seen at that early stage in her life, and the number of people in white uniforms, men and women, the rows of beds with people in all stages of illness, and the clinical smell would stay with her forever. She sensed the panic in her mother, and later her father, as Cornelia spent day after day with her head wrapped in bandages. Nobody said anything, but all shared the same concern – would Cornelia be able to see again?

Through good fortune, medical skill, and the resilience of youth, she made a complete recovery. And Anna knew what she wanted to be when she grew up. She would be an eye doctor like the ones who had saved her sister's sight.

In some children, this would have been a passing phase, along with those other ambitions of all young girls: one day, a princess; the next day, a ballerina; then a model, an actress, and so on. But Anna was different. Her sense of purpose remained solidly in place from that day forward, until the age of eighteen when Anna achieved the highest marks in the whole of her school at the Abitur (A-Level) exam. To be more accurate she received the joint highest marks, since Stefan Schicker achieved an equal mark. The school presented two awards – one for the highest-scoring female pupil and one for the highest-scoring male pupil. (It makes more sense in the original German language).

Stefan also intended to pursue a medical career and was delighted to be accepted at the Medical Academy in Dresden. But Anna was not happy. She had applied for a position at the Charité – Universitätsmedizin Berlin, which was, in her mind, the best place to study. The Charité traced its origins to the year 1710, and more than half of all German Nobel Prize winners in Physiology or Medicine had worked there, so she was not far wrong. She had desperately wanted to become one of the more than 8,000 students studying there and had completely overlooked all the obstacles and practical difficulties in obtaining a place.

It was her father who noticed her disappointment. He had been travelling frequently in the few months before Anna had made her application, attending various university seminars and symposiums across Europe. He felt some justifiable guilt at his absence at a vital time for his beloved daughter. He told her he would do what he could and asked her to try and enjoy the summer – the break between school and the intense world of medical study might be the last break she would have for a long time.

She did enjoy the break. For a few months, there was no studying – unless you included the two-person field courses on human biology (practical) with Stefan, which they both enjoyed.

Meanwhile, her father set himself a task. He had a position, some authority, and plenty of contacts. He would use them to get his daughter what she wanted. He phoned people, called in a few favours, and had some quiet words in the ears of some of his more senior contacts.

Securing the offer was the easiest of the two tasks he faced. He had a contact at the Charité whom he had met at a symposium in London, and he was able to use his influence to find the right person in the organisation who could issue a conditional offer. The more difficult task was to find accommodation for his daughter for her long stay in Berlin. Her stay would last many years, and there were few sources of funds. There was Anna's remuneration for her work periods during the mixed practical and academic stay, some contributions from the State, and the eternal 'bank of mum and dad'. However, even the combination of all these would be insufficient to meet the soaring cost of even the most modest accommodation in the nation's capital city.

His breakthrough came when he was told of a couple at the institute who were cohabiting but had not informed the authorities. They rented out the smaller of their two apartments, which was strictly prohibited. Anna's father was able to persuade them that it would be far better for them to rent it to his daughter, despite her being sadly unable to match the rent they were currently receiving. They understood the alternative of his 'friends' being made aware of their current situation would be much less favourable to the young would-be landlords.

So, Anna received the wonderful news from the Charité that a place was available for her, and the surprise news from her father that he had some good friends in Berlin who would be renting her a small apartment at a very reasonable rate. She quite literally did not realise how lucky she was.

Her parting from Stefan did not involve the drama usually associated with the end of a first love. Both had their minds so concentrated on what lay ahead instead of what had passed, as enjoyable as it had been, that their brief affair ended swiftly without a backward glance. This first relationship with Stefan proved to be a template for many of Anna's future relationships with men.

Anna moved to Berlin in 1985 and settled into her new home and her new life. Her flat was modest but sufficient, and her new landlords were perfectly civil, but Anna could never understand why their dialogue with her was always so formal – even to the point of frostiness. She wrongly attributed it to the fact the Berliners must just be unfriendly to strangers. She had very little other interaction with the people of her new hometown since her new life could be summed up in the idiom 'her nose was kept to the grindstone'.

There were reasons that the Charité had such an excellent reputation. It had excellent facilities and first-rate staff, and although its candidate selection was not entirely based on merit, it still recruited some of the most able students in the country. But once recruited, the students had to work and study hard. And Anna was determined to succeed. She wanted to not only obtain a basic medical qualification but to achieve her goal of one day specialising in ophthalmology, so had to be in the upper quartile of candidates.

The task of becoming a doctor in East Germany was particularly onerous. After four years of study, she had to reach a qualifying level in both Russian and English languages to achieve the Sprachkundigenprüfung. This was the only part that Anna had some advantages in. Her father had insisted on the family learning some basic Russian from early childhood, and in later life, Anna, like so many of her friends, listened to English language pop music regularly on the West German radio stations that could so easily be picked up in Berlin. Another huge advantage of having her own flat!

Working in the Charité, which she was allowed to do in the later years of study, also meant that she would interact with some of the patients in the private wards. These patients were usually foreigners, which meant they either spoke English or Russian. The private wards were not widely publicised by the hospital, but they were known to a select few. The hospital kept many secrets, including the source of some of the bodies that the students were able to witness in anatomy classes. The body of every person who died attempting to cross the wall was brought to the Charité for an autopsy.

But even in her bubble of hard work and dedication, she was not immune to the events going on in the world, her own country, and her adopted city of Berlin. She was aware of some of the illicit meetings that started soon after she came to Berlin, and continued throughout the late 1980s, and the Monday demonstrations that began in late 1989, but she did not attend any of them. However, as the crisis deepened, on November 9[th,] 1989, she was joined in her small apartment by several friends, all watching the live broadcast of the leader of the SED party, everyone eager to discover what form the government's announcement would take. Later they joined the many revellers on the streets, witnessing first-hand the flow of people through the open checkpoints and celebrating into the early hours of the night that the Berlin Wall fell.

November 10th was Anna's first and last hangover experience, but life, study, and work continued. The effects of the new liberalisation changed her life as they changed the lives of so many others, gradually but continuously over the coming years. But there was still a qualification to be achieved.

Eventually, she completed all her medical studies and achieved her lifelong aim of being a doctor. (She was grateful that the additional task of completing a final paper on Marxism-Leninism, compulsory in earlier years, was no longer necessary). There was a huge party for all the graduating students, and her parents and sister visited Berlin to witness her presentation.

She was no longer a student. She was now an employee of the Charité. A new century was just around the corner.

-

Cornelia was pleased and proud of her sister's achievements; if there was any sisterly jealousy, it remained hidden. But she recognised an opportunity for her own escape from the smothered surrounding of her parental home and prevailed upon her sister to allow her to come and spend some time with her at her apartment in Berlin.

During her stay, she sprang her surprise on Anna, asking if she could make her stay more than just a visit, as she had been offered a job at a school in Berlin. Anna realised that she had been manipulated by her sister – the offer of a job could only have come after Cornelia had made an application and attended an interview, of course. But how could she refuse her sister?

Cornelia moved in the following week.

Living in Berlin in the 1990s was a unique experience. There was social turmoil on every level and in just about every aspect of life. People who had wanted to leave the city for years grabbed the opportunity – some still fearful that the situation could change yet again. And people who wanted to return to the eastern half of Berlin – a much smaller number than those who wished to leave, but a more problematic group – returned. A small consequence of this was the ease with which Anna found a job. A larger problem concerned those whose property had been 'taken' by the state when the city was partitioned and who now wanted to reclaim it.

However, the main change that the two sisters, particularly Cornelia, noticed was the incredible party scene that pervaded Berlin. With so many empty apartments and a whole generation of young people suddenly experiencing freedom for the first time, the city became a permanent party for those who wished to join in.

Anna was too preoccupied with her job to become involved. The early years of being a doctor are an intense learning experience, with every procedure and situation being handled by the doctor for the first time. And with Anna's determination to become a specialist in ophthalmic medicine still driving her, she had no time for distractions. Not so Cornelia, who was drawn into the web. Over the course of many months, she moved from occasionally missing a day at work due to 'illness' to the edge of losing her job and a dangerous dependence. The consequences might have been bad for her, but she was saved just in time when a change in her sister's situation rescued her.

Anna heard about an opportunity in the ophthalmology department of the Klinikum der Universität in Munich. It suited her career path perfectly and after attending an interview she was offered the position.

Cornelia travelled with her to Munich and attempted to find work at a school. However, she found that the Bavarian government, in common with other state governments in former West Germany, had taken steps to restrict the influx of teachers from the Eastern side of the country seeking better-paid jobs in the West.

Despite the efforts of the central government, including the revaluing of the Ostmark currency of East Germany at parity with the West Germany mark for wages, there was a disruptive flow of people from east to west. The passing of the new law (the Gegenseitige Anerkennung von nach dem Recht der DDR erworbenen) made it difficult for a teacher from the East to teach in a state school in Munich, and, after a few failed attempts, Cornelia decided to return to Dresden, where she took a job in the same school that she had attended as a child. The move conveniently coincided with a deterioration in the health of their mother, and Cornelia became a part-time carer as well as a full-time teacher.

Cornelia's move relieved Anna of many worries. She had not only been concerned that Anna was in danger of 'going off the rails' but also worried about her parents' welfare. Like so many senior citizens of the DDR, they faced many social and psychological difficulties as their whole world changed so rapidly in front of their eyes. But now Cornelia was there to look after them, and Anna was free to develop in her new role.

She worked in the Innenstadt campus of the combined University hospital, housed in a collection of solid, classic four-story buildings in the centre of Munich. Her whole life was spent within a stone's throw from the Hauptbanhof (the central railway station), in an area well populated with shops, bars, cheap accommodation, and a small run-down red-light area.

Life was more relaxed than the frantic atmosphere of Berlin, and she enjoyed the cosmopolitan life of a Western city for several years. It proved the ideal transition before her final career move. In 2003, she successfully applied for a position in London at Moorfields Eye Hospital.

6 Not Again?
November 2022

The prof had delayed taking action for a few days, looking for an opening to do what he felt was unavoidable. All the time he felt the frustrations caused by the delay and the dangers inherent in procrastination. Finally, an excuse presented itself. It was not as good as he would have liked, but it would have to do. He shuffled the papers into the required position and called his assistant on the phone.

"Please can you come in, Margaret - I need your help to solve a problem."

Margaret Walters immediately stopped what she was doing and entered his office. She hated this part of her role – the need to drop everything when the prof asked for her – but she was grateful that he obviously knew she disliked it and so kept such requests to a minimum.

He asked her to sit in the chair normally reserved for patients and held out the file he had been reading.

"There appears to have been a mix-up," he began. "It occurred before you joined me, so you don't need to worry about how it happened or who is to blame, but I need your skills to help overcome it."

She nodded, suppressing a small smile. He thought she had some skills after all – not that he showed it too often.

"I've just been reading the notes for Mister Henry Graham before his appointment later this afternoon, and I suddenly thought they looked familiar. It seems that they may have been duplicated and placed in the file of a Mister Graham Henderson." The prof paused to give Margaret a chance to react, but she did not take it, so he continued, "I have dug out Mister Henderson's file – he apparently came to see me a couple of weeks ago - and thankfully there is very little difference in the two reports. But I really should inform Mister Henderson about a couple of slight nuances."

Margaret risked a brief "Indeed", not understanding what might be entailed in a 'couple of slight nuances' but guessing that her communication skills would be shortly called upon in some way.

"Could I ask you to draft a letter to Mister Henderson asking him if he could pay us another visit? We need to make sure he understands that the visit is merely dotting i's and crossing t's and that there is absolutely no need for him to be concerned in any way. I feel that you would be so much better at drafting such a letter."

"Certainly, professor," Margaret replied. "Is there a date or time you would like to set the appointment?"

"I'd like it to be as soon as possible. I recall that Mr Henderson finds it most convenient to have a late afternoon appointment, so perhaps you could offer him a choice from my diary?"

"Certainly. I'll draft something for your approval. Was there anything else?"

"No. Thank you very much, Margaret."

-

When Graham opened the invitation for a return visit, he thought it might cause him more consternation than any of the professor's other patients experienced when they received letters concerning eye surgery that really had occurred. He had never gone under the prof's knife but was beginning to dread their meetings. At the last one, he had given his opinion that the episode of time travel that he had experienced was likely to be repeatable, and subsequently had the distinct impression that the professor would attempt to travel back in time to discover what had happened to his assistant.

Thinking of the likely reasons for the prof putting on this show of him needing a further appointment meant that he had probably failed in his attempt at time travel and wanted to discover the reasons for his failure. Either that or, which was probably worse, he had succeeded, and now wished to embroil Graham in the outcome. Wanting more than ever to put a line underneath this whole episode, he selected the earliest appointment from the selection offered and telephoned the hospital to book it.

-

The look on the prof's face as Margaret showed him into the office confirmed that something was wrong. Undoubtedly, the professor was doing his best to make Margaret think that he was giving the patient a pleasant 'nothing to worry about' look, but Graham could see through it. He had to keep up a dialogue of 'Thank you for coming to see us so quickly, I'd like to apologise for the inconvenience and assure you that there is absolutely nothing to worry about. How was your journey, ...' Until he was sure the door was firmly closed, and Margaret was out of earshot. Then the conversation changed.

"It didn't work," was all he said. His appearance portrayed abject misery.

"You mean you tried to repeat what happened to me? To travel back in time?" Graham asked.

"Yes. It was quite simple, really. I told everyone that I had done some calculations and thought there might be a chance that the communication could work at a lower signal strength if we took a measurement that was just off-centre. I persuaded them to let me run a test and got permission from the company you visited to allow me to conduct a brief measurement in their offices. I told them that we were setting up an interdepartmental wireless link with the government office on the floor below them. In fifteen minutes, I would be able to ascertain that it couldn't affect their office wireless network. I asked Margaret to do a test run of the communicator from this office while I stood by the window in the financial company's office opposite."

"But we know that it only worked when the signal was at full strength – why did you think it would work on lower power?"

"I didn't. I stayed behind in my office one evening before the test and modified the transmitter to bypass the attenuation controller. Margaret and everyone else thought she was doing a five-minute test at fifty percent signal strength, then five minutes at sixty, and then five more at seventy percent. In fact, the dial she was twisting had no effect. It was running at full strength the whole time."

"I have to be careful how I ask this question," Graham said. "What were you thinking of? While you were standing in the window exposing yourself to the transmission?"

"I remembered what you said about recreating the thoughts and emotions of a particular day, so I tried to think of the day when we ran our very first test and got such great results. We were convinced we had taken a significant step to helping many blind people see. I tried extremely hard to think of the joy and the sense of achievement I felt on that day."

"And then you woke the next morning to find that nothing had changed?"

"Sadly, yes."

The prof's face, which had briefly become enlivened as he retold his feelings on the day of his first experiment, now lapsed into the miserable expression it had previously shown.

"Do you have any idea why it didn't work?" Graham was not particularly interested but felt he had to ask.

"I can only attest to the scientific aspects of the experiment. I tested and retested everything, and everything worked as it should."

"So, the only difference between my successful jump and your failed one is the person involved…" Graham interrupted.

The prof didn't answer – but his shrug said it all. Graham dreaded what might come next.

The prof drew a deep breath and launched into his prepared speech. "It's obvious that despite my best efforts, I cannot replicate what you did. I must resort to begging you to help me. If I cannot discover what happened to Anna, I cannot continue my work. She was so important to me – and I know of no other person to turn to. There is also something else that I should add so you have the complete picture. As I said, we kept our relationship completely professional. But over the years we had conversations about what was happening in the world, and I know that Anna had certain political views. I fear that once she discovered the reasons for our second experiment – that we were being used as a weapon she might have had feelings that made it difficult for her to continue with the programme."

"Are you saying she might have wanted to leak some information about your experiment?" Graham asked.

"I don't know. It is possible - and I fear that this might explain why our security team will say nothing to me about it. Maybe they knew about these sympathies of hers. Maybe they know exactly where she is. Maybe they are even the cause of her absence. I just do not know. If you were to go back and find out what happened, and I could know what had happened to her – no matter what it was - everything would be fine. It's the not knowing that is eating away at me. You are the only one who can help me. Please, will you go back one more time?"

It was exactly what Graham had feared, and he had his answers prepared. But he paused briefly to make sure that he gave them maximum impact.

"Prof, you cannot seriously expect me to spend fifty years back in time so that I can solve a problem from a few weeks ago," was his first line of defence.

"Do you need to go that far back? As you say, the problem only occurred a few weeks ago. Surely there is some other point in time you could jump to, isn't there?"

"Well, the only date that we know will work is the one that has already been successful. But you are right, there may be other dates. I have had plenty of time to think about this. I even talked about it with Carol back then. We agreed that the date had to be something significant. A date when the person involved was experiencing some strong feelings that they could recall and replicate."

"Surely there must have been some other times in your life when this happened to you," the prof prompted, and Graham knew he was being drawn down a path he feared to tread.

"Yes. There was the birth of my first child – that was certainly one."

He paused as he remembered sitting alone on a Saturday night in the hospital waiting room, his wife out for the count after a caesarean operation performed under general anaesthetic, leaving him clutching a swaddled tiny baby. Realising that this baby was unlike any other that he had ever held. This one carried his name and, more importantly, his genes.

This baby would be formed into an adult by him and his wife. For many years, this tiny being would be completely dependent on the two of them.

Graham sat quietly in the prof's office, lost in thought for a few seconds. He knew this was the type of emotional impact he would need to make the jump.

"Could you not try to travel – what was it you called it, jump - back to then?" the professor asked, interrupting his reverie.

"Prof, I've considered this. I'd be thirty years old and married – so yes, it would cut the time difference for the jump from fifty to forty years. But there would be consequences. Imagine it. I would have virtually no short-term memory at all. Neither personally nor professionally. I'd know nothing about my job – the products, fellow employees, customers, and so on. The things that I worked with every day. I'd be useless. Personally, I'd have no memory of conversations I'd had with friends or family in the previous days, weeks, or even months. My mind would be remembering all of them through a telescope from forty years away."

"But this time, it would be different. You could prepare for the jump. Memorise the lottery numbers. You'd start your life with a fortune."

Graham did his best to explain to the prof why he was less than thrilled at starting his third life in the midst of his marriage. With all the mental stress of the 'jump', the risk that it didn't work correctly or that he forgot the lottery numbers. And then the challenge of spending the rest of his married life knowing what was going to happen in the world, with his partner not knowing. Would she understand if he told her about the jump? Surely, he would have no choice but to. And would the relationship survive?

He must have succeeded in his arguments because the professor changed his tack to the positives that Graham could experience with a planned jump back to his eighteen-year-old self.

"Just imagine being eighteen - but with a small fortune. A lottery jackpot. And the knowledge of how to invest that money to create a major fortune for yourself. What a life you could lead! There must be loads of ways you could spend your time. You could visit anywhere in the world – places that have been spoiled in the last fifty years – you could see them as they once were and never will be again. Travel first class…. Are you a music fan? You could see performances that will never be seen again. The first Glastonbury. Or sports events – football games, Cup Finals, Superbowls, World Series. Please say you will at least think about it….."

Graham had to admit there was much that he would like to experience. The prof had obviously been rehearsing the arguments. Of course, there would not be much fun attending a Cup Final for which you already knew the result – but Graham certainly would like to see a Superbowl or an Aussie Rules Grand Final where he did not know the outcome (which he didn't for almost any year). And the thought of experiencing some hedonistic pleasures was severely tempting. Who would not want to exchange his seventy-year-old body for the eighteen-year-old version? Not to mention the women of a similar age he could share his bed with. It was noticeable that very wealthy men always seemed to have the most beautiful women on their arms.

But he had to make sure that the prof understood the downside. He also knew that there was one other date in his life that he thought he might be able to jump back to, but he decided to keep that information to himself for the time being.

"Prof, last week I saw my children and grandchildren for the first time in fifty years. You're asking me to go another fifty years before I see them again. And you must remember that this time-travel lark is not all beer and skittles." His strength of feeling made him choose the phrase even though the prof might not understand it.

"You're asking me to go back to a life of loneliness. Unable to share what is probably the most important fact about myself with any colleague or companion in case they think I'm crazy. A life where I will get frustrated every day. Frustrated that I have no mobile phone and there is no such thing as the internet, email, or Google. Don't get me started on what it's like to go into a restaurant back then. It's great to afford a fancy five-star meal, but it's ruined when the people at the next table all light up their cigarettes. And don't even think of going into a pub – or a railway carriage. It's not fun."

He thought about outlining some of the difficulties that might present themselves when he made the jump back again, or some of the risks that were involved in any jump, but instead paused to allow things to cool off a little, which gave the prof a chance to reply.

"Please, I can only ask you to give it some thought. I am a desperate man, and if there is anything I can do to help, you know I will do it. I truly believe you are the only person who can help me."

The prof looked at his watch and recognised that they had overrun the allotted half an hour again.

"I will contact you one more time to hear your final answer," he said, obviously feeling less than confident that he would hear an answer he wanted to hear. Once again, they had gone past Margaret's clocking-off time, so the prof walked him back to the lift and wished him farewell.

-

Graham's thoughts on his journey home and for the next couple of days meandered around two topics. The first was the temptations laid before him of a second, planned jump. The prof had hit many of them fair and square - but had omitted one. He wondered if he could contact Carol as soon as possible after she landed from her jump. She had jumped in 2012 and landed in 1982. He had met her in 1992 – and those ten years between her landing and their meeting had been very difficult for her. If he could somehow make contact with her just after she landed, he could make things so much easier for her. She and he could possibly even begin a life together. They had spent a few very pleasant years together the last time around - before their time had been cut short. It was certainly worth a thought.

His other thought was the alternative date for a potential landing. He had not mentioned it to the prof, but in all his time spent thinking about the subject – and in his hundred-and-twenty years of combined lives there had been plenty of time for such thought – he had concluded that there was one other potential date. He had been putting it to the back of his mind because although the timescale for the event suited his purposes rather well, the strong feelings associated with that date were distinctly unpleasant.

Graham's wife, Mary, had been killed in a road accident in 2017 after enjoying lunch and a few glasses of bubbly with friends. While walking from the restaurant to the car park, an elderly driver lost control of his vehicle, which mounted the pavement, hit his wife, and killed her.

Graham remembered that day and the one after. But his memory of that period was far from clear. Those were the days of maximum shock, grief, and pain. But they were not the days he was thinking of when he thought of a possible landing for his jump. For days after Mary's death, his thoughts and feelings had been all over the place. He could never attempt to replicate them. The day he was thinking of came a year later. Exactly a year later.

He had spoken very little to anyone about the shock of losing the woman he had been married to for over forty years. They had never pretended that their marriage was perfect. It was not made in heaven nor full of hearts and flowers. He and Mary had often joked about the messages they heard on the radio as couples pledged their undying love, their gratitude for how someone had completely changed their life, how they loved them more and more every day of their life and other such phrases which seemed out of place when not contained in a 'chick lit' novel. Neither of them believed these claims to be true. Theirs had been a constant, caring, close relationship that lasted almost their entire adult life. Filled with overcoming life's problems, the raising of two children, and, latterly, the joy of grandchildren.

On the rare occasions he did speak about it, he described her loss as akin to the loss of a part of your body. It was as if your left hand had just been severed. There was a short, sharp period of pain, followed by a dull ache that never quite disappeared. And the constant feelings that lay somewhere between frustration, annoyance, and anger as you were constantly reminded that a simple everyday task was going to be different. Something perfectly normal and easy to achieve with two hands became surprisingly difficult when attempted with one hand. That was how it felt for a long time. Every day, there would be something – seldom anything important – which caused him to say to himself, "I must tell Mary that", or "I wonder if Mary knows that", or even "I'll have to ask Mary when/what/where that is."

He had lived in a fog for a whole year. His children had done their best to help him out of it – but they had their lives to lead, their problems to overcome, and their children to raise. He perked up enough when they met to fool them that he was OK. But he wasn't. Underneath it all, he was mentally sliding down a dangerous slope.

The recognition of his problem came on the first anniversary of Mary's death. First, he recognised how unusual it was that he felt that the date was significant. He was not one for remembering anniversaries; that had been Mary's forte. But he remembered the significance of this day as soon as he awoke. And then he asked himself why he was remembering it. He didn't have any plans to commemorate the day. He was not going to visit her grave to lay fresh flowers or go to church or anything like that. It wasn't the way he (or they) did things. 'Then why are you remembering the day?' he asked himself. 'You've always struggled to remember dates. You never commemorated the day you met Mary or your first date or anything like that. You know the birthdays of your children and your brother and sister – but apart from that? No. One of the first things you had to do after Mary died was to find out the birthdays of all the rest of the family – your son-in-law, your daughter-in-law, and even your grandchildren. Not to mention all your cousins, nephews, and nieces. Remembering them was Mary's department. So why are you so hung up with this being the anniversary of her death? You're just wallowing. Self-pity is not at all attractive, I can tell you.'

This was how he began a day of giving himself the biggest kick up the arse he could manage.

'You've not even cleaned up after her' was how he saw it and said it. He had done all the legal stuff – that was all completed within weeks. He'd dealt with the bequests in her will, closed her accounts, and settled all the financial, administrative, and legal matters – and he'd made sure that her jewellery was passed to their daughter and granddaughters as she had wished. Mary had left instructions about that. But after he'd done that, he postponed everything else. The first action after his self-administered kick was to start to deal with all the rest of her possessions.

So, despite the general subject matter, much about that day had been positive – it was a day that involved many strong feelings that he believed he could replicate. But he had to ask himself did he want to relive it? Or, more to the point, did he feel he should relive it?

He sympathised with the prof's problem. Graham had the distinct impression that the prof did not open himself up too easily to too many people. He was probably a bit of a cold fish. But he had seemingly opened up more than a little to this Anna woman – and, in his way, he had also opened up to Graham. Could he turn him down – with the knowledge that he was probably the only person on the planet who could help? To have such an opportunity to help another human being and refuse it. Was that something he could carry around with him for the rest of his life? He was beginning to think the answer to that question was 'no'.

7 Anna Does London
2003 – 2012

London was everything Anna thought and hoped it would be, and her first year in the city whizzed past at a speed that surprised her. As she started her twelve-month review meeting with Louise Hillier, the HR manager at Moorgate Hospital, she expressed these very thoughts.

On the work front, she could not be happier. She had developed a remarkably good relationship with Professor Karbajanovic. She found him to be a great teacher, a considerate doctor, and a thoughtful manager. She was extremely happy with their working relationship, and when asked if there was anything that could be improved, she could only say that he was often so deep in thought about his work that he was less communicative than she would like. But she was more than happy to have this lower level of personal interaction since the work was so important.

On a personal front, she told Louise that she had moved out of the temporary accommodation the hospital had provided when she started the job and was now living in a studio flat that was smaller than she would like (a feeling that most Londoners share about their accommodation) but hoped to move into something larger when she was fully established.

Louise made a polite inquiry about her personal life for professional and personal reasons. She was of a similar age to Anna and wondered if the challenges of being a single woman in a city like London – hard enough for an English woman, let alone a foreigner – were causing any problems for Anna. In response, Anna admitted that there had been some issues – she had had to rapidly increase her knowledge of the English language to understand the everyday slang of the average Londoner. She had not formed any friendships outside of work but hoped that this lack of social interaction – probably her only concern – could change as time progressed.

Acting as a friend rather than an HR representative, Louise suggested something to Anna that would profoundly affect the rest of her life. She suggested that Anna should investigate a dating agency called Select Few. Louise admitted that she was on the books of the agency herself and that it was unlike any other agency she had heard of. A strong vetting system ensured that the agency's users got what they wanted out of it. The men had not only to be completely 'clean' in every sense of the word but also wealthy enough to treat a woman in the old-fashioned way. "None of this modern 'going halves on the cost of a meal'", was how she put it.

In other words, the man would pay for every date. The woman needed to be interesting and mature enough to be a fascinating companion to justify her date's expenditure. She reassured Anna that it was not in any way a 'Sugar Daddy' site – but a site for people who looked for certain aspects to be present in a relationship and were willing to accept, possibly even welcome, the fact that other aspects would be absent.

Louise told her she had enjoyed an interesting and rewarding series of encounters. Some men were obviously looking for only one thing – but were generally respectful enough to acknowledge that it was the woman's choice how the relationship proceeded, if at all. Others – quite a few actually – were genuinely looking only for good company on either an occasional or a frequent basis. To sum it up, Louise said she had spent many enjoyable hours in places she might not have been able to access on her own – and had eaten many wonderful, expensive meals. She gave Anna the contact details.

A few weeks later, Anna signed up and soon began to enjoy all that Louise had promised. There was, however, one significant difference between the two women. Anna had been brought up in a society in which capitalism had been almost eradicated. As a result, she had always had a slightly different approach to some of its finer points than those who had known nothing but capitalism since birth.

She regarded membership of Select Few as a capitalist venture and decided to embrace it fully. She learned that some of the men she met would enjoy taking her to a restaurant of their choice, one where they were known. Others would ask her to suggest a place to eat, preferring the anonymity of an unknown venue. Anna had found La Isola Bella, an Italian restaurant close to her flat to be the perfect place to eat on the rare occasions she treated herself. She chose to take one of her earliest dates there and was pleased that he thoroughly enjoyed the meal, bought a bottle of one of the most expensive wines on the list, and tipped well. She sensed a commercial opportunity and dropped into the restaurant for coffee the morning after. Massimo Sereni, the manager joined her and asked if she had enjoyed the meal.

"It was wonderful. And my colleague enjoyed it too," Anna reported, "and I hope to bring him again soon."

He smiled, and Anna continued, "Massimo. I believe that sometimes a restaurant pays an introductory commission to people who bring customers to their restaurant. This is common in London, no?"

Massimo was quick to guess the direction she was heading and remembered the size of the previous night's bill. "Yes, this does happen sometimes," he cautiously replied.

"Good. You see I might be able to bring colleagues here quite regularly. It would be good if I could drop in for coffee the following day and see if there was a small consideration for me."

Anna could use the English language surprisingly well when she chose to, and the first commercialisation of her new membership began. This was in addition to what one might consider the normal perks of her position. In the month before her birthday, she told two of her dates about her forthcoming celebration and received a small present from each of them. Pondering the fact that she would only be able to enjoy this benefit twice a year – her birthday and Christmas - she decided that it should be possible for her to have more than one birthday per year – provided that she made sure always to use the same birthday when meeting the same date.

Accordingly, she noted her 'birthday' on the index card for each of her dates – yes, she did partly conform to the racial stereotype of the efficient German and kept an index card for each date. And she memorised the key data. In addition to being a real Cancerian, sharing her birthday on 25th June with George Orwell, she would also be a false Arien, sharing a March 25th birthday with Elton John and a false Libran whose birthday of September 25th coincided with that of Mark Hamill and Christopher Reeve. 'After all,' she thought, 'if you get to choose your birthday, then why not share it with Luke Skywalker and Superman?'

There were other occasional benefits. One of her early dates was with a partner in a firm of stockbrokers. Anna did not have to pretend to be fascinated with his table talk of stocks and shares, investments, indexes, and so forth. She genuinely wanted to understand this world that was so foreign to her, and her attentiveness was rewarded on their second date when he presented her with an account that he had opened for her (with preferential dealing rates, of course) in which he had deposited fifty pounds worth of a promising share. Over the years that followed, whenever she dated someone from the financial world, she sought their investment advice and was able to multiply the size of the account many times.

Among her longer-lasting arrangements was Christopher, who helped her significantly increase the size of her wardrobe. She accompanied him to several of his company's dinners, award events for his industry, and the occasional social event. They became friends – and only ever friends - because, as one might genteelly put it, she would be of no interest to him if she were the last woman on earth. But the nearest she ever came to a long-term relationship was with Paul.

Paul was larger than life in every sense of the phrase. He was over six feet tall and big with it, but his immense energy and personality helped disguise his bulk. Going out with Paul always seemed to involve meeting several of his friends, of which he apparently had many – all of whom spent their evenings in the same bars and restaurants as he did.

Anna often joked that she was never quite sure what his real name was. His friends so often referred to him as Del-boy, Arthur (Daley), or Swiss Tony – names which she understood referred to characters in TV shows who were known to live on the fine edge between legal and not-so-legal business practices. He told people that he was in the asset management business, and one night after he had consumed one or two too many glasses of cognac, he told her how he had started his business.

Born in the East End of London, clever but not well educated, he had been employed, like all the best yuppies, selling stocks and shares for a major financial institution. He enjoyed considerable success as his personality, quick wits, and hard work brought him financial rewards. Then, one day, a client asked if he could help with a confidential problem.

"I need to sell some shares quickly for cash. A lot of cash," he had said.

"No problem," Paul replied, "you know we can have the money in your account before the close of business today."

"No, I mean real cash. Folding beer vouchers. Pieces of paper with the Queen's picture on them."

"How much are we talking about?"

"Fifty thousand."

"I can see why you described it as a problem. Can you give me an hour or two to see what I can do?"

"Yes – but please don't take too long. I need to move quickly."

Paul didn't waste time asking why it was so urgent or why his contact needed cash. He focussed on how he might be able to help and profit from giving his help. Putting the transaction through official channels was out of the question – any transaction involving more than ten thousand in cash was closely tracked, and he knew that this would not be what his client wanted. For the same reason, Paul knew anyone he spoke to would face this ten-thousand limit. But he could raise that ten thousand – and he was pretty sure he could find four friends who could do likewise.

'If one of them asked me for a very short-term loan of 10 K, would I do it?' he asked himself and rapidly answered, 'Yes, if there was something in it for me.'

He was confident that most of his friends thought very much like him – and that for five hundred quid they would let him have ten thousand for a day or two – no questions asked. He confirmed it with a few telephone calls – made from his mobile phone outside the offices with no danger of being overheard, of course.

Before going back to the client, he calculated his costs. 'Four times five hundred, plus a grand for transaction fees and a grand for myself; four grand total,' his arithmetic went. He returned his client's call.

"I can raise you fifty grand, but there'll be ten percent deducted," he told him.

"In that case, it'll have to be a sale of fifty-five grand's worth. I need to net fifty grand. Can you do that?"

Being this close to such a profitable deal, Paul confirmed he could. It took him a couple of hours to make all the arrangements, and the following morning, he met his client at the nearest Starbucks and handed him a large holdall.

The profit on the deal—almost two thousand pounds—was the spark that lit Paul's business. Six months later, his client repeated the transaction, and Paul assumed that one or two other calls he received for similar deals were the result of personal recommendations.

Not all the transactions were as straightforward (or as close to illegality) as his first. They involved people wishing to exchange an asset in one form for an asset in another form. His biggest breakthrough was when a colleague asked him to help with a deal with a client in the newly emerging East European market. They wished to raise some capital, but the only asset they had to exchange was a quarter of a million euros worth of tractors.

Paul contacted an old school friend who had not wanted a job with the risks involved in the financial markets and had opted for safer employment in the government department for overseas aid. He was the only person Paul could think of who might know something about anything agricultural, and his hunch proved correct.

Over lunch at a restaurant whose price levels shocked his companion, Paul learned that when Britain gave aid to a foreign country, it was not given in any financial form – it was given in the form of goods that could be useful to that foreign country. The type and amount of goods chosen from a shopping list supplied by the receiving country. Thus, the British government could help needy foreign nations while providing support to its key domestic industries. Providing trucks and buses was a favourite method.

Paul also learned that the Foreign Office was keen to aid Eastern European countries joining the European Union. This type of action simultaneously assisted the Foreign Office's aims of being pro-Europe and anti-Communism. So, the problems caused by the strict rules that the goods needed to be of British manufacture might be overcome.

It was not as straightforward as he would have liked, but the information he gathered was well worth his investment in lunch for two (and another dinner for two to be claimed by his guest - and companion - at a future date). A little more lobbying of key contacts enabled him to arrange for the tractors to find their way to Central Africa and a substantial sum to find its way to Paul's bank account.

-

There was a time when Anna thought her relationship with Paul might go further. They had been away for a long weekend, which Paul was honest enough to tell her was arranged so that he could disappear for a couple of hours for a business meeting. The location more than made up for it. Montreux in Switzerland was one of the most beautiful places she had ever seen. Fortune favoured them with bright, clear, sunny days for the weekend they were there, and they enjoyed the simple pleasures of strolling along the lake shore in both daylight and at night.

She noticed, but was not concerned by, Paul having a long conversation with the hotel concierge which seemed to relate to some problems with their passports. The conversation was entirely in French (which Paul spoke surprisingly well) and she left him to resolve it while she examined the artworks displayed in the hotel lobby.

She also thought nothing of the story; he later told her that the hotel was concerned that paparazzi were around the hotel trying to photograph someone who wanted their presence to go unreported. She assumed this was why they were photographed a couple of times as they entered or left the hotel. It did not in any way spoil the few days of their stay.

But all thoughts of a lasting relationship ended a few weeks later. Unusually, they went to a restaurant of her choice because Paul had said he wanted the chance to talk to her uninterrupted over dinner. But it was not for the reason she thought it might be—in fact, it was quite the opposite.

Paul told her that he had an opportunity for a considerable expansion of his business, but one that would necessitate him being away for quite some time. And even when he was back in the UK, he would not want anyone to easily establish who his close contacts were. So he was, very reluctantly, having to end their relationship.

"I wanted to give you a farewell gift," he said. "It's not very romantic, but I believe it is something you will one day come to enjoy."

He took an envelope from his jacket pocket and placed it on the table but did not yet give it to her.

'Only a man of his size could hide a large, well-stuffed envelope like that in his inside pocket', Anna thought, distracting herself from the shock of the news and the curiosity of what the envelope might contain.

"You see, Anna, I believe one of the reasons we have got on so well is that deep down we are very similar. We spend our lives making deals, sailing close to the wind, and taking risks. You cut your deals with boyfriends and restaurant owners, and I cut them with financiers and government employees. But we are both out there looking for the main chance. The deal that will make everything OK."

Anna wondered if he had found out about her deal with Massimo, or whether he was just guessing shrewdly. Ultimately it didn't matter.

"So, I've got you this," he continued, pointing at the envelope but not yet passing it over. It's just a boring bank account with a thousand pounds in it. But it's a very special account. It won't earn you any interest - but it's with a Swiss Bank. You'll need to use a series of numbers to access it. And nobody and I really do mean nobody - financial, government, or anything else – will ever know if you put money in or take it out. And there's a German Passport that goes with it. It's got your photo in it – but not your name."

He smiled and pushed the envelope across the table to her.

"I believe that one day you might find them useful," were his final words.

She looked at the brand new passport in the name of Anna Dreier.

"Anna Dreier?" she asked. "Couldn't you come up with something better than that?"

"I thought you'd better keep the same first name for convenience. And then I thought that if you had a husband or brother, then he would at least be useful."

Anna gave him a puzzled look.

"Useful. Herr Dreier. Get it? Herr Dreier, hairdryer," Paul explained.

It was a dreadful joke and because English was her second language it took an extra second to get it. There was only one possible answer.

"Paul," she said with mock seriousness, "Don't give up the day job!"

Anna thanked him and put the unopened envelope in her handbag. She had no idea where these thoughts of his had come from – and did not want to follow his train of thought. She was sure it did not lead anywhere nice. She merely thanked him in as bland a way as she felt she could.

Nothing else was said about the envelope, and much later, their evening ended as an evening between two lovers who were about to face a long separation should.

Paul left very early the next morning as he always did. He had always said it was because he wanted to be at home in front of his computer screens by seven a.m. when the pre-opening trades started on the European stock exchanges and there were still one or two business hours remaining (depending on the time of year) on the exchanges in Singapore and Hong Kong. But Anna knew it was more than this. Paul wanted to cram as much life into every day as he possibly could – and only a start before six a.m. made this possible in his eyes.

Once awake, she had time to examine the gift he had given her the night before and to ponder the things he had said about her. She was certainly cutting deals as he had put it. The restaurant owner, the multiple birthdays, the whole idea of dating 'useful' men. Was she really taking risks? Probably. But she was not so sure that she was looking for the big deal that would make everything OK. The truth was that she did not know what she was looking for.

But the separation was permanent. She never saw Paul again, and if any of her future dates took her to a restaurant frequented by Paul's friends, none of them ever made themselves known to her.

She took a holiday shortly after the break-up and didn't date anyone for a few months after returning. Eventually, she was reminded that her job, fascinating and rewarding as it was, could not consume her whole life. She remembered what her long-term financial goals were and resumed her relationship with Select Few.

Within a couple of years, she felt ready to take the next significant fiscal step and get onto London's financially challenging property ladder. She knew she had enough to fund a property deposit, which influenced her choice of potential dinner companions for the next few months.

Sure enough, one of them, an estate agent, told her that he had just the thing for her. An elderly lady had recently passed, and the family wanted to sell her apartment as quickly as possible despite it having recently been uncared for. (Anna loved the English language. The old lady was 'elderly' not old; she had 'passed' not died; and the property was 'uncared for' not run down.) But a visit to the property was arranged, and she immediately knew it would suit her perfectly.

It was in a suburb of London called Whetstone – she even loved the name of the area. She thought it wonderfully English and slightly odd. It was not far from where she was currently living and while parts of Whetstone were very attractive, some parts were quite ugly. And this was where the flat was located.

The property was the upper floor of a fairly large house that had been converted into two maisonettes (another new word for Anna to add to her English vocabulary). It was located on a busy main road and the agent warned her that since the property was leasehold rather than freehold it might be difficult for her to get a mortgage. But this did not worry her. It was conveniently located close to the tube line that went directly to her place of employment, there were plenty of shops and restaurants nearby, and a short walk away there were parks and gardens she could walk in.

It was quite a large flat for the money – and she could take her time to bring it up to date. Besides, she found some of the old furniture which was included in the sale to be rather cosy and comforting.

Another dinner companion was in the financial world and assured her he could get her a mortgage on favourable terms, even for a leasehold property, and that the normal introductory fees would be waived. (Anna discovered the meaning of the word 'waived' for the first time and loved its sound. There was a German word for the procedure, but the translation would be 'destroyed' or 'eliminated'. English was so much more prosaic!)

And so, Anna became a property owner – albeit one with a severely depleted bank account and a need to be frugal in her spending for the next few months. It was not until nearly a year later that she was able to make the property look even moderately appealing. It helped that a new dinner companion, who happened to be in the property management business, sent one of his teams to her apartment to give it a new coat of paint. Without charging her a penny, of course.

-

She enjoyed her job. Every day was different and there was a wonderful feeling that the team she was part of was doing good work and helping people. In addition to the day-to-day work that the Professor was involved in – improving the sight of so many people with complex problems – he continued to work on his research project to bring sight to people whose optic nerve was damaged so badly that there would appear to be no hope of sight ever being restored.

He explained his project in simple terms to anyone who would listen.

"Once upon a time, you had to have a cable connecting your computer to a router to access the internet. Then, someone created wireless networking, and you could connect to the internet without having that direct connection between your laptop and the router. Well, think of the router as your brain and your laptop as your eyes. I want to help people with no cable to still be able to see, so long as their 'laptop eyes' work."

He had been working on the project for many years, making slow progress. By 2010, he had built a camera with a wireless transmitter attached to it, transmitting images in a way that mimicked the signals being sent along an optic nerve. He could blindfold a sighted person and get them to 'see' an image transmitted by the camera. But there was still much progress needed. The quality of the images needed to be improved – the ultimate aim being the successful transmission of moving images. Also, the size of the device needed to be reduced before it was even approaching practicality. So, the professor sought additional government funding and achieved some level of success.

Unfortunately, some of the aspects of the project that were of most interest to the government department that provided the funding differed from those of prime concern for the Professor. He was allocated two additional people and sufficient funds to purchase the equipment he needed, but the testing had to include increasing the power of the signal being sent from the camera so that it could be operated remotely. Of course, the professor did not need remote operation. The distance between the transmitting camera and the receiving brain would only need to be a few inches for his purpose. But he had to play along so that he could make progress.

There was also some reorganisation needed in his department as there was now deemed to be a security aspect to their research. A man named Martin Knight was now frequently seen on site and some of the ancillary workers in the department were replaced with other hospital staff because they were deemed to be a security risk. Martin also arranged for a remote office to be set up in the office block on the other side of the street so that transmissions could be tested across a distance of fifty meters.

The first test was held on October 7th, 2012, and the tragic aftermath of this event was the lowest point in Anna's life. They had tested the transmission in the usual way – sending the signal from the camera with its results being tested both by registering the signal on a receptor unit that the new employees had constructed, as well as checking to see if the blindfolded human volunteers were able to see the image that the camera was capturing.

The first test, held at 9:30 am, was a failure. All the equipment was checked to confirm it was functional, and, having established this, the Professor instructed Anna to rotate the dial and double the transmission power. Again, no signal was received in the room across the street. One more check was performed, and at 11:00 am, the third test was conducted. Anna rotated the dial to redouble the strength of the signal, and the test was successful. The electronic receptor picked up a signal, and the two human guinea pigs reported seeing what the camera had captured.

There were brief celebrations, and the rest of the day was spent recording the results. The following morning, the tragedy unfolded. The three government employees and hospital workers all failed to report for duty, and it was soon discovered that all of them had died in their sleep the previous night.

Anna felt particularly awful. It was her hand that had turned the dial. It didn't matter that she was only following the proper procedure, nor that someone else would have turned the dial if she had not been there. She was offered time off to recover from the shock but insisted on working harder than ever. Doing more to help more people was the only way she felt she could atone for what she had done. She also spent a lot of time with the Professor during this period. They were the only two people at the hospital who knew exactly what had happened, and they gave each other much-needed mutual support.

All work on the project ceased, and the inquiry process began. Postmortems, a thorough medical investigation, and a security inquiry were held, and all parties were exonerated. Martin Knight was never seen again. But a year later, with the shock wearing off, a new government security person, David Allinson, introduced himself and began persuading the professor to recommence his research. He stressed the crucial aims of the project. "Surely there could be few better aims than enabling the blind to see again," she heard him say in a snatch of overheard conversation.

Anna thought long and hard about it and finally agreed to resume work with the professor. They vowed to be even more careful in the future.

Gradually, Anna's life returned to normal, and after a pause when she felt that she could not reasonably spend any social time with anyone, she resumed dating.

8 Brands Hatch
November 2022

Graham did not know what the form of his next communication from the prof would be – but he knew there would be one. This time it was an email. He did not recognise the name or email address of the sender, but once he began reading its contents, it was obvious whom it had come from.

> Graham – I know you said that your love of motor racing does not extend to Truck Racing, but nonetheless, I thought I would let you know that I am treating a couple of my nephews to the event at Brands Hatch next weekend and I've booked a box in the main stand so we can enjoy the day in style. They are the car-mad ones and will probably be running around all the displays and so forth for the whole day, leaving me alone. If you care to drink some of my champagne, please feel free to drop by - I'm told my name will be shown on the outside door of the box and you need merely to knock to receive a warm welcome. I hope to see you there!

"Yes, I bet you do bloody hope to," he said aloud as he read it. He briefly wondered why the prof had chosen this rather strange meeting place but then remembered part of their very brief conversation – that part used as a cover whenever the prof thought they might be overheard. He had once remarked on Graham's address in North Kent being close to where his sister lived and, on another occasion when he spoke about grandchildren, the prof compared it with his own relationship with his two nephews.

He looked up Brands Hatch on the internet and saw that the truck racing event, the last event of the year at the circuit, was scheduled for the coming Saturday. He entered the date in his calendar.

"I am going to have to say yes, aren't I? Not just to a meeting at Brands Hatch but also to go back in time to find out what happened to his bloody

Anna! I'd better start putting some thought into what the fuck it is that I'm going to do, hadn't I?"

He felt better after loudly uttering a couple of expletives and pulled a piece of blank paper and a pencil across the desk. Everything would eventually be typed and printed, but first thoughts were always best noted with the old-fashioned tools.

A few minutes later, he typed the following summary into his computer and printed it. This, and any other additions he could think of, would form his agenda for the meeting on Saturday:

> How/when to jump?
> My background story
> Money – Lottery? ***
> Anna Plan – date for first contact
>   Background info from Prof. Any Suspicions ???***
>   What am I looking for?
> How to signal Professor on the other time plane
> John Bishop? When? How? What to tell him?
> Return date?

And then, to make himself feel that he had at least done some research into his forthcoming 'project' he found an internet site that listed the lottery results for previous years. He would probably need some funds for whatever he was going to do. There might well be travel involved; he would probably need the assistance of a private detective at some point; some palms might need to be greased; and then there were always the unknown unknowns as Dick Cheney had referred to them. He would need more funds than he currently had, and the obvious place to find them would be the lottery.

He needed to find a set of numbers that had been selected as close as possible to his landing date but which were easy to memorise, because he would not be able to take any notes back there with him. He soon spotted the ideal combination:

7 November 2018 Winning Numbers: 4,5,9,40,46,59

Ideal. Just when he would need them, and easy to recall. The jackpot was around six million, enough to fund any plan he came up with, and since it had rolled over, he wasn't directly depriving anyone of it. He would create an automatic entry to every lottery draw as soon as he landed. And, as his plans began to form in the back of his mind, he looked for a second memorable draw for the middle of the following year. He found:

26 June 2019 Winning Numbers: 5,7,9, 24,32,44

Not quite as easy to memorise, so he would have to work on that. These numbers would fit two purposes. If, for any reason, his original win either did not happen or was insufficient, this set would be a backup. Also, if he needed to recruit someone to help him find Anna, he might need to prove his time-travelling credentials. And he could think of no better way to do this than to provide someone with a set of winning numbers for the lottery.

The jackpot for this second set of numbers was £12 million. This one had not rolled over, but he reasoned that even if he had to split it, the original winner would still have more than enough money to celebrate and squander. And it was not as if any of this was real!

He reasoned that the money he was going to win, and was hopefully going to help someone else win, was no more real than the fifteen hundred pounds you receive when you start a game of Monopoly. It is the money you need to take part in the game. And the only way that Graham could keep a level head right now was to think of what he was about to do as a game. A game he would agree to take part in very soon. One that would last about five years, and all being well, one which would end with him returning to where he started, unharmed and unchanged in any way, with enough information to placate the prof. He now knew which two sets of numbers would be on the standing order lottery ticket he would buy online when the game started.

He looked at the list again. He guessed that the date for the jump would be as soon as it could be arranged, and it would show good intent if he presented a full plan. They dared not risk visiting the finance company together as there was a possibility that Graham would be recognised as one of their clients. He would suggest to the prof that he should organise a visit to the solicitors' office across the street from the hospital to carry out the same wireless network checks. Accompanied by Graham, posing as his assistant. During this set of checks, the prof would arrange for the beam to be activated from his office, and Graham would attempt to make the 'jump'.

He would suggest this plan to the prof on Saturday at Brands Hatch – and quiz him heavily on every snippet of information he could gather about Anna. Including her full HR file from the hospital. And he needed to make sure that the prof got this to him at least a couple of days before the jump so that he could memorise the contents and make sure he knew everything it was possible to know about this woman for whom he was about to set out on what might be a wild goose chase.

-

When he arrived at the prof's executive Suite at Brands Hatch on Saturday lunchtime, he was introduced to the prof's two nephews – he guessed their ages to be about thirteen and fifteen. They certainly showed the typical situation of the young teenager – keen to take up the offer of a free day out at a car racing event, but awkward in the company of their uncle. They positively itched to go out and look at some of the exhibits – preferably with the accompaniment of a large burger and chips and without the company of any embarrassing adults.

When the prof asked, "Would you like to go and get a burger while I chat with my friend?" there was only the briefest hesitation – just enough time for the handing over of sufficient funds to satisfy their hunger.

"Is it OK if we go and look and some of the cars and trucks?" the older one asked.

"Yes. But be back by three, OK?"

They departed rapidly, and the prof turned expectantly to Graham.

He spoke before the prof had a chance to. "OK. I'll do it," was all he had to say to produce an effusive and slightly embarrassing hug from the prof, who seemed close to tears.

"I am so very, very grateful," he said, doing his best to choke back the emotion he obviously felt.

The next two hours were filled by quizzing the prof about everything he knew about Anna while simultaneously availing himself of the free food and drink on offer to box-holders. There were repeated apologies from the prof for how little he knew about his close colleague – their relationship having been so focussed on work matters. Graham had to act as grand inquisitor. There were plenty of snippets he gleaned, but extracting them was worse than pulling teeth.

At the end of the session, he knew that Anna was born in East Germany, had left there in the nineteen nineties, and then spent a few years in Munich before coming to London for her first job at the hospital. She became his assistant soon afterwards.

She was a very organised person – but the prof knew little about her home life beyond the fact that she lived alone in an apartment. He had never visited until her disappearance but assumed that she must be as organised and detail-oriented at home as at work. She was well-read, both in English and German and, he assumed, probably possessed plenty of books. The only family he knew of was her younger sister, who lived in Dresden.

According to the prof, she was friendly with several of her fellow workers, almost all female, but did not appear to have any particularly close friends at work. Eventually, Graham extracted the fact that Anna did have a social life. She was registered with some dating agency, he recalled, and very occasionally spoke of one or other of the interesting gentlemen she had met – but it seemed as if she used it as a source of social life, rather than a serious search for a life partner. Graham stressed that it was vital that he knew which agency she was with and extracted a promise from the professor that he would discover this.

Lastly, he asked the professor the standard investigator's question, "Was there anything unusual in her behaviour in the time leading up to her disappearance?" After thinking for several seconds, he did recall one thing. He had asked Louise Hillier in HR, who was the closest that Anna had to a friend in the hospital, if there was anything she could remember. She had remarked that Anna had been dating the same person for a long time. This was unusual for her because most of her dating relationships only lasted a few months until her partner realised she had no intention of making any long-term commitment. But this guy had stayed with her right through lockdown and beyond. He was reasonably sure that this conversation had taken place only a few days before he last saw her. However, the professor was unable to give any detail whatsoever about the man concerned.

Graham made notes on his phone of the key facts – but by the time he had asked every question he could think of, was disappointed by how little he had gathered. The only shred of a lead was the person Anna had been dating at the time of her disappearance.

Lastly, he asked the professor for the piece of information that he would need as a signal.

"You need to tell me one fact. Give me one piece of information that only you know. Something you have never told another living soul. Because when I meet you back in time, you won't know me. I may need to prove to you that I'm a time-traveller and that I am there at your request. The only way I can do this is by telling you something I could only have found out from you."

The prof thought long and hard before he came up with an answer, He delivered the information slowly and quietly. "I keep a photograph of a young woman in a blue dress in my family bible."

Graham did not push to find out the name of the woman in the picture, but from the look on the professor's face as he revealed this information, Graham was reasonably sure that the person in the photograph was the same person they had been discussing. Anna. It had been a wrench for the prof to even let him know of the photo's existence, and that would be enough to fit his purpose.

Having exhausted his information gathering sooner than he had hoped, there was time left for the prof to ask about his plans.

"May I ask if you will be travelling to the same date as last time - or have you another date in mind?" he asked.

"If you don't mind, I'll keep that to myself. I'm trying to replicate my previous jump as closely as possible, so I'll not say, if you don't mind."

"But what is your plan when you get back there?" The prof was too interested in the outcome not to push for more information.

"All I can tell you is that I will try to make contact with her via the dating agency. And if I need to, I'll contact our friend John (or Martin) to see if he has any information or can get me some. It'll be a challenge because, like yourself, he will have no recognition that we had previously met, and I'll have to persuade him to believe my crazy story. I may also need to find a private detective to help, but I won't know until I get there. I'll have to react to whatever it is I find."

The boys returned, and the two adults had to spend some time watching the racing – which they both found to be rather dull after a few minutes. They kept up the pretence of enjoying it and listened with as much enthusiasm as they could muster to try to match the boys' obvious excitement.

When they eventually made their way back to their cars at the end of the day, Graham reminded the prof of the importance of him receiving Anna's file and the agency name as soon as possible. Having heard the outline plan, he agreed that they should meet in the lobby of the office building opposite the hospital at 10:45 on Monday morning, nine days away.

Graham returned home. In his way of occasionally talking to himself about important things, he could be heard to say, "What have I done? What the fuck have I agreed to?" more than once in the next few days as he walked around his home.

-

A copy of Anna Mueller's personnel file was delivered to Graham's house on Wednesday. It was less helpful than he had hoped. It confirmed her date of birth, March 25, 1965, and her place of birth as Dresden, then in East Germany. He recognised this as the same city where her sister now lived, according to the prof, which made sense. There were details of her university, first medical appointment (in Berlin, he noted), and subsequent employment dates at a hospital in Munich before she obtained a job at Moorfields. Her medical qualifications were listed and had obviously been verified. Still, most of the information in the file was either in German and/or medical technical speak, so it was not of much help.

The photograph looked like it had been officially taken when ID cards were first introduced, several years ago. It reminded him of the old joke 'I've been so ill recently I've begun to look like my passport photo.' It would not be much use in helping him identify her. Unhelpfully, an attached note contained the message: 'Not sure of the name of the dating agency'.

"Twenty bloody years she's worked for him, and he still knows fuck all about her," he exclaimed in frustration. Apart from helping him to discover her date of birth and her home address, the file had been largely worthless. Hopefully, he would be able to find a better likeness of her when he found out the name of the dating agency and accessed it – but that would be in a different lifetime.

-

Graham had reached his decision on his destination date. He had been tempted to return to his original landing date of 1970. Partly because he knew it had worked before – and in a situation filled with so many uncertainties, each known known was not easily relinquished. And he could not deny the temptation of being a teenage millionaire, and the life of pleasure he could envisage rolling out before him and the opportunity to prevent some of Carol's suffering.

He had been comfortable in his real life – a good job, well paid with plenty of overseas travel. He had been close to some real wealth – he'd been on business trips to entertain and lure clients: Posh restaurants, casinos, even the occasional lap dancing bar. But never in a situation to really throw lots of money away. But he'd been there and seen others do so. And he'd been invited to a couple of sales reward 'conferences'. Three days in five-star resorts. But that was as far as it had gone. He'd walked through the business class section of planes on his trips to the US headquarters and wondered what it would be like to actually enjoy a flight at the front of the plane instead of just enduring it in the cheap seats at the back.

He had been wealthy in his second life – but had not reached the full potential a pre-planned jump could give him. It had taken many years to gather the wealth that he could, with pre-planning, achieve within days of landing this time around.

He had even sketched a plan for his potential second landing in 1970. There was no national lottery back then, but there were the football pools which he had re-familiarised himself with on his last jump. All he would have to do before the jump was to look up the date when only eight football matches resulted in a scoring draw, remember the names of the home teams and then enter those on his football coupon. That would virtually certainly result in him winning a jackpot. In 1970, these were about £300,000 – worth over ten million pounds in 2022 terms. The UK stock market wasn't fantastic back then, but he could surely find some shares that had doubled in price in each of the next few years. He should be able to complete his college degree and be a twenty-one-year-old millionaire. Then there would be only a few years to wait for the nineteen eighties, the launch of Apple, Microsoft, and so on. Shares that grew tenfold in value and more within the year. Yes, becoming a thirty-year-old billionaire was not beyond possibility.

What stopped that train of thought was thinking about his grandchildren. He had only recently seen them at his birthday party – his first contact with them for fifty years – and did not want to wait another fifty years before seeing them again. However, he thought to himself, when the delightful little tots that they are now, turn into spotty, quarrelsome teenagers in a few years, maybe he would rethink it. He would not rule out a future return trip. But for now, he would stick to his original plan and go back just four years. To the first anniversary of his wife's death.

-

Having committed to memory the few facts he had gathered about Anna and the two sets of lottery numbers, he met the prof in the ground floor lobby of 179 City Road on the morning of Friday, December 1st. A few minutes later, they were alone in the conference room of Mulgrave, Shervin, and White - Solicitors. The prof was pretending to take readings and entering them into his iPad.

Graham stared out the window and tried to remember his thoughts and feelings of that day back in October 2018. The first anniversary of his wife's death when he had given himself a severe talking to.

To replicate how he had started his first time-travel jump, he spoke his thoughts about that day four years earlier, loud enough for the professor to hear. He was not sure if the prof was listening to what he was saying or if he was too embarrassed by Graham's revelations of inner thoughts and feelings to respond. Maybe he thought it important to leave Graham uninterrupted to ascertain the conditions for his jump were optimal. But he remained silent. Graham reckoned he had completed all he could vocalise and remembered that the signal test was scheduled to last only fifteen minutes, so he broke his chain of thought.

"I guess we will both have to wait for tomorrow morning to see if this was successful or not," he said and received little more than a grunt in acknowledgement.

Returning to the reception area, they shook hands and went their separate ways. Graham did his best to repeat the steps that he had followed after making his first jump. He had lunch in the same pub – alone this time – took the train home, walked back to his house from the rail station, pottered around his house, and had a light evening meal.

'I hope it's a good sign that I'm feeling as knackered as I did last time' he thought. 'I guess I'm either heading for a jump, or I'm just getting older and can't take the strain. I'll know one way or another when I wake.' These were his last thoughts as he drifted off to sleep.

9 First Report
September 2014

David Allinson was nervous about making his first report to the Colonel about the project that he had been managing for almost a year. He was pleased with his progress and was sure that he had not bothered the Colonel unnecessarily in the past twelve months. But his instructions had been clear. "Make sure that security is watertight, and if you encounter anything out of the ordinary in this respect, bring it directly to me." He was sure that what he had recently been informed of qualified under this heading. He knocked on the Colonel's door at five-thirty as instructed.

Timothy Williams was well aware that he had acquired the nickname of the Colonel. He had been selected for the job of head of the Service – it was not the type of job that was ever advertised – for several reasons. His years of experience in the Police, culminating with a well-respected and successful stint as head of the counter-terrorism branch, were crucial. But perhaps even more so was his background. Generations of army service were in his family – all at high rank. Such was the level of expectation in his family that his decision to join the police force rather than one of the armed forces was seen as rebellion.

His life experience had given him capability and a certain bearing. For those men in grey who effectively chose the head of the Secret Service, he was what they were looking for to re-establish the form of discipline they believed had been missing for years.

He remembered that on his first day in his new role, he had briefed his secretary on some immediate actions that needed to take place in and around his office and some of the daily routines he wished to establish when she had asked, "What am I to call you?"

The question had been unexpected – in the police, senior personnel were always addressed either by rank or just plain 'sir', but he was quick to discover that this did not apply in his new role. He hesitated before answering and his secretary continued, "I'm happy for you to call me either June or Mrs Davis, whichever you feel more comfortable with. But are we to address you as Mr. Williams, Commander, or something else?"

"How did you address my predecessor?" he asked, and she replied, "He asked us to use his first name." The tone with which she answered his question made it abundantly clear that she was very unhappy with this relaxed attitude.

"I'd prefer to be addressed simply as 'sir,' if that is acceptable," he replied.

"Oh, yes, that is completely acceptable, sir", she replied, coming as close to smiling as she was capable.

"And one more thing, Mrs. Davis. I believe you have the ability and the authority to pass on this instruction to everyone else who reports to me."

The nickname of the Colonel was established soon after this, and when he heard about it, he was not displeased. 'Coming from the police, there are plenty of other nicknames I might have acquired that would be a whole lot worse,' he reasoned.

He called David into his office as soon as he heard the knock. He knew there was no chance this meeting would be a complete secret, but setting the time at the end of the working day kept it from being openly advertised. He beckoned him into one of the easy chairs and offered him a drink. David knew that the Colonel's refrigerator contained nothing other than a wide range of cold, fizzy drinks and asked if he might have a coke.

"I've been keeping an eye on your reports from Moorfields. Everything seems to be going very well?"

"Yes sir, things are progressing – slowly I'm afraid, but there is movement."

"And now you've found something out of the ordinary, I assume?"

"Yes sir. I organised a thorough sweep of all the people involved in the project when I took over, sir. The only question mark was over the main assistant to the professor. Her background gave me a little cause for concern, so we dug a little deeper."

"She was originally from East Germany if I remember right?"

"Indeed sir. So, we checked her background and have recently discovered that her father was mentioned in the Rosenholz Files."

This brought back memories for the Colonel. He had been in the field when the issue of the Rosenholz files first surfaced. They contained information, including the names of employees and helpers of the Hauptverwaltung Aufklärung, the primary foreign intelligence agency of the former German Democratic Republic, or East Germany as most people knew it. And he remembered with some regret that during the German reunification, the files ended up in the hands of the CIA under unclear circumstances.

"Interesting, I'm not sure if we knew that about him before now. What was his real job?"

"He was a university lecturer, sir. Doctor of History, specialising in twentieth-century European History. He rose to become head of the department."

"I assume he travelled to meetings and symposiums?"

"Yes, sir. He probably travelled as frequently as anybody from that part of the world at that time."

"And no doubt did his best to recruit sympathisers and gather information – which was why he was in those files which the Stasi so obligingly left behind after their demise."

"Exactly. We're keeping an extra close eye on his daughter just in case. I didn't bring it to your attention at the time, but it was in my regular report. And I also checked one step further. Miss Mueller appears to have a much healthier financial situation than one would expect. She owns a nice maisonette and has all but paid off the mortgage on it – and it's not easy to do that on her salary."

"But your report did explain it."

"Yes sir. It seems she is an active member of a website known as 'Select Few' – a glorified sugar-daddy site if ever there was one –so I checked her contacts and found what I expected. Frequent dates with a string of men older than herself; all holding senior positions in commerce, finance, real estate, that sort of thing."

The Colonel inwardly shuddered at David's use of the phrase 'real estate'. 'Another Americanism creeping into our vocabulary', he thought. 'Why can't he just say 'property' or 'estate agency'?' His concern went unspoken, and David continued.

"But recently we have come across something of an anomaly. She has recently dated this man." He placed a photo, whose blurred detail meant that it was no doubt obtained surreptitiously, on the Colonel's desk. "He uses the name Karl Kominski and purports to be a senior public servant, but we can find out nothing about him. He's a complete blank."

"Which leads you to assume he is not who he pretends to be," the Colonel allowed himself a brief smile. "It appears that your ability to find out who she is dating and what information they place on their profile is very thorough. I will not ask about your methods."

David took this as a compliment, and both smiled and relaxed a little.

"So, you would like me to see if I can find out anything about him?" the Colonel asked.

"Yes sir."

"I will see what I can do. And in the meantime, what are you doing about the young woman?

"We've slightly reassigned her duties, sir. She's a very valuable member of the medical team, but we're making sure that she only sees that side of the project and is not involved in the stuff we're interested in."

"Splendid – seems like you've got things under control."

The meeting finished with some brief chatter, and both men swallowed the last of their soft drinks.

"I'll contact the other lot and see if they know anything," the Colonel said to David as he showed him out the door.

Moments later, he was on the phone with his opposite number in 'the other lot' arranging a meeting over coffee first thing the next day.

In his first meeting with his new boss, the Home Secretary, Timothy Williams made no secret of his dislike of the Secret Service's structure. He told his new boss that he thought it was outdated and needed complete renewal to meet the needs of the modern world.

"It's like Manchester United playing in Europe and using one team and one manager for the home leg, and then a completely different team and a completely different manager for the away leg," was how he had put it, knowing his new boss's reported liking for football.

He had pushed his opinion one step further in reply to the expected platitudes.

"It may have suited the way the game was played in the old days," he continued. He had already picked up the habit of referring to the secret world as 'a game'. So many of his colleagues used the term. Any references to his new world as a trade, a profession, a business, or anything else were far outnumbered by references to it as a game.

"But it's different now. Back then it was a game of two sides – them and us – played out on a board with a section for Europe and another for the Middle East. Nowadays there are far more players and far more board squares. The oil countries have their teams. So do the Chinese. Not to mention several others. And the devil is that while you might be playing *against* some players on one part of the board, those same players are on your side on a different part of the board."

But he had to comply with the existing structure and the rules that accompanied it. So, he continued to figuratively manage Manchester United only when they played at home. Today he would share an early coffee with the man who was the manager when they played abroad.

"I'd like to know if you recognise this chap," Tim asked as he placed the photo on his desk.

"You could have emailed it to me, you know," Fergus replied.

Fergus Kelly – the manager for away games, or the head of 'the other lot', as Tim sometimes referred to him, was more usually known as 'The Irishman'. Inevitable in the light of his name, but it was five generations and almost a hundred and fifty years since the most recent ancestor of his had wiped the last of the County Mayo mud off his boots.

After generations of his family using more normal 'English' first names, it became fashionable for those of Irish descent to revert to giving their children names from the old country. Hence Fergus had a brother, Sean, and a sister, Roisin, both of whose names shared the two characteristics of an Irish name. They were not pronounced how they appeared and had an accent on one of the letters – so obscure that Fergus could not tell you what it was or where it occurred in either of his siblings' names.

He picked up the photo that Tim had placed on his desk and re-photographed it with his mobile phone. He continued pressing a few buttons on the phone while talking to Tim.

"We don't use the services of a little old lady with an incredible memory anymore, you know. We prefer to use electronic brains." He was referring to Timothy's well-known dislike and distrust of electronic means of communication – born of his time spent in the data division of the police a few years previously.

Fergus pressed a few keys on his desktop keyboard and looked at his computer screen.

"Karl Kominsky is the name he uses. He's a recent recruit to Georgi's team, but we haven't seen him make an appearance on the field yet."

Timothy ignored the slightly smug expression and gave his input.

"I think he's about to take part in his first game," he replied. "Is there any way you could find out if this is the case?"

"I'm due to have lunch with Mr. Golovin next week, I'll let you know if I can find anything out."

"You have lunch together?" Timothy was surprised.

"What's wrong about lunch with the Russian Cultural Attaché?" Fergus asked, using the job title that Georgi Golovin officially had, according to the Russian Embassy website. A title that almost nobody believed.

"Anyway, wasn't it you that said we play the game on different parts of the board, and sometimes we are on the same side?"

Timothy was slightly taken aback that his confidential words, spoken to a senior government minister, were being quoted back at him almost verbatim, but he decided to say nothing.

"It would be good to know if he's following team orders or doing a bit of free-lancing," he replied.

A week later, Timothy received a call from Fergus.

"I thought you might be interested in what I gleaned from Georgi."

"Of course I am."

"Well, apart from him insulting me by saying that he looked forward to having lunch with me because it allowed him to find out where the best value for money lunch could currently be found in London's West End, implying that my expense allowance was a little lighter than his, I was able to get a few pieces of information. It seems they are interested in your East German lady and that Karl is keeping an eye on her once a month across a restaurant table. Special exemption granted."

"Anything else?"

"No, but I will let you know if anything else arises."

"Likewise."

10 Gathering Intelligence
2014

There are many ways in which those involved in the process of gathering intelligence go about the task. The internet age has allowed for a great deal of information to be gathered by even untrained people. Much of it can be discovered without the researcher leaving their desk, possibly without even leaving their home.

However, the very ease of gathering the information makes it more important that the person seeking intelligence – as opposed to just obtaining data - knows *where* to look. That, as they say, is what separates the men from the boys, or, in less sexist terms, separates the successful from the failures. And one good place to begin is by looking in the same place where your rivals are looking.

The word 'rivals' is more appropriate here than 'enemies'. Spying is not really a team game. If it is a game, it's a unique one where sometimes a player can be on your side, and the next minute can be your opponent. So, with very rare exceptions, it is a game where it is everyone for themself.

So, when the UK secret services were less than careful about the many resources they deployed to ensure the security of the Optic Nerve project (subsequently renamed Project Petra) run by Professor Karbajanovic at Moorfield Eye Hospital, they should not have been surprised that other organisations also showed interest.

This being London, where there is a higher representation of members of the intelligence community per square mile than anywhere else on the planet, one group in particular noted the surprising number of people they recognised being seen in the vicinity of the city's premier eye hospital. Perhaps the only surprise is that only one other organisation noticed.

Having noticed this anomaly, internal and external resources were then deployed to investigate, and they confirmed a significant presence of known British Intelligence personnel at the hospital. Then, the online research began, and several threads were explored. The possibility that there was a patient of significance at the hospital was investigated and then eliminated. The presumed intelligence operation had been going for too long for it to involve one patient. After all, this was an eye hospital, and people were not expected to remain in-patients for more than a couple of months, even for the most serious conditions.

This left the main theory that some confidential research of scientific interest was taking place there. The type and size of the deployment of domestic intelligence personnel made this seem most likely. Investigation of this alleged project was not given the highest status by the investigating foreign agency, so the resources made available were limited. The case officer was granted one internal person and one external. She set them both to the task of research, to identify who in the hospital might be involved in a project that could fit the information they knew.

After months of careful digging, the answer emerged that it must be something led by Professor Karbajanovic, and the next stage of investigation commenced—the investigation of the Professor himself. A few days of background research showed that this was not likely an easy task; he was a cross between a workaholic and a hermit. Unmarried with no partner, his immediate family was limited to a sister and her two children, and he had seemingly no interests outside his job and no known weaknesses.

However, his assistant was more promising, and resources were switched to examining his staff. The internal researcher was able to discover that Anna Mueller was a key member of the professor's team. Her background seemed auspicious. Discovering that she was born in East Germany raised their hopes, but caution had to be exercised. Experience showed that those who had left the former Communist state were likely to be either very pro- or very anti-Communist. They were rarely indifferent to it. A fervent anti-Communist was unlikely to be a useful resource for them.

When they delved deeper and found her name on a list of subscribers to an exclusive dating agency, the avenue of approach was obvious. This discovery earned the researcher some praise from her boss – a clear example of lateral thinking and the use of all resources the memo said. The memo did not mention that the membership of this elite dating agency was information that the agency had no right to possess and had been obtained by methods that they were, strictly speaking, not allowed to use.

However, the researcher did not exactly receive fulsome praise from her colleague Karl when he was told that his next task would be to join the same agency and begin dating the target. He was naturally delighted to know that he would receive plenty of assistance in honing his dating profile from both his boss and his female colleague.

He had seen Anna's profile picture, and she was more than attractive enough despite being some ten years older than him. Even worse, he had been told this would be a slow-burn operation. He needed to be fully prepared to date the woman for months, possibly even years.

As far as they could determine, the project that the professor and Anna were involved in had been running for a few years. There had been a setback in 2012, which resulted in the project being placed on the back burner for a time – but recent changes in policy in the UK government meant that the project was moving forward again. It was now on the front burner, but nobody ever used that expression. Karl's task would be to get as close as possible to Anna, to establish a relationship, and to find out if there were any ways in which details of this project could be discovered.

With every part of his profile having received approval, he was allowed to take a few 'practice swings.' He was coached all the way, from his initial online contact to his exploratory emails and request for a date. Neither of his first two dates was ever to suspect that they had been dress rehearsals for a long-term intelligence operation. His conversation over dinner was recorded and analysed by his new advisers. When they were satisfied that he was as ready as possible, he approached Anna Mueller online. With both being cautious – Karl for professional reasons and Anna because that was just the way she was – their email dialogue lasted a month before she finally agreed to meet him.

Karl was pleasantly surprised with their first date. He offered Anna the chance to choose the location of their rendezvous, and she chose a pleasant Italian restaurant on the northern edge of London. She was every bit as attractive as her profile picture – which was a relief to Karl. His experience of dating agency meetings was limited to the two trial dates from the pages of Select Few, and he soon discovered that some ladies used profile pictures that were more than just flattering. They were as far from being accurate as was his profile. Anna, however, was not only pleasant to look at but was also very relaxed and easy to talk to.

He was well-rehearsed in his false profile and his reason for signing up with the agency. The story was that he was a government employee whose job was highly secret. Unusually for a government employee, he was also well rewarded – hence the false wealth shown on his profile could be justified. But the crucial point he had to convey to her, very late in the date when they had reached some level of confidence in each other, was his particular reason for wanting to date her. His first task was to confirm the analysis that his team had made of her.

"I hope you don't mind me asking this, but I do have a question. I'll be delighted to give you a complete and honest answer to the same question if you wish, but what I want to know is why you are a member of this dating agency. You are an attractive, intelligent, and very personable lady. One who would easily attract many men, which makes it difficult to understand why you find it necessary to use such a method of finding a date."

"Oh, it's very simple," she replied. It was not the first time she had been asked this – although it usually came at a later stage in the dating process and was asked in a more roundabout way.

"I've told you that I love my job. I'm privileged to be able to find intellectual stimulation in my employment, to work with some wonderfully stimulating colleagues, and to genuinely help people because of what I do."

Karl nodded at each point she made.

"But I also enjoy the finer things in life, Karl. Eating good food, attending the theatre or the occasional concert, wearing nice clothes…"

"And nice jewellery and expensive perfume," Karl continued.

"Indeed," she smiled. "But sadly, the health service does not provide me with enough funds to achieve this, so I look to the friends I meet through the agency to give me this slice of life. And I retain enough romance, even at this stage of life, to hope that one day I may yet find my Mister Right."

Anna felt she had given enough and took up Karl's counter-offer. "So, why are you a member of the agency?"

Karl felt that Anna's answer had almost perfectly fitted the analysis that his team had provided. Putting it very bluntly, she was in it for the money. He proceeded with the second stage of his strategy.

"Unfortunately, when you are in such an important confidential part of the system as I am," he said, stressing the word confidential, "You are subject to certain levels of scrutiny." The last word was also stressed.

"This is understood, of course, but there are certain parts of my life that I really wish to keep private. So, there needs to be a barrier of some sort. Maybe a smoke screen would be a better description. I am, by nature, a very private person, and if I choose not to show myself, it elicits suspicion. If I were to be seen going out from time to time with an attractive lady, there would be less attention paid to me, you understand?"

He paused to make sure that Anna was still following him, and her sympathetic nod and smile indicated that she was.

"I find you to be the most wonderful company. And I hope you are not offended by my suggestion. I would dearly love it if you could accompany me on a date once a month or so. I'd be happy for you to choose the venues for our meals or to suggest a show or a concert you wish to see. I only ask that you behave as a girlfriend would behave in public. There would be no demands on you other than this. I am sure that you understand that the very reason that I wish to erect a smoke screen confirms that I would never make any such demands of you."

Anna was about to reply, but he held up his hand to stop her and continued to speak. "I trust you will not be offended, but I am asking you to give up some of your time – and there is never a chance that I will be the Mister Right you may be seeking. I am more than happy to compensate you for your time. Would an envelope with two hundred pounds in it at the end of our evenings together be acceptable to you?"

Anna had never been so directly propositioned, but her surprise was more pleasant than it might have been. She was so quick to think, 'Two hundred a month. That would make some dent in that mortgage, wouldn't it? I'll soon be well on my way to paying it off if this continues.'

"Well, let's see how it works out, shall we?" she answered.

They dated about once a month from that day forward. It could never be called a relationship – but it was a fixed point in both their lives and, free from the restrictions of any normal relationship that might have acted to shorten their time together, they found the time spent together to be relaxed. However, the sharing that appeared to be happening was false. Anna told Karl little bits about her work that he reported back and pieced together (with the help of his colleagues) over the months. The story he told Anna was of a completely fictitious job.

And Anna's reporting back was different. She chatted from time to time with Louise who had introduced her to Select Few all those years ago.

When Anna was asked about her 'latest' – which was how Louise always put it, Anna gave a guarded reply.

"It's a little odd," she said. "Very pleasant but odd. He asked me to go out with him once a month so that it looks like he's in a relationship – but he has no interest in being in one."

"You mean he's gay? Surely this is not your first?"

"No. It isn't, and he isn't."

"Are you sure?"

"Look, all my life I've dealt with it. Straight guys always look at my breasts first and my face second." She made an exaggerated gesture of flipping her head down and then up which made Louise laugh. (She had wanted to say 'tits' instead of 'breasts' to make her point more forcefully but chickened out at the last minute. She hated the word. She didn't mind 'boobs', 'knockers', 'baps', or any of the other silly names men used to label this part of the female anatomy, but she hated the word *tits*.)

"Well, I've not got the firepower you have in that department," Louise replied with a downward nod of her head and a smile, "so I'll take your word for it. But if he's behaving oddly and you're concerned, please be careful."

"I'm more puzzled than concerned. But I'll be careful, you can be sure of that."

11 The Tallest Church Spire in the UK
March 2018

Two events – or three, depending on how you count them – which occurred in March 2018 had a significant impact on the life of Karl Kominsky.

The event that is familiar to the wider world is a complex story related here from a British point of view. If the same story were viewed from another perspective, it might be told differently, but since it occurred in the UK, it seems sensible to report it from a domestic point of view.

According to the British version of the story, on March 4th, 2018, two young Russian men, whose real names were Alexander Miskin and Anatoly Vladimirovich Chepiga, travelled under the aliases of Alexander Petrov and Ruslan Boshirov, respectively, to the British city of Salisbury, and visited the home of Sergei Skripal.

Sergei Skripal, a former Russian military officer and double agent for the British intelligence agencies, had taken up permanent residence in the UK and, in early March 2018, was being visited by his daughter Yulia, at his home in Salisbury, a small historic town in the West of England.

Miskin and Chepiga placed a quantity of a Novichok nerve agent on the door[knob of the front door of Sergei's house in an attempt to assassinate him – an attempt that proved to be unsuccessful. The two visitors returned to Russia the next day.

Russia disputes this version of the story, and the two men, when subsequently interviewed on Russian TV, claimed that they had been visiting Salisbury to see the famous Cathedral. Their choice of a place to visit was quite logical, even if their story was not. Salisbury Cathedral boasts a spire that is 123 meters high, which became the tallest church spire in the United Kingdom in 1561 and has remained so until the present day.

The timing of this whole event was particularly unfortunate for Karl Kominsky. The previous day he had requested permission to immediately return to Russia for compassionate reasons. Karl's mother had been taken into hospital, and he had received a message from a friend that his mother was almost certainly dying. Normally, his request for immediate compassionate leave would have been granted, and the necessary paperwork was being processed when the news of events in Salisbury broke. Knowing that there would be a reaction from the British government, but not knowing what it would be, the Russian Embassy issued an internal edict that all travel was immediately banned for all employees.

By the time the travel ban was lifted a few days later, Karl's mother had died. He was able to attend the funeral but had not been able to say his last farewell to his mother while she was still alive. The impact on him was devastating. His mother was the only human being with whom he had ever formed an emotional connection in his forty years on the planet.

Karl was not a bad man. He was admired by his colleagues for his professionalism and, although quiet and withdrawn, seemed to get on well with everyone. But nobody would ever include him on their list of friends, and nobody ever had done. It was not that he did not like people – he just never formed any emotional attachment to anyone. Just as this unusual personality trait had made him the ideal person for the false relationship with Anna (he regarded every meeting with her as a work task to be completed professionally – and that was what he did) it also meant that his enforced inability to say goodbye to his mother affected him deeply. She had been the only person in the world to whom he related on a personal level, and he was not allowed to say goodbye to her. His professional dedication to his job meant he never showed it, but the scar was deep and permanent.

He knew, deep down, that his employers did not really care for him. Moreover, he was truly alone and therefore had to decide his long-term aims. Whatever they were, he should take whatever steps were necessary to achieve them.

He was allowed a few days off from his duties; many of the activities were placed on temporary hold anyway until the storm caused by events in Salisbury had blown over.

Karl spent much of this time walking around Hyde Park, which was only a few meters away from his accommodation in central London. The 350 acres the park covered gave him ample space to walk and lose himself in thought as the depression passed through him.

It was a pleasant change from the urban life he lived. But the park's ordered neatness only increased his longing for the vast open untamed space that had been part of his early life in Russia. He had no desire to return there now, other than the immediate wish to say a farewell to his mother. But his desire to live somewhere that had access to vast wilderness started to gnaw away at him.

He also spent time walking around the gardens of Grosvenor Square, close to his home and office. He was struck by much of the symbolism. The huge building that had once been the Embassy of the USA was now being redeveloped, and the main contractor was neither an American nor a British company. It was Arab-owned, as presumably would be the luxury hotel that the building would become in a couple of years. This made him smile – a symbol of what the world was becoming, perhaps.

Then, there were the gardens within the square. A huge memorial to the American forces who had fought alongside their British Allies in World War Two was now dirty and overgrown with moss. The dedication carved into the paving stones was now so cracked and broken that it was almost illegible. You could read so much into these things if you wanted.

After the funeral, Karl mastered his grief, buried his doubts, and returned to his duties, including the monthly meeting with Anna. He apologised to her for having had to cancel their original date and explained why. It was a rare occasion when the whole evening with her was spent talking about him. After their date, he had nothing to add to his growing pile of information about her and openly admitted it in his report to his superiors.

12 The Princess and the P.D.
September 2018

When Karl attended his mother's funeral, he began a long overdue process of asking himself what his life goals were. He was now truly alone. If he had any living relatives, he was unaware of their existence, and they were so distantly related that it was unimportant anyway.

Throughout his life, he had not had a clear sense of direction. He only knew the next step: pass the school exams, apply for military college, work hard, follow orders, and use the skills that you have been provided with. Be loyal.

But the trip to and from his mother's funeral gave him thinking time. The long train journey from Moscow to his home-town reminded him of what it was about Russia that he loved and missed so profoundly. The wide-open spaces. Panoramic views that seemed to go on forever. Big skies. A landscape that made any human being feel truly anonymous and insignificant. He longed to be back in this environment, away from the crowded streets, and incessant traffic of London. He just wished to find somewhere with wide open spaces but accompanied by plumbing that worked, an electricity supply that could be relied on, and without the need for a multiple-hour train journey to rejoin the twenty-first century.

-

He had progressed into the Secret Service from the military while posted to East Germany. It was noted that he had a truly remarkable ability to pick up a foreign language. Within weeks he was able to converse fluently with the local military and the local citizens. To his superiors, his accent seemed indistinguishable from a native. He was assigned to intelligence operations, taken out of uniform, and later transferred to his current role.

When the number of people in his division stationed in Germany was drastically reduced in the early 1990s, Karl was transferred to the UK in the hope that his ability to pick up a new language quickly would be useful. It was, and he soon conversed with existing staff and the locals as if he had spoken English all his life.

Karl had always known, deep down, that he would have to make his own way, to shape his own future. His motivation was reinforced, and the first steps became possible when he received an unusual assignment.

-

Karl held no particular views about the oligarchs in Russia. He had even glimpsed one or two of them in the course of his duty. It was a waste of time to concern oneself with them. It was as pointless as having an opinion about the weather. It was what it was. Oligarchs came and went. If he thought about them at all, it was to think of them using a word he had heard in England – 'chancers.' People with the good fortune to be in the right place at the right time and the flexible moral code that allowed them to maximise their good fortune. That was it. He did not expect his opinion would change if he knew more about them. He was about to find out if this was true.

-

Christina was the daughter of Maksim Komlichenko, one of the richest Russian oligarchs in London. She had spent most of her childhood in the UK, so when she completed her A-Level exams at her private school in the summer of 2018, her wish was to do what her contemporaries did and go on to take a degree course at a British university. Her chosen course was History of Art, and the university she wished to attend was in Surrey, about forty miles south-west of the central London apartment where her father lived with the latest of her stepmothers.

Her father wanted only to please his daughter. So he arranged to allow her to attend the university so that she could enjoy making an independent life for herself - but with the additional security measures necessary for the daughter of such a high-profile father. He rented a house close to the university and contracted two bodyguards to provide her with twenty-four-hour security. His close association with the government allowed him to call upon state resources for help.

Karl and his younger colleague, Ruslan Silyanov, were selected for the duty and were briefed by their boss, Georgi Golovin.

"You two will be Private Detectives for the next year". Handing them both a copy of the briefing dossier with Christina's name and picture on the cover, he continued, "You'll be guarding a very special young lady. You'll live in the annexe of the house she is renting. You will watch her from the day she starts university to the day she returns home for the vacation. One or other of you will be within two meters of her twenty-four hours a day, seven days a week. Understood? The only possible exceptions to this are when you guard the only entrance to a room in which she is either alone or in the sole company of someone on our trusted list of contacts. In other words, one of you is to be stationed awake outside her bedroom all night, and if she goes into any room at college or anywhere else and there is more than one person in it, you go in there with her and stay there. Is that clear?"

They voiced their consent, and their briefing ended with the words, "It's up to you how you apportion your duties between you. If you fuck up and anything happens to her, you better wish that you are killed in the process, because it will be much better for you than what would happen to you otherwise."

After leaving the meeting, Ruslan suggested that they split the working day into two shifts from midnight to midday.

"Not the best time to do the changeover, Karl said. She'll likely be at university at noon and still out somewhere at midnight if she's like most eighteen-year-olds. Probably better to split at 6 pm and 6 am."

"But that means one of us gets to go to school with her every day and the other gets to party with her every night," Ruslan countered, fearing that as the junior member of the protective partnership, he would be drawing the short straw."

"You don't fancy the day shift then?"

"No fucking way" was the succinct reply.

"Well, isn't it very lucky for you that I'm a sad, tired old man who'll volunteer for the day shift?"

Ruslan could hardly believe his luck. "But you had better be wide awake when I take over from you outside her bedroom every morning, or I'll have your balls on a skewer," Karl responded as a statement of his seniority.

And that was how it worked out. Karl rose at about five every morning and took a brief run through the peaceful woods surrounding their charge's house, before showering, changing, and going to meet his colleague in the corridor outside Christina's bedroom, where he was usually regaled with details of the wonderful restaurant, or the exclusive party they had attended the previous night.

Christina would emerge from her bedroom at about eight am, and Karl would join her for breakfast. Shortly after, they travelled to university together. He offered to drive, but Christina insisted on driving – the car had been a congratulations present from her father. A white Range Rover with the palest leather interior imaginable and every possible accessory fitted. During some of his copious free time one evening, Karl went on to the appropriate website and worked out that the car had cost more than a hundred thousand pounds.

He accompanied her to her lectures and tutorials – the university had been made aware of her special requirements and was only too happy to accommodate the needs of their celebrity pupil, anticipating some reward from her father in a future endowment. He tried his best to follow what was being presented and discussed, but he found there were so many words that were unfamiliar to him that it was too difficult. But Karl was not so easily put off – he asked Christina if she could take some time when they were alone together on their journeys to and from the college, over breakfast or occasional other moments, to explain some things to him and she was happy to oblige.

So, he took a small notebook and pen into the lectures and tutorials and noted words that were bandied around – like impressionism, cubism, and so on. Later, he would ask about their meaning, and Christina would patiently explain. He also took the opportunity to ask her to explain some of the slang terms that she and her friends used. Thus, he learned that it was common to use a word to mean its opposite, so that 'bad' meant 'good' and so forth. On one occasion, he asked her the meaning of a word one of her friends used. "What does 'peng' mean?" he asked, and she chuckled.

"It means something is really good. Beautiful. Lots of rizz," she replied, knowing that she would also have to explain 'rizz'. "Where did you hear that?" she asked.

"The boy with the red hair," he replied.

"And what was it he described as 'peng'?" she asked and caused Karl to blush slightly.

"I think we both know," he replied - and this time Christina blushed.

-

Sometimes, Christina would visit her parents on Saturday, accompanied by Karl – his responsibility for her protection beginning and ending at the doorway of her parents' apartment. He saw very little of the apartment – being ushered to the kitchen shortly after arrival and spending the whole of Christina's visit talking to the kitchen staff. Even so, he had never seen such luxury – even in his occasional visits to Embassies and government official residences.

His first visit occurred about a month after his duties commenced, and he was taken aback when Christina's father sought him out and spoke to him briefly.

"Christina tells me you are doing an excellent job," he said, speaking his mother tongue and revealing in his diction to his fellow countryman that he was a man of very ordinary background. No Moscow-influenced words or accent showed up in his speech.

"She tells me you have gone out of your way to do your duty and to make her feel comfortable. I wanted you to know that she is very precious to me, and I am very grateful that you are taking extra care of her. I only know one way to express my gratitude." He accompanied the last sentence of his brief speech by handing a small packet to Karl, turning on his heel, and leaving the room.

Karl recognised that the envelope could only contain one thing but did not examine it. He put it immediately into the inside pocket of his light leather jacket, the one that was always either on his back or within one meter reach. The small packet would help balance the other inside pocket, which contained a small, light handgun. Later, when he was alone, he opened the envelope and found twenty £50 notes. He wondered briefly if this was a one-off gesture or the start of a regular reward. The gesture was repeated a month later, and Karl understood that he now had a problem. A good problem, maybe, but a problem, nonetheless.

His possessions could be searched at any time, and while he had been able to keep one packet hidden on his person since receiving it, a growing number of such gifts would be challenging to hide. The act of hiding them took him across some metaphorical bridge to a different status. But it was what he had resolved a few months back when his mother had died. He would join the 'chancers'. He would never be an oligarch he laughed to himself – but he could take this first opportunity to feather his nest for the future.

Once he put his mind to it, the method was ridiculously simple. But first, he needed a little help from a co-conspirator, and that opportunity came a few days later.

"Can I ask you a question?" Christina asked on their drive back to the house from college.

"Of course," he replied.

"What exactly are your instructions concerning me?"

"I am to keep you safe at all costs from any and every threat".

"Do you have to accompany me absolutely everywhere?"

"The only exceptions are when you are truly alone in a room with no other entrance and are accompanied by just one person, provided that person is on the list of safe persons."

"And that list of safe persons?"

"Your family, servants, employees, and staff members of the college."

"Can anyone be added to this list? What if I wanted to study with a fellow student?"

Karl began to see the direction the conversation was heading.

"If you could give me the name of that person, I am sure that he can be checked out, and if he is OK, we could add him to the list.

Cristina digested this careful reply before voicing her follow-up question.

"Are you also tasked with reporting on my activities?"

"No, I have never been asked to do that."

"And what would you do if you were asked?"

"I would be as truthful as possible but only offer the requested information. For example, if you were studying with a fellow student, I would say so. I would not see a need to report anything more closely than that."

Christina was silent for a moment before continuing, "Could you add someone to the list for me?"

"The boy with the red hair?" he asked, and she blushed slightly before answering.

"His name is Cyrille Dupont. He's from France."

"I am sure we can get his details from the college. I will let you know if there is a problem."

Cyrille was duly checked out and added to the safe list. When Christina accompanied him to his flat a few days later, Karl told them he had to check that nobody else was on the premises and then would wait in the kitchen until they had finished studying.

When he accompanied Christina on her next shopping trip, he asked if she would please wait in the bank while he met a member of the bank's staff, and of course, she agreed.

"Can we put this on the same list as your studying sessions with the red-haired boy?" he asked, adding, for clarification, "Only you and I need ever know that it happened."

Christina smiled and nodded.

It had been simple. Like all the embassy staff in his line of work, Karl carried a UK driving licence with his photo and the details of a perfectly ordinary citizen, just in case he needed to 'prove' that that was what he was. In his case, he was Peter Eastwood, who lived in Slough, a town he had never even visited. Taking this driving licence into the bank, he intended to open an account into which he could deposit his bonus – which looked like arriving every month.

A minor setback of needing to prove his address was overcome by apologising that he had not updated his licence and providing a utility bill from his new address. He had taken a utility bill from Christina's house, and with a smartphone and a laptop, produced one with his name instead of hers on it. If the bank were to use this address to communicate with him, any mail could be intercepted as he was first to the mailbox every day anyway.

The assistant bank manager was happy to open both a current account and a savings account for him - and to explain that a bank card would arrive by post in a few days, which could be used in the machine in the branch to withdraw money or to deposit cash or cheques at any time.

-

By the end of the summer term, Christina's romance was still alive but had to be placed on hold as Cyrille needed to return to Paris, and she had to accompany her parents on their Caribbean vacation. Karl's bank balance had grown to five figures, and his knowledge of modern art was significantly enhanced. It was a dreadful disappointment for him to learn in September that he would not be resuming this duty.

"Did she fail her exams?" he asked his boss.

"No, she did not fail. It was others who failed," was the cryptic reply.

"It appears that her father no longer qualifies for state assistance with family security," Georgi continued. Karl immediately understood what this meant and why it had been expressed in such a roundabout way. He considered replying but kept his thoughts to himself.

'I guess he has a double problem. Having to pay for her security is a small problem. The bigger problem is that he will need increased security if he is no longer close enough to power to be provided with state assistance…' he thought.

-

Karl never saw Christina or her father again. His introduction to the world of the super-rich oligarchs did little to change his opinion of them, but it created an opportunity to take an important first step to determine a different future for himself than he had previously envisaged. More steps would have to be taken to take him away from his previous path. For that opportunity to happen, Karl would have to wait for a few months to pass, a change of responsibility to happen, and a major global pandemic to occur.

13 Here We Go Again
October 2018

Graham woke and looked around him. Every morning since his retirement, there had been these few empty seconds at the beginning of the day—a few seconds during which he was not sure what day it was and what, if anything, the day held in store for him. He put this feeling down to the fact that most days were, to be honest, pretty empty.

The exceptions weren't terribly interesting either. But a doctor's appointment, a necessary supermarket visit, or a planned lunch with a friend gave the day some definition and seemed to allow the brain to kick in more quickly. Just like it had in the old days when each day was defined by the work to be done in it. But there was nothing in the diary for today, and so a few seconds passed until he remembered this was a Tuesday and that he had been out in London with the professor the day before.

A glance around his bedroom told him that the jump had occurred. Traces of his late wife were evident in several places. He checked the screen of his phone, which lay at his bedside. 'At least this part is easier this time around,' he thought. 'When I underwent this time travel lark before, I had to go out and buy a newspaper to find out what day it was!' The screen told him it was October 17, 2018. Exactly one year since his wife died, which meant that he had successfully travelled four years and two months backwards in time.

He got up and gathered his thoughts while switching on the coffee machine and pouring a bowl of cereal. The only positives he could come up with to start his day, and he was in the habit of trying to find positives to start most days, were that this day would not be as bad the second time around. This was the day he had given himself a severe talking to. A real kick up the backside. But that was back then, so he didn't need to do it again. He just had to get on with the task of clearing his house and clearing his life. Although he still missed her every day of his life, it was five years further forward. Seven years of acclimatisation had happened, and the pain had dulled.

What had to be dealt with first was the practical stuff. And he needed to do it more quickly than before because he now had some additional major tasks to undertake and a timetable for their completion. And although those tasks did not start until the middle of next year, there were preparations to be made – and once started, he knew these tasks might well encompass more of his time.

He breakfasted, showered, and dressed. He also removed the beard he had grown – partly because his wife had never allowed him to grow one while she was alive and partly out of sheer laziness. 'I could do with a haircut too', he thought, looking in the mirror. 'It'll be bad enough to go without one during lockdown, so let's at least look our best while we can!'

And then began the task of removing the clutter. First, he went through the CD racks. A few could be considered as belonging jointly to him and Mary, but most were quite distinctly either his or hers. The pile of hers was placed in a cardboard box for the benefit of the local charity shop. He remembered that when he had completed this task before, he had driven up to the shop, deposited the CDs, and then called it a day. But this time he intended to do more. He made a sandwich and ate it before going on to sort, box, and deliver the books.

Only then did he pause and remember his two online tasks. He opened his laptop and bought a permanent subscription for two sets of lottery numbers for every future draw – both weekend and mid-week ones. 4, 5, 9, 40, 46, and 59 were chosen to produce a jackpot in the next few weeks to fulfil his own need for funds; 5,7,9, 24,32, and 44 were there for use in the middle of next year. He was almost certainly wasting money by buying the ticket now, but this was the best way to ensure he didn't forget to do it in six months or, even worse, forget the winning numbers.

His sketchy plan was that he would need some funds to pursue Anna to wherever it was. And if he needed to enrol someone to assist, there was no better way to establish his time-travelling credentials than by producing a set of winning lottery numbers.

He also thought he should do a brain dump of the key information that was still at the front of his mind concerning his quest. If he did not do this, much of it might fade from his memory before there was a chance to do what he had come back to achieve.

He got paper and pen and wrote the key information about Anna: her date of birth, the town she grew up in, her current address, the professor's details, and, critically, the description and location of the photo of the woman in the blue dress that he had told Graham about as his secret code.

He also noted down some of the key dates that he had memorised as they might influence his planning: March 23rd, 2020, the start of the lockdown; June 21st, 2021, the official end of the lockdown; and February 24th, 2022, when Russia invaded Ukraine.

Then he sent a message to his family on their What's App Group, telling them he wanted to have a Zoom call one evening soon to discuss a couple of things.

As expected, he received calls from both his children that evening – no doubt aware of the date being the anniversary of their mum's death and concerned as to what he wanted to discuss.

"I just wanted to let you know I was aware of the date, and that it has caused me to have a bit of a think. I've been keeping myself a bit too much to myself recently and I wanted to let you know that I've given myself a severe talking to, and I'm going to do my best to get out a bit more."

Both his children were obviously pleased to hear what he had said and did their very best to encourage him. Relieved, no doubt that he was identifying his problems and seemingly taking steps to address them.

On the group call a few days later he began by saying, "I managed to have a bit of a fall over the weekend while I was pruning the apple tree." He interrupted their expressions of concern to reassure them that he was OK.

"Don't worry, I've been to the quack and had it checked over. No damage done it seems. They do say that where there's no sense, there's no feeling. But I knocked myself out for a few minutes, so I wanted to get checked out. The only problem I seem to have is that my short-term memory is all over the place. So, if there's anything important you've told me or that I've promised to do over the last few weeks, then you probably need to remind me because I've almost certainly forgotten it."

It was a well-rehearsed routine. He had told the same story when returning from his previous time-travelling jaunt. It was one of the curses of this activity that when you arrived you would have next to zero recall of events in the recent past of whenever it was that you landed. Both on the outward and the return journey.

Neither his son nor his daughter could think of anything recent and relevant to him. A sad testament to the emptiness of his life, he thought. His son asked him if he had watched the most recent game on Monday Night Football. "Good example," Graham replied. "I can't remember."

"Then you can count yourself lucky," his son replied. "It was dreadful."

He decided to move on from this topic. "I also want to let you know that I've got an idea for what to do at Christmas."

He had their attention. Last Christmas had been difficult. It had come too soon after his wife's death, and despite everyone's best attempts, the three days that his children and grandchildren had spent with him between Christmas and New Year had been uncomfortable for everyone. Graham knew the passing of a further year would make it easier this time, but it would pose additional problems. The grandchildren were growing, and the house was simply not big enough to hold all of them, night and day.

"I'm looking at Airbnb to hire a large farmhouse near here for three days. Something with at least half a dozen bedrooms and some outdoor space."

His children agreed it was a great idea but were concerned about the cost."

"Don't worry," he replied. "One advantage of living like a hermit is that you save a lot of money."

The call ended soon after, and Graham was confident that his white lie about his fall had worked. He had covered his tracks by actually visiting the doctor and getting checked out. The practice manager at his local GP's surgery was a school friend of his daughter, and he needed to make sure that just in case the two of them spoke, his visit to the doctor was on record. Luckily the doctor listened to his description of the fall and the 'symptoms he was suffering' and told him that no immediate action was necessary – but to make another appointment if any other symptoms arose. Graham was certain there would not be any.

-

He had to remind himself that as far as the staff at the charity shop were concerned, these recent visits were the first he had ever made. In his previous life, he had already visited several times when clearing his wife's possessions and was on first-name terms with some of the staff. He had to start all over again.

He noticed a few changes to the parade of shops in his village where the charity shop was located. A couple had not survived the pandemic, but here they were, back in existence in this rerun of his life. He kept reminding himself that he was five years back in time and not to make any stupid mistakes. It had been so different the last time around. Travelling back fifty years meant that there was no chance of forgetting it had happened. Everything was so different. But now the changes were more subtle and there was a danger of forgetting.

And then, visiting the supermarket, Graham experienced the first noticeable difference. People were standing so much closer to each other! Although the world he left was two years past the pandemic and its concomitant two-meter rule, he had not realised quite how much difference the pandemic had caused in people's everyday behaviour and how those changes had remained post-pandemic.

People in the checkout queue in front of him were standing right next to each other, as they had once done. He even noticed that people engaged in discussion with friends and colleagues in the aisles and outside on the pavement seemed to be a good few centimetres closer to each other.

-

Over the next few weeks, Graham was more active than he had been in a long time. After conferring with his daughter and daughter-in-law, he was able to clear his wife's belongings – handbags, costume jewellery, cosmetics, and so forth. He visited the charity shop so often that he was able to strike up a relationship with the shop's manager, Elizabeth, a woman aged about sixty (he guessed). He noticed how surprisingly attractive she was. She appeared to have embraced some of the effects of ageing and had dyed her hair to a uniform shade of steel grey which hung loosely on her shoulders. Coupled with a trim figure and an energetic disposition, her days of turning men's heads had not yet passed, he thought.

She asked him the obvious question as to why he was clearing out so much stuff, and he told her that he had finally decided that it needed doing since his wife had passed more than a year ago, and he needed to move on.

She was sympathetic, relating how she had gone through much the same process a couple of years earlier when her husband had passed. Graham was able to ask her about the prospect of future relationships in a way that both helped him prepare himself for the possibility (since he foresaw it might be part of his plan to find out about Anna) and established that she had not taken any steps in that direction herself.

He asked Elizabeth if the shop accepted perfume and cosmetics and she assured him that they were perfectly acceptable if they were unopened.

"I thought I'd ask since I've never seen any for sale in your shop, and I have found a few back at home."

"I'll let you into a secret," she said in a mock conspiratorial manner, "It's because the staff always buy them before the public gets a chance. One of our few perks is cosmetics at half price. Always plenty of those around just after Christmas."

"And do you join in?" he asked.

"Only if there's anything by Chanel," she replied.

Graham made a mental note and included several unopened boxes of 'smellies' in his next visit.

-

In November, he received an email from Camelot letting him know that his ticket had been successful. A jackpot of just over three and a quarter million pounds was on its way to him.

He waited until Christmas to let his children know his good news. He decided not to let them know the exact amount – and surprisingly, they didn't ask. Perhaps it was because he had forestalled them by letting them know they would each be receiving a quarter of a million. "Enough to pay off the mortgage" was how he explained it. And there were new bikes for all three grandchildren waiting for them at their Airbnb stay. There would be more to distribute, he hoped, when his quest was finished.

On that score, he had looked up the availability of an apartment in central London that might be needed for his plan. Having a base in the city might be useful and would add credibility to his cover story of being a high-worth individual. He found a company renting out extortionately priced apartments in the centre, overlooking the River Thames. They were aimed at high-flying businessmen, which is how he would portray himself, so he rented a fully furnished one for four years. It would come in handy for some of the plans forming in his mind.

He was sad to think he would soon have no excuse for the chats with Elizabeth that he had begun to look forward to. Whether it was the increased feeling of well-being that comes from having a healthy bank balance or the slight feeling of 'I don't care anyway' that time travel produces, he couldn't be sure – but on his next visit to the charity shop, he surprised himself by asking Elizabeth for a date.

"Nothing fancy. But maybe we could have a drink at the Crown – or perhaps even a meal?"

The Crown was a large pub-restaurant in the village where they both lived. Far too large for such a small village, but very popular, pulling in trade from several miles around and offering casual employment to some members of the local community.

"A meal together would be very nice," she said, and they settled on the following Thursday as the evening that was empty in both their diaries. His diary offered a much wider choice of empty evenings than hers, but he kept quiet about this. He offered to pick her up, but she said the short walk from her home would do her good.

Although they were both extremely rusty at the dating game, their many conversations over his black bags of second-hand goods meant that they already knew enough about each other to start conversations, but they also knew so little that there was plenty to talk about. So, the evening went well, and they agreed to repeat it the following week.

From there, it became a weekly event. Always rounded off the same way – Graham driving to the pub because the distance from his house to the pub was twice that of Elizabeth's. He insisted on driving her home, and she always accepted. A brief kiss was exchanged as he dropped her outside her front door. It was the centrepiece of his week, but he feared it carried less significance for her. He felt he was on the same list and at the same level of importance as the weekly meeting of the Women's Institute.

Two months into their dating relationship, an event occurred that could only happen on a 'senior' date. At the end of the evening, when he pulled up outside her house, she invited him in. Luckily, he had already talked to her during the meal about how much he was looking forward to seeing his granddaughter in her school play the following day. So, when he told her he would have to leave home before six the next morning to miss the morning traffic and get to his granddaughter's school in time, she understood him politely turning down her invitation. A younger man might have let passion rule his actions. The older man knew the importance of a good night's sleep before an early start.

"I hope you're familiar with the American expression of 'taking a rain-check'", he said. "I'll definitely accept the invitation next week – if it's still there."

"It'll still be there," she smiled as they kissed goodnight, the kiss lasting slightly longer than it had done on any previous occasion.

The following week, he parked his car in Elizabeth's drive (both literally and figuratively). They adjourned to the bedroom, and both explored the difficulty of what might be described as participating in a complex dance routine that they had each only practised with the same partner for many years. But somehow, they made it work, and Elizabeth lay back in bed and smiled. "That was all right, wasn't it?"

"I think that sex over the age of sixty is not unlike seeing a dog singing," replied Graham in a well-rehearsed witticism he had heard some time back. "You shouldn't remark whether it is good or bad – just marvel at the fact that it happens at all." This reply earned him a playful slap.

The following morning, he woke to an empty bed and the sounds of Elizabeth moving around downstairs. After splashing some cold water on his face and finding a hairbrush to tame his thinning, greying, but still unruly mop, he dressed and looked around the room. A couple of photos of Elizabeth and Harry, her late husband, were on display, and they caused him to do a quick double-take.

He was surprised at how much alike he and Harry were. Not in a 'Oh my God, it must be my long-lost twin brother' way you might find in a Harlan Coben novel. More like a 'We look remarkably similar and could well be brothers' kind of way. He mentioned it to Elizabeth when he joined her in the kitchen.

"I'd honestly not thought about it," she replied, "But now you mention it, I suppose you do look a lot alike." But she didn't dwell on the issue, moving on to ask him whether he would like anything to eat and reminding him that she was due at the shop in a few minutes and that he had to be gone before she left. "I've got into the habit of setting the burglar alarm before I leave," she explained.

"It's OK. I'll eat when I get home," he replied before tackling the awkward issue of whether there was any change in their relationship after the previous night. After a little careful verbal fencing, they agreed that he could cook Sunday dinner for the two of them so that Elizabeth could see inside his house for the first time.

Apart from the fact that, on Sunday, they both did something during daylight hours that neither of them had done in daylight for a long time, the day was unremarkable, and Graham drove Elizabeth home in the late evening.

In the following weeks, their relationship continued on this slightly unusual basis. They spent Thursday evening on their date at The Crown and the night at Elizabeth's house. Sundays – day and night - were spent at his house. Occasionally, there was a second date during the week – cinema, theatre, or whatever, and maybe they would spend the night together, maybe not. They spoke about the oddness of the arrangement and realised that they were both happy with this strange understanding – each having a few clothes and toiletry items at the other's house – and were not keen to change it for the time being. They agreed it might change at some point in the future, but for now, neither wanted to completely cohabit.

Graham wondered whether he was doing the right thing by entering a close relationship. Did he want to burden himself with even this minimal extra responsibility when he had a complicated task to complete? Did he need to incur the added difficulty of explaining his inevitable unplanned absences? Was it a relationship doomed to failure unless he let Elizabeth into his time-travelling secret? He decided that with the complexity he would soon be facing and the loneliness he felt, he deserved some comfort. And the issue of time-travelling might well solve itself one way or another in just a few years when the date on this current plane of time caught up with the date on the plane he had just left.

One Sunday evening, they discussed in depth their feelings about the loss of their respective partners, and how they had adjusted. Graham thought that Elizabeth was slightly overzealous in expressing how well she felt she had completely removed Harry from her life.

He conducted a small experiment the next time he slept at her house. While she was preparing breakfast, he opened the drawer of the cabinet at 'his' side of the bed and found it to be, as expected, an untouched 'man drawer', full of the minutiae of Harry's life that it had always been. A box of cufflinks, a few coins – some foreign, some British pre-decimal – an old diary, a passport, and assorted trash. He thought this confirmed his opinion that Elizabeth had not removed him from her life as totally as she protested. Maybe he would check sporadically to see if it had been touched, and perhaps when it was emptied, she might be ready to deepen their relationship.

But he did more than just look and think. For no logical reason, he picked up Harry's passport and pocketed it. When he reached the foot of the stairs, he transferred it to the pocket of his jacket, which hung in the hall. If anyone had asked him why he did this, he would probably have thought of no better excuse than that he was acting in the way you were told to act in those old computer adventure games he had played more than a lifetime ago. *If you see something useful lying around while you're playing the game, be sure to pick it up. It may come in handy later in the game.* After all, he was playing the ultimate enhanced reality game of all, wasn't he? And you never knew when it might be useful to have a passport of someone looking so much like you that you could use it. He filed it carefully at home, where neither Elizabeth nor anyone else could ever stumble across it.

He was delighted that Elizabeth showed no interest in politics. It spared him from having to talk about Brexit. In normal times, he enjoyed discussing politics – but the whole Brexit issue had turned him off completely. And now he was forced into reliving it. Some days, there was absolutely nothing else in the news. It had been bad enough experiencing it the first time around, but the re-running of the debates, politicking, and posturing was something that he couldn't face.

Elizabeth also showed little interest in football – which was a more serious setback – so when he tried to talk about the historic occasion when two English teams met in the final of the UEFA Cup, he was met with a blank stare. Instead, she was more likely to try to engage him in discussing the tragedies and triumphs that she found more pressing, like the recent demise of Debenhams, where so much of her shopping hours had been spent and so much of her current wardrobe acquired.

She would probably have worried if she knew how concerned he was when she expressed such pleasure at the birth of the latest royal baby. He had no axe to grind when it came to the Royal Family. All in all, he thought they were probably a good thing for Britain in their role as a bulwark against dictatorship and the generators of so much tourist revenue. However, his earlier experience of Carol, his partner during his second life, and her obsession with one particular member of the royal family made him suddenly concerned.

Carol had had such a traumatic experience of travelling back in time that her parents had virtually sectioned her. She had subsequently identified heavily with Princess Diana and became obsessed with her. She had cajoled him into taking action to prevent the car crash in Paris that had ended Diana's life. When Diana died in a different accident a couple of months later, Carol suffered a severe breakdown.

'Is there something about me that attracts these pro-Royal women?' he wondered. But, as time progressed, he understood that Elizabeth's pro-royal tendencies were of the much more normal kind, mostly involving a liking for babies and weddings.

Their relationship progressed to both their satisfaction, and they even spent a short foreign holiday together. But his attempts to get Elizabeth interested in sport were less than totally successful. He was an armchair fan of many sports and a more than occasional spectator. But this aspect of life was severely altered when he became a time-traveller.

There's very little pleasure in watching a sporting event when you know exactly what the result will be. Rare exceptions exist, for example, when you know the team you support will both perform well and win. But most of the time, sitting through a game you've already seen is not worth your time. Since travelling back in time, he had switched from watching

Premier League football to following his local minor league team for just this reason. The standards were lower, but he had no knowledge or memory of their results, and so could attend their games with the normal involvement that comes from not knowing the result. But he went to the games alone.

He tried to use his knowledge of the results of upcoming fixtures to enlist Elizabeth as a sports fan. He knew that the World Cup Cricket Final would produce the most exciting finish to a cricket match in cricket's two-hundred-year history and wanted very much to experience it this time by being at the ground rather than in front of the TV set. But Elizabeth was not prepared to forsake her charity shop colleagues on the busiest day of the week for cricket, so Graham took his son to the game and enjoyed it as much as he expected.

The whole idea of watching sport changed once he became a time traveller. Of course, he did not remember the score or the details of every game – but he did remember the outcome of the important ones. But it was more than that. Watching sport had a false feeling about it. You knew that you were in a sense watching something that had already happened, whereas all the people around you were watching a live event. Very few games of any sport provide enough entertainment to be viewed in their entirety after the game has finished. But he hoped to get Elizabeth to accompany him so that there might be something they could enjoy together if their relationship was going to be long-lasting.

He was surprisingly successful when he suggested that Elizabeth might like to join him at the first-ever game of Major League Baseball which was scheduled to take place at the London Stadium.

Whether it was the novelty value, the proximity of the stadium to their home, or the fact that he told her that the star outfielder of the Boston Red Sox was related to Meghan Markle, he wasn't sure, but Elizabeth agreed to accompany him.

He had picked up a liking for baseball during his first life during several business trips to the USA and had once been taken to a game by one of his US colleagues. The showmanship, the exuberant presentation of the game, and the high skill levels of the players hooked him completely. And he was confident that he could explain the game more easily to his companion than he would have done if she'd agreed to go to cricket.

He had been at the inaugural game in the UK in his first life and clearly remembered its high-scoring excitement. It was tied at six runs each after only the first inning and the New York Yankees finally won an exciting high-scoring game.

Elizabeth was an immediate convert, and they agreed that one day they might see a game together in the USA.

Graham could not be happier. They were approaching a six-month anniversary, and the only thing that saddened him was that he was going to have to tell her his first white lie.

"I'm going to be away for a couple of days next week," he told her over Sunday evening dinner.

He knew it was not essential to tell her about the proposed trip since he had arranged for it to take place on Tuesday and Wednesday so that it didn't cut across their time together. But she just might have driven past his house and wondered why his car was missing on two consecutive days.

"I told you that my old firm asks me to help out occasionally with special projects - and this is one of those times."

"Where are you going?" she asked.

"South Wales," he replied.

At least this part of what he had told her was true.

14 It's Not Unusual

June 2019

Graham began his journey to South Wales with some trepidation. There was a higher level of uncertainty about the whole thing than he was comfortable with. His task was to persuade John Bishop, the member of the British Secret Service he had worked with during his second life, to help him. The task would be to find Anna a couple of years in the future when she would disappear. He had decided to begin the task well in advance.

He was confident that John would be found in the same place he had been living after his retirement when Graham had visited him last time around. An ex-colleague had been able to check the Register of Voters and found a Thomas Woodward – the alias John had been using – living in a house named Pen y Bryn in the village of Llangennith in South Wales. This just had to be the same person! But there was still the challenge of persuading him to help – and that might prove to be very difficult.

He and John had a cordial, maybe even friendly relationship for several years, but that was on a different plane of time. On this plane, they had never met. And he had to persuade this man to help him find a woman that he may not even remember when she runs and hides. He would have to hope to get a foot in the door before he had the chance to offer the lottery numbers as proof of his time-travelling story.

That was one of the reasons for starting the task now. He was reasonably confident that he would be able to prove his time-travel credentials to John by giving him the winning lottery numbers. He had memorised numbers that were drawn relatively soon after his jump because the longer the delay, the more chance that the numbers drawn might change. Another reason was that he might need some time for the story to be accepted and for John/Tom to conduct some background checks on both Anna and Graham.

The first time he'd visited John, when he had sought his help during the pandemic during Graham's second life, he had travelled in more comfort – first class rail from London to Swansea followed by a long taxi ride to the village on the Gower coast where John had made his retirement home. But that had been in different circumstances. And literally in a different life. On that occasion, John had been expecting his visit and Graham knew that a long conversation would ensue, so he had prepared for an overnight stay. This time he could not even be sure if John would open his door.

Once he got to his destination, he would need the flexibility of having his car available in case his plans had to change, including the possibility that he might have to start a search for Tom in a different locality. So, no chance of a relaxing first-class train this time. Anyway, he was quite looking forward to taking his new car for its first long drive on British roads.

He'd decided that a new car was a permissible self-indulgence from the proceeds of his lottery win. His car would need to be renewed at some time, so why not now? A new car might well help his disguise of being the successful, self-made businessman that he was going to portray.

It was not the car's first long drive, just its first on British roads. The first long journey had been the trip from Munich to Kent. That trip occurred when Graham finally got around to doing something he had always wanted to do.

During a business visit to the BMW facility in Munich during his first life, he discovered that anyone who purchased a new vehicle could collect the car from the main plant in Munich. New purchasers kept their pre-arranged appointment with a company representative, and their vehicle was driven up a ramp to an indoor area where the company employee showed them their new car's features before they drove off (presumably into the sunset) proudly piloting their new set of wheels.

He had never got around to fulfilling his wish to do this in either of his previous lives, but now that he had the time and the money to enjoy this, he had made the necessary arrangements when he bought the new car. He had finally achieved it a few weeks ago, with Elizabeth keeping him company for what had become their first holiday together. It had been a highly enjoyable day, the company doing everything it could to make their customer feel special. And when Elizabeth described the tour of the plant as one of the more unusual dates she had ever been taken on, he knew that she had the right sense of humour for him.

They had flown out to Munich and spent a day in the city, enjoying the Glockenspiel, Marienplatz, and the old city. In the evening, they enjoyed steins of beer and a plate of Schweinhaxen in the Hofbrauhaus. There had been the inevitable oompah band and they had joined in the choruses of 'In Muenchen liegt ein Hofbrauhaus' and the seemingly endless repeated toasts of 'Ein Prosit, ein Prosit, der Gemütlichkeit' before they had tottered off to bed, Elizabeth being slightly tipsy after consuming a whole litre stein.

The next day, they boarded the S-Bahn to the BMW plant and collected a brand new 5-series (complete with just about every available option), which he had ordered three months earlier. They had made two stops on the way back home, each lasting a couple of days. They had stopped in Cologne (the cathedral, the Rhine, and a visit to a work-friend of Graham's) and Bruges (lace, chocolate, canals, and a bar that sold hundreds of different types of Belgian beer) and completed a very pleasant short holiday.

Having met so late in life, he and Elizabeth had plenty to talk about during the drive, and this break had helped them move their relationship forward. They now spent every weekend together and, with their regular Thursday evening date still in place and occasional joint events, their life was lived, slightly chaotically, in and out of each other's houses. Graham felt sure that if he pushed, they could transition to full cohabitation. However, he was not sure that now would be the right time for that push, as several tasks would necessitate him being away from home, and it was not going to be easy to explain his absence to a live-in partner.

He had chided himself for starting the relationship. 'You're on a mission, not a vacation. If you let her get closer, you'll have to justify why you're away from home,' had been his train of thought. 'You can't even use the excuse that you only live once because that's plainly not true in your case!'

But he justified his decision – which had been made with heart rather than head – by thinking how lonely he would be. And wasn't he doing all this for the best of motives?'

This brought his thoughts back to his impending meeting (he hoped) with John Bishop aka Martin Knight aka Tom Woodward.

"Straightforward, really," he spoke aloud to his empty car. "All I need to do is convince a guy who has lived a life of secrecy and has never met me, to believe a preposterous story about time travel and go out of his way to help me find a woman who vanishes after the event, when, if she is still alive, she has hidden so well that even the security services can't find her. Nothing unusual there!"

He spent the journey listening to some of his favourite relaxing CDs and rehearsing the speech that he planned to give to Tom tomorrow. Eventually, he pulled up in the Fox's car park in Llangennith. It was just as he remembered it. He checked in and was shown to his room, which was typical of a British country inn: clean, comfortable, cosy, and slightly cramped. He leafed through some tourist brochures helpfully left on the bedroom table before setting out for his evening stroll.

He walked down to the coast to experience a refreshing blast of sea air before returning to the village and walking the half mile to the start of the driveway to Tom's cottage. There was the sign, hand-painted and barely legible, Pen y Bryn. The cottage was not visible from the road, and Graham dared not walk up the drive. He would be driving up there tomorrow.

Returning to the Fox, he went back to his room and 'freshened up' before going down to the bar for dinner. He was pleased to rediscover that the local draught beer was as tasty and as well-kept, and that the shank of local lamb was as delicious and as perfectly cooked as he remembered.

He moved from his table to a bar stool to enjoy a second pint after his meal. The only other customers were a couple of locals who were in a deep discussion, so the landlord engaged Graham in conversation.

"What brings you to our remote part of the world?" was the obvious conversation starter.

He gave his prepared reply. "I'm going to visit an old work colleague of mine. I don't know him all that well, but I'm hoping he can help me trace someone we both know but haven't seen for a while."

"Who's this old colleague of yours, then?"

"His name's Tom, Tom Woodward. He lives in a cottage just up the road. I checked out where it was when I went for a walk." Graham stopped and waited to see if the landlord would respond. He remembered that when he had been here in his last life, the landlord had recognised Tom and had spoken to him by name. He now hoped to find out from this conversation opener whether Tom was indeed a local resident.

Graham never knew whether Tom Woodward was the real name of the multi-alias man he was seeking or if it was one final joke he was playing on his contacts. Tom Woodward was, after all, the actual name of one of South Wales's most famous exports – the singer and Las Vegas star Tom Jones.

"He's a man who likes to keep himself to himself," the landlord continued, referring to the other Tom Woodward. Graham was delighted that the first hurdle had been overcome. Tom was here. Graham reasoned that his host would naturally want to protect one of his locals from unwanted intrusion.

"Yes," he replied. "He always was that way. As I said, I didn't know him that well. I was on the financial side, and he was on the security side, so our paths only occasionally crossed, but like you say, he was a cautious guy. But I'm hoping his memory is better than mine and he can help me find the person I'm looking for."

"Close colleague, was he? This person you're looking for."

"*She* was. And I hope I can find her because I'm writing a book, and she could be very helpful."

Refills were needed for the other customers, and Graham reached the bottom of his glass and rejected the temptation for a third pint, knowing he would need a clear head the next day. His chat with the landlord was over.

-

It was tough refusing the full English breakfast (or, rather, the full Welsh breakfast since it was served with optional laverbread), but Graham did not want too full a stomach to slow him down during his meeting. So, after a light breakfast, he drove the short distance to Tom's cottage.

Having negotiated the narrow driveway, he emerged onto the paved area in front of the house and parked his shiny new motor next to Tom's more modest and much older small SUV. The cottage appeared much as he remembered it, but he did notice that the property next door was in a ramshackle state. The last time he had been here, it had been fully restored to the same standard as Tom's cottage.

'Maybe Tom's retirement pension was not sufficiently well funded to complete the purchase and renovation of both cottages,' Graham thought. 'He did much better for himself the last time I was here – back then his pension must have benefitted from the helpful input from a time-travelling colleague giving him investment tips.'

He tapped the ancient knocker against the door and waited a minute before Tom opened it, dressed in his gardening gear.

Graham took a deep breath and began his rehearsed speech.

"Tom, my name is Graham Henderson and I'm hoping you can help me, even though you don't know me. I'm looking for a man I used to work with. His name is John Bishop."

There was no response from the man who had opened the door. Tom's long experience of interviewing people from all walks of life told him that maintaining silence would usually bring more information out of the mouth of the other person, so he waited for Graham to continue.

Graham knew this and was prepared for this response, and so continued. "I'm also hoping to contact another ex-colleague, Martin Knight, whom I believe you might know. I was given your address by a mutual contact – Professor Karbajanovic."

There was a brief sign of a reaction on Tom's face. Graham had deliberately lied, saying that the prof had given him this address and Tom must have wondered whether he had ever told the prof his address.

"I'm sorry – those names don't mean anything to me," Tom replied, much as Graham had expected.

"Look, I've driven a bloody long way to see you and I've got a story that explains everything. Can I ask you for half an hour of your time to hear me out before you decide what to do?"

Tom took one final look at Graham and his car before deciding to metaphorically let down his drawbridge. He opened the door, stepped back, and said, "I guess you'd better come in then," in his slight Welsh accent.

Graham followed Tom into the sitting room. He tried to remember exactly how it had looked on his last visit and concluded that it was not quite as well furnished or fitted out as he remembered. Tom indicated one of the two large chairs for Graham to sit on before positioning himself in the other.

Graham assumed Tom's silence meant that he should launch into his tale.

"On October 8th, 2012, I had a meeting with my financial adviser at his office in City Road, London, opposite Moorfields Eye Hospital." He was beginning the story with a lie (his meeting had been ten years later, but he needed to simplify the tale). He also needed to include a few items of colouring (like including that he was meeting his financial adviser) because if he stuck to the necessary facts his story would not seem natural, and it might be harder for Tom, professional as he was, to digest everything.

"During the meeting," he continued, "I briefly reminisced with him about my eighteenth birthday, almost exactly forty-two years previously. After a pleasant lunch, I went home and fell asleep quite early."

He paused and checked that Tom was attentive. He was, which was good because here came the killer line.

"The next morning, I woke, not to my sixtieth birthday as I should have done – but to my eighteenth birthday. That's right, I had travelled back in time." Another pause for a possible response – but there was none so Graham continued.

"I lived my whole life over again. During that life, in the late nineteen seventies, I met a man by the name of John Bishop. I worked for a financial organisation, dealing with the Middle East and John worked for a government department, dealing with the same area. We exchanged information regularly, and to our mutual benefit, I might add." Graham adopted a chattier style to his monologue, hoping to gain some feedback, and briefly paused again. Tom was paying attention to his every word but made no response. He correctly sensed that there was more to come.

"I should explain that this all took place on what I've come to think of as a different plane of time. So of course, none of it is familiar to you. Even if I threw in extra detail like our lunch meeting at Simpson's in the Strand and the pints of draught Bass in silver tankards, you would be quite right to not remember any of it."

Mentioning the venue where they had shared lunch and the unique nature of the drinks served there was quite deliberate. It was not unlike a boxing match with a canny opponent. Graham hoped to soften him with a series of well-directed body punches.

"Anyway, John and I lost touch over the years until I re-established contact many years later. By this time John was working with Professor Karbajanovic, taking care of security for his experiments at Moorfields Eye Hospital. I guess it was part of that security for John to change his name to Martin Knight. He told me about the experiment on October 8th,

2012, and the terrible after-effects. The death of the people who had been in the office building and one floor below me."

Graham now took a couple of risks. He paused his story, hoping it would help his host digest a lot of information, much of it being somewhat difficult to swallow, in a short time.

"Look, I'm grateful for you hearing me out, but is there any chance of something to drink – I'm not used to talking this much."

After a brief pause for thought, his host asked, "Tea or coffee?"

"A cold drink if you've got one. Glass of water, or perhaps a Diet Pepsi?"

Graham thought he could see a small frown appear on his host's poker face. Not surprising, after all. He had unusually asked specifically for Diet Pepsi, having remembered from his visit all those years ago that the fridge had been well stocked with this particular drink as it was John Bishop's favourite soft drink. Another body punch had been landed.

John brought in two ice-cold cans, and Graham tugged the ring pull and took a swig.

"Thanks. Where was I? Oh yes, John told me about the events of that day. How the professor had sent a beam from one building to another, and all the people who had received a dose of that beam had died. He even told me about the rather scary fact that in the postmortems, their brains had shown 'unusual levels of low-level electrical activity.'"

Having landed another punch using the very phrase that John had once used to describe the incident and how it had badly affected him, Graham paused again to look at his host's face. He could see some slight signs of concern. He had decided to use the telling phrase, not wanting to cause pain but to substantiate his story.

"When I heard this story from John, I put two and two together. I reckoned that there was a connection between this experiment and what had happened to me, especially since I'd been in an office one floor above the place where the beam was being aimed. The office from which some poor civil servants went home that night and never woke up the next morning."

Graham paused again and looked at John. "This is quite a story," was the only response. But he had John's undivided attention. The direction of their conversation now needed to alter as he was shortly due to switch from retelling past events to actively seeking co-operation.

"So, John introduced me to the Professor – or simply The Prof, as we always called him - and I told him about my experience. I'm unsure what use it was to him, but I felt he needed to know. Now, as I said, this all happened on a different plane of time. And I continued on that plane – through to 2022, when the prof ran the experiment again."

Seeing a slight look of puzzlement cross Tom's face, he explained, "Yes, despite knowing the consequences of the previous experiment. In fact, it was exactly because of those consequences that they reran the experiment. Or perhaps I should say that they will rerun the experiment – because I'm speaking of a different plane of time. We haven't yet reached 2022 on this plane of time.

There's going to be a helluva lot of tension between Russia and the West at that time. More than usual. The government's going to take the extreme step of getting two government employees, known to be passing information to Russia – double agents, I think they called them – and allocating them to the prof's project. They'll sit in the office in City Road, transcribing some messages in the Russian script – which I believe was the excuse they get given for their participation in the experiment. They were told that it was necessary to check if the beam could transmit messages in another character set. And of course, neither of them will wake up the next day. A clear message to Russia. Not only that we know that they were double agents, but that we were determined enough to take drastic action and that we had a weapon that was capable of being deployed in a city centre and would cause the targets to appear to have died many hours later from natural causes."

Graham took a long swig from his can and watched Tom, who seemed to be physically digesting the last few minutes' worth of information.

"Which brings me to the last part of my story – and my reason for being here today," Graham continued and wondered if he noted a look of some relief on his host's face. Presumably, grateful that there was not even more to the story.

"After the events of this date in the future, I was asked by the professor to help him with a task that only I could complete, and then only if I got some assistance from others. He persuaded me to come back in time again and ask for your help. But of course, it would be completely unreasonable of me to ask for your help – especially as it might need you to reveal something about yourself to a stranger. So, I know I need to do something to try and prove that this outlandish tale has some element of truth in it."

('As if the Diet Pepsi, the lunch at Simpson's, the multiple aliases, and the quote about unusual levels of low-level electrical activity aren't enough', Graham thought to himself.)

"Here's what I propose to do. I'm going to give you a piece of evidence you can verify for yourself – and trust that once you have verified it, you will decide that I am not completely mad, and you'll help me do something to help the prof.

"By the way, if you ask the prof himself about this, he will be unable to help. Like I said, I've come back in time, and as far as the prof is concerned, he hasn't ever met me, nor asked me to help him."

Graham reached into his back pocket and took out two pieces of paper.

"It's one hell of a story. And I don't expect you to automatically take it all in and believe every word. I wouldn't. But I'm going to leave you with two bits of paper. The first is my card, which has my name, mobile number, and email address on it. The second is the one that doesn't exactly prove what I've said – I don't believe that's possible anyway – but it's the one that I'm hoping will convince you to pick up the phone and call me."

He handed the two pieces of paper to John.

"A lottery ticket?" John asked. Graham smiled. 'Even the most seasoned professional can ask a question whose answer is bleeding obvious', he thought.

"A ticket that covers the same set of numbers for all the draws next month," he explained. "After all, what sensible time-traveller would deliberately embark on a journey into the past without knowing the winning numbers in the lottery? And to be clear, I'm gifting this ticket to you. It's yours. And any money that it wins is yours to claim and to keep. I suggest that when the end of the month comes around, you either check it online or visit a lottery kiosk where you're not known. Don't use the local post office unless you want the whole village to know you're a multi-millionaire.

"All I'm hoping is that when you've won your jackpot, you'll believe that there is some truth in my story - and we can sit down together and see if you can help me to help the prof. Is that fair?"

John took a moment to respond. "I guess so," he said before asking, "How come the ticket is for a whole month?"

Delighted with the first feedback he had received during the meeting, Graham explained, "I had to memorise the numbers before I came back. I know they will win sometime in July, but I couldn't remember exactly which draw they came up in, so I bought a ticket to cover the whole month."

"I guess that if I win a few million I will owe you a call," Tom replied.

Graham stood up and made to leave.

"But don't hold your breath," were the parting words from his taciturn host.

-

Driving back to Kent, Graham went over the meeting in his mind. He had found Tom (or John) and had been able to tell his story in full. He was confident he would receive a call when the ticket came up next month.

'That meeting probably went as well as I could expect,' was his conclusion.

15 A Couple (of) Lunches
August 2019

A week into August, Graham was beginning to worry that he had not received a call from South Wales. He had been confident that even Tom, with all his security concerns, having digested the seemingly impossible tale, would still do him the courtesy of calling back. He was beginning to plan what his actions would be if he didn't hear anything when Tom finally called.

"The numbers came up, so I'd better hear the rest of your story," were his first words. "And I've got a few questions I'll need to have an answer to, if you want my help," Tom continued.

"No problem," Graham replied, trying hard not to show the sense of relief he was feeling. "When can I come down?" he continued.

"As soon as you like."

They agreed on the following Tuesday for their next meeting – Graham did not want to forgo his Thursday evening out and wanted to avoid both weekend and Monday morning traffic issues. He could afford the comfort of first-class rail travel this time around and promised to be at Tom's house around midday.

He was pleased to experience a little warmer reception and to be told that there was some bread, cheese, and bottled beer available for lunch. A polite inquiry about his journey and his point of departure filled the small-talk gap while they took their lunches into the lounge.

"If the prof wants his problem solved and you've told him about your time travel adventures, how come he hasn't come back himself? It'd make more sense since he and I know each other," was how Tom shifted the talk to the agenda for the meeting.

"Good question," Graham answered. "He told me he tried – and if I know the prof at all, I'm sure he tried more than once. But it seems he couldn't achieve it."

"So, you're the only one who's capable of this time travel then?"

"Seems so," Graham replied. He had so many avenues to go down with Tom he decided to edit Carol out of his story. He wanted to close off this potential blind alley.

"OK – we might return to that later," Tom continued. "But if you say that this problem concerns something that is going to happen in October

2022, how come you're asking for my help three years before it happens?"

"There's a couple of reasons for that. First, I need to find out what happened in the months leading up to October 2022, so I was always going to need to see you some months before, and I didn't know how easy it would be to find you. Secondly, there is a limit to my time travel capability. It seems that I can only travel back to certain specific dates. And the nearest one of those was late last year. I had to choose a lottery jackpot win that was due to happen as soon as possible after that date. Believe it or not, me coming back in time sets off a kind of wave of events that can change future events. It could even alter the lottery numbers, so now was the optimum time. But there's also a huge third reason, and that's the first big piece of news I have to give you."

Graham went on to tell an increasingly incredulous Tom about the impending pandemic. He remembered he had given the same speech to the same man when he had visited during his second life. The reaction was much the same. It wasn't entirely one of incredulity. As a member of the Secret Service, Tom had been briefed more than once about the possibility of a major pandemic and the chaos it could potentially bring. Not only that, but being an avid science fiction reader, he had also read several books that were based upon the idea of a worldwide pandemic, including 'The Stand', 'Contagion', and even 'Earth Abides'. So, he listened carefully while Graham outlined the events that were to come.

Having covered all the key points, he summarised, "Next year is pretty much a write-off for most activities – yours, mine, and the person that the prof wants some help with."

Tom took the opportunity of a break in the dialogue to clear away the plates and offer Graham a cup of coffee which he accepted. As he brought the two cups into the room from the kitchen he asked pointedly, "What is it that you say the prof wants me to do?"

"You may remember the prof had an assistant, a lady by the name of Anna Mueller? I don't know if you ever met the lady, but you'd remember her if you did. Striking is how I'd describe her."

Graham looked over at Tom. If he had ever met Anna and was not reacting to this prompted memory of her, then he truly was ice-cold, Graham thought. Tom showed the merest response of having remembered her.

"Immediately after the rerunning of the experiment, she disappears. Seemingly, the prof was quite attached to her, both professionally and emotionally. He asked around, including the people who had been seconded to his team to deal with security matters, but nobody could tell him where she had gone. He assumed that either they knew where she was and were deliberately not telling him or that she truly was a remarkable woman and had managed to elude even them. So, he asked me to see if I could repeat my trick and travel back in time and either stop her disappearing or, if I couldn't do that, at least find out where she had gone. Which brings me to the reason for my visit to you."

"You want my help to find her?" John asked. But only after Graham had used the same interview technique that John had used earlier, keeping quiet for a long time.

"That's the gist of it," Graham replied. "Use your old connections to find out what you can about her. As far as I can tell, there are two possibilities. Either they know what has become of her, and they're not letting the prof know. Or she has somehow managed to evade their surveillance and has gone somewhere they don't know."

"The second of those alternatives is unlikely," Tom replied.

"And the first of them is unpleasant," Graham replied.

Graham related what he knew about Anna, as had been told to him by the prof. It was not much, and Tom remarked on this. But he promised to do what he could and to let Graham know what he could find out.

"Give me a few weeks. I'll have to resurrect some old communication channels. And I'll need to do it carefully because the last thing you want is to let them know you're looking for her."

Tom called the number of the local taxi company, and they engaged in some more relaxed conversation while they awaited its arrival.

"Now you've got some money, you should get some work done there," Graham said, pointing at the window overlooking the sea. "You know a wall of glass with sliding doors and a patio immediately outside it would look good," he said and waited for Tom's response.

"I was thinking of that," he said and then noticed that Graham was smiling.

"You have to remember I've been here before. When you had retired with quite a bit more money. I can promise you that a wall of glass looks good there. And last time you had done up the property next door for your sister and her family. Nice touch."

Something close to a smile crossed Tom's face.

-

Two weeks later, Graham received another call from Tom. He had some information about Anna and surprisingly suggested that they meet in London.

"Let's have lunch at Simpson's, just like old times," he suggested. They set a date, and Graham pondered this warming in Tom's manner. 'Just like old times' was perilously close to a joke, he thought. Which was very unlike the Tom (or John) that he knew.

Over lunch, he not only learned some key information about Anna but also began to understand why Tom was warming to the task. This quest was getting Tom's juices flowing in a way that they hadn't been for some time.

"A bit of an enigma, this woman," he began once their orders had been placed. "She has only one living relative as far as anyone can tell. Her sister, who's a teacher living in Dresden, which is where the family originated. Her parents are both dead.

"She's been in the UK since about 2005. The odd thing is that she owns her own flat – and that doesn't add up. She bought it about fifteen years ago and seems to have paid off the mortgage in record time, even though she has no visible income other than her salary – which ain't enough to live off and pay off a mortgage of that size that quickly.

"She appears to have no close friends. Her social life revolves around a dating agency called Select Few, which she joined about ten years ago. Now, seeing as how this is a site that seems to exist to pair wealthy men with attractive women, I would guess that she has a sugar daddy somewhere. But if she has, then nobody knows who he is."

Graham was pleased to hear that Tom had found the name of the dating agency – more than the professor had been able to tell him, he thought. He asked a few more questions to see if Tom had more than this to report and was disappointed to discover that he didn't. They agreed that the best way for Graham to discover more about her was to try to date her via the 'Select Few' website.

"Mind you, I don't know if you're wealthy enough to meet their requirement," Tom said and Graham was not sure if this was a genuine concern he was expressing, or another sign of the sense of humour that seemed to be emerging.

"Don't worry," Graham assured him. "I prepared some funds for this task. You're not the only one who has had some luck on the lottery."

This revelation moved the conversation onto the topic of time travel. In hushed tones, Tom began to ask a series of questions on the subject.

"How do you think this time travel actually happens?" was one of the first. Graham decided to answer them as best he could. The only previous conversations he had been able to have on the subject were with Carol during their ill-fated relationship in his second life. And even then, the conversations had been very brief. Carol had had such a bad experience that she shied away from revisiting it whenever they talked.

"I honestly don't know," Graham replied. "The way I understand it is that this ray that the prof transmitted during his experiment affects the human brain in a way nobody quite understands. I know that they believe the brain does a kind of re-boot exercise whenever we sleep. It has a huge amount of information it has gathered during the previous day and has to decide what to keep and what to throw away. And the stuff it keeps has to be filed in such a way that it can be accessed in the future. If you've ever seen the animation of a computer doing a disk defragmentation, it gives you an idea of what is happening. Well, I reckon that the prof's ray disrupts this in some way. Those who were unfortunate enough to receive its full power just didn't reboot their brain the next day. I was on the edge and didn't get the full blast. So, it just messed with the mechanism and my brain rebooted on a different day than it was supposed to."

"And you are the only one this happened to?"

Graham shook his head and explained about Carol, who had an identical experience to his – but landed on her wedding day.

"I was very lucky when I first did it. It didn't matter that my short-term memory was completely buggered because I was in a totally new environment. But for her, it caused major problems, which, to be honest, she never fully recovered from."

In response to further questions, he told Tom about her obsession with Princess Diana and how, in response to Carol's requests, he had tried unsuccessfully to prevent Diana's early death. This led to a brief discussion about how a time traveller affected the environment in which he landed. Graham began to realise that Tom had more than just a passing interest in the subject and interrupted his narrative flow to find out more.

"I've always been fascinated by the subject," Tom admitted. "Ever since we read "The Time Machine" in an English class at school, I've read everything I can lay my hands on. Science Fiction in general, and time travel in particular."

"Hence the grilling," Graham smiled.

"Yeah, hence the grilling. I don't reckon I'll get to meet too many people who've actually done it. Why do you think you were able to travel back here, and the prof couldn't?"

"You understand that all you're going to get from me is my opinion, not scientific fact, don't you?"

Tom nodded.

"Well, I've always been a bit of a chameleon. Responding to my surroundings and changing to meet them. It was useful in business because I had to work with so many different types and nationalities. And often get them to change their ways of working. People remarked on how I seemed able to get on with almost anyone. And when I did some amateur dramatics, I was told I was pretty good at it. I found it easy to pretend to be someone else. So, I've got something malleable up here," Graham pointed at his head. "And perhaps the prof's brain is a little less flexible."

They went on to discuss the effects that a time traveller might have on the environment he lands in.

"As far as I can see – it's limited. And in a way that I don't fully understand. Obviously, my mere presence causes change. If we weren't here, this meal wouldn't be taking place. Simpsons would be short of the money we're paying them. As would British Rail for your ticket and God knows what else. All from just one person on one day. If you took a taxi here from Paddington this morning, you've changed the entire day for that taxi driver. Not only that, but you've also changed the day for every other taxi that picks up from that rank for the rest of today – because they'll start the day with a different fare from the one they would have had if you'd not been there. If they are creatures of habit and always go to the same place for lunch at the same time every day, then you've only changed their day until lunchtime. Maybe changing the work pattern of scores of taxi drivers makes no difference – but it just might.

"So, every day I'm causing change to happen on this plane of time. But there is a limit to the amount of change that can be made. When I stopped Princess Diana from getting killed in that road accident in Paris, she died from another accident a few weeks later. And when I stopped the tragedy at Hillsborough, there was a major road accident the same evening that killed almost as many people as the original event."

Tom's face bore the expression of a man who has a hundred questions to ask and does not know which to start with.

"Yeah, there's a lot I could tell you. But it'll take more than a lunch to cover it all - if you really want to know. And we haven't even talked about 9/11." Graham thought Tom might be in danger of exploding from the pressure of so many unanswered questions.

"You changed 9/11?" Tom asked.

"Yes, with your help. But it's too long a story for now – maybe I'll tell you some other time."

The conversation paused as they worked their way through a delicious plate of roast beef and a bottle of expensive claret. When they took coffee in the lounge area, Tom returned to his inquisitor role, enjoying his unique chance to speak with a time traveller.

"You said that you might cause the lottery numbers to change. How could that happen?"

"I don't know, but I could picture a scenario where it might happen."

Tom did not have to say anything. His quizzical look was expressive enough to encourage Graham to continue.

"Well, I haven't tried to program a computer since I was nineteen, and that was a long time ago. But I do remember that there is no such thing as a true random number generator, so I assume that the lottery folks have found a way to achieve this.

"If you asked me to use the lottery company's computer to generate random numbers for the two weekly draws, I might come up with something that looked at the list of numbers that people chose the previous day. I'd ask it to do something like picking the tenth, twentieth, thirtieth, fortieth, fiftieth, and sixtieth numbers from the list and then discard them. Yes, there would need to be additional complications in case the same number got chosen twice; then another manipulation because the numbers that people choose aren't spread evenly – there's a bias towards numbers up to thirty-one because people choose birthdays. But the essence is that the random numbers would come from data that already existed in the system.

"And don't forget the computer also has to choose random numbers every time someone asks for a lucky dip. So, what I'm saying is that if the numbers are chosen in any way that uses existing data to provide them, then it's possible that even buying just one ticket that wasn't bought before, or not buying one ticket that was bought before, can change the whole shebang.

"Maybe a taxi driver who pulled a lucky hundred-pound fare from Paddington today decides to buy a lottery ticket with it, whereas the guy who should have got that fare would not have bought a ticket. And that's before you start spending your lottery proceeds. Once you start work on converting that cottage of yours, some builders, electricians, and plumbers down on the Gower are going to have some money in their accounts pretty soon – maybe quite a lot of money. And maybe a local car dealer is going to sell one or two more new cars than he might not have otherwise. It's a series of small ripples, but can you see what I mean about unforeseen changes?"

Tom gave a very pensive nod, and Graham took the opportunity to return the conversation to his plans.

"Tom, I enjoy discussing time travel with you, but I need to talk a little more about the next steps. Assuming I manage to get accepted by this dating site, I'll meet Anna and see what I can find out. Unless you hear anything from any of your ex-colleagues, which I expect is unlikely," he continued.

"Yeah, you could say that" Tom interrupted. "They don't exactly send out a newsletter to tell everyone what's happening."

"Like I said, if you don't hear anything else, you'll hear from me if and when I've got some more information. I've got no idea what she might be planning – if she's actually planning something. But I'll try to find it out and if I need more help – and I expect I will need some help – then I'll get back to you. But remember, the rate of progress for the next few months is going to be glacial. From March next year until the middle of twenty-twenty-one, it will vary between being difficult to get around to being downright bloody impossible. There'll even be a period of time when they will be turning back cars on the Severn Bridge unless they've got a valid reason to travel. So, I won't exactly be able to pop down and see you."

This warning was still churning through Tom's mind as they parted a short while later, agreeing only to re-establish contact when there was something worth talking about.

16 Keeping Secrets
October 2019

Graham and Elizabeth took a holiday cruise together and got to know each other better. If you had asked Graham, you would have been told that all was well. He was preparing to broach the subject of how they would spend Christmas, and when and how he would introduce her to his children.

So, it came as quite a surprise when Elizabeth told him she wanted to end their relationship. He had always known that she was a woman capable of strong passion and reasoned that the unfortunate companion to this trait was a propensity to make sudden, unpredictable decisions.

Recovering from the shock, he tried to persuade her to change her mind. She hadn't even explained why she wanted to break up. When she tried to explain, once again he heard a story that he had heard on multiple occasions in his second life. Each time it was slightly different, but the message was always the same: 'I can't shake the feeling that you're hiding something from me'. Or 'I don't know what it is, but there are times when I just know you're not telling me the truth. Or not telling me the whole truth.' Or other variations on the same theme.

This time, it was expressed as, "You are not being totally honest with me. There's a part of your history that you have completely blocked from me."

Even Graham, with his determination to find something positive in every situation, struggled to do so. The best he could come up with was that he would now not need to worry about hiding his forthcoming attempts to find out more about Anna. The next step in his plan was to establish contact with her in some way.

With his relationship with Elizabeth now a thing of the past, at least he could choose any day of the week for his activities.

He received a call from Tom and asked if he had made any progress.

"Of a sort," was the cryptic reply. "I've finally got through to someone who can maybe let me know what's happening, and he's agreed to meet me for a drink next week."

"In London?" Graham asked.

"Yes. So, it would make sense for us to meet the following day. Much as I love the big city," Tom said with a huge slice of sarcasm, "I don't want to outstay my welcome."

After Tom's informal appointment with his former employers, they met for lunch the next day– at the usual venue.

Graham vetoed Tom's attempts at discussing Brexit. He was aware that certain key steps had taken place in parliament that week, but this was a story of which he felt he knew the ending – and it was not a happy one. Instead, he asked about the progress of work on the cottage.

"Coming along nicely," Tom replied. He no longer bothered to try and hide his South Wales accent.

After a few more questions elicited some detail about what he was doing, Graham felt it was now OK to ask about the real reason for their meeting.

"There's been a few changes at the old firm since I left," Tom started as soon as drinks were in front of them, and their meal had been ordered. "It took me a while to get through, but it was worth the wait. It seems that the professor's project was put on ice for a while – for obvious reasons – but they started it up again about a year later. There was very little appetite from Government for the first year or so, so the medics were working alone. But that's changed. It's now been going about five years. Anna and the prof are still running it, but on a slightly smaller scale. No more transmitting beams across the road – they do all the research in the lab in the main building. Interestingly, my old lot has kept up the lease on that other building, 'just in case' according to my contact, but I'm not sure I know what he means by 'just in case'. I'm not even sure he knows what he means by that either." Tom paused and took a swig of his beer, which gave Graham the chance to interject.

"Were you able to find out anything more about Anna?" he asked.

"Yes, and that's the interesting bit. You knew she grew up in East Germany, didn't you?"

"About all I do bloody know about her." Graham moaned.

"When they restarted the project, my old friends appointed a new young chap to look after it – you do understand that all of this is never to be repeated, don't you?" Tom seemed to suddenly realise that he was perhaps being a little too expansive to Graham and worried whether his loose tongue meant that his skills were getting rusty – or he was just getting old.

Graham was forceful in his reply.

"Tom, I've got no intention of sharing this information with anyone. Remember that you are speaking to someone who needs to be guarded about everything he says to anyone. All the time. I've just lost another girlfriend because she thought I kept too much to myself, so I'm not likely to blab anything you share with me."

"OK, keep your shirt on. Well, this new fellow decided quite rightly to recheck the records of everyone on the project and it showed that your lady friend had a bit of history. Her dad was a university lecturer who travelled around Europe back in the bad old days when East Germany didn't let too many of its citizens cross the border. It seems he did a bit of recruitment for the other side. My old lot would probably have liked to have her kicked off the project, but that couldn't happen. So, they decided to keep a close eye on her and to restrict her access to the real sensitive stuff. Just in case she turns out to be a chip off the old communist block."

Conversation paused as their main course was served but resumed as soon as the waiter was out of earshot.

"But they decided to let her stay and to keep a close eye on her. It's a good tactic, in my opinion. If you know you have a weakness and keep a good eye on it, it's better than blocking the hole and then always having to find out where the next leak develops. Because there's always a leak somewhere."

"And did they find out anything while they were keeping a close eye on her?"

"It seems that your Anna is not averse to a bit of male company. As I told you last time, she's on the books of an online dating agency. Well, it's called Select Few. She's been a member for years and has used her many meetings with well-heeled gentlemen to er .... feather her nest, shall we say."

"Yes, I remember that the prof told me she was on the books of a dating agency and that maybe she had been keeping the company of one particular gentleman for a long time."

"And that, as they say, is where the story gets really interesting," Tom appeared to be enjoying his return to the world of intrigue. "Because this fellow she's been seeing is one of us – or should I say one of them. And I'm not referring to his sexual proclivities. He's Russian."

Graham considered this piece of information carefully. Tom had been spending more time talking than eating for the last few minutes and was quite content for there to be a lull in the conversation so that he could concentrate on enjoying the roast beef.

Graham finished his meal – he had always been a quick eater - and while waiting for Tom to catch up, he mused.

"So, you're saying that our Anna, who we all thought was whiter than white, is not only dating a Russian spy but that she has been doing so for some time?"

"Yes. It's the 'for some time' bit that has our friends intrigued. If he was just trying to find out about the project, he would have dated her, found a way to get the information, and then broken the connection. Either that or he particularly enjoys her company."

Graham gave him a look, and Tom smiled. "Yes, just joking. There's no way this is happening without the full knowledge and approval of his superiors. We must assume that she is taking much longer to crack than they thought – or that they have decided to keep the project under long-term surveillance in this roundabout way."

"And what do you, and more importantly, your old friends, think is happening?"

"They think it's the latter of these two options. She is unlikely to spill her guts. Not if she's as close to the prof and the project as we all believe she is. And the Russians don't know the full story. They probably know there's 'something going on,' or else why would we have our people around the hospital for so long? No, they're keeping a watching brief."

"So, their plan is just to watch and wait?"

"Seems so"

"OK. We'll see if I can add any information into the mix when I've spoken to Anna."

Tom almost choked on one of his last mouthfuls. "Now that, my friend, is not something I expected to hear from you. And not something I'd recommend you do either."

"Look, I've come back in time five years, I've risked my life going through that dodgy beam of the professor's, and who knows what damage I'm doing to my brain. All to do a favour for a man who seems to deserve some help because I'm the only person who can help him. I'm not going to chicken out now. I have to go and see her."

"Well, just put it on record that I've advised you against it. Dating ladies who are dating Russian agents can be very dangerous for your future lifestyle. Just ask Mister Profumo if you don't believe me."

Graham pondered his friend's witty reference to a scandal of the nineteen sixties, knowing that Tom had guessed correctly that he would understand his reference. Back in the days of politicians with scruples, John Profumo had resigned as a government minister because it had emerged that his girlfriend was also dating a Russian spy.

Graham asked a few more questions to see if there was anything else that Tom could add to what he'd said, but there was nothing else of substance.

"I was wondering how to make contact with her, and you've given me the answer. I'm going to sign up for this dating agency and try to get a date with her. I'll let you know how I get on."

As they moved into the lounge to enjoy their coffees, Graham wanted to get an answer to something that had been bothering him.

"Tom, you've accepted my story more fully and more easily than I thought you would. Even after the lottery win, I expected to get more of a grilling from you."

"I guess it must be because I read so many science fiction books. I was always fascinated by time travel, so I must just be susceptible."

Not being totally convinced, Graham pushed a little further.

"Which ones have you read?" he asked.

"Loads. 'The Time Machine', of course. 'Replay'. The ones by Adrian Cousins because they're set in the UK and don't take the subject too seriously. That Stephen King one about the Kennedy assassination."

"'11.22.63'"

"Yes, that's it. Didn't like that one much. I've just finished 'Wrong Place Wrong Time'. I liked that one – very clever."

"Interesting. I suppose that would make it easier for you to believe my wildly improbable story. I used to read things like that myself, not that I read them any more – now that I'm living the life!

Anyway, on this particular plane of time," Graham said, clumsily turning the subject back to their joint concern. "I'll let you know how things go if and when I meet Anna," Then, responding to the old-fashioned look he was getting from Tom, he added, "And yes, Dad, I'll be careful."

17 Important Dates

January 2020

A few days after his lunch with Tom, Graham signed up on the 'Select Few' website and answered the questionnaire. He did not fear any investigation into his financial record or his past. He had no CCJs or criminal convictions. And he felt even more normal for having a sprinkling of speeding offences. He'd attended multiple speed awareness courses and once paid a fine. Other than that, his record was clean. More importantly, he could report a net worth that would meet their criteria. But he would not be honest about how it was acquired. They didn't ask that – but if Anna did, then his story was that it had come from the sale of his business.

He also noted some of the questions asking his opinions on various matters. Of course, he answered, it was the man's role to pay for the expenses of any date. And no, a woman who accepted this type of hospitality was completely right to do so. Even if you didn't know what kind of dating agency this was when you started the questionnaire, you certainly should do so by the time you finished it.

He answered the questions in exactly the way he thought they would want him to answer them, even when some of his answers did not entirely coincide with his true beliefs. He was here to gain admittance, not to express his real opinion.

It took a couple of weeks before he was accepted, and received a helpful, chatty email telling him how to behave when contacting the ladies on the site. Initial contact would be by anonymised email. The ladies' profiles included a photograph and a first name by which they wished to be known and as much (or as little) about themselves, their work status, age, and so on, as they chose to reveal.

Graham briefly wondered if the delay in getting approved was caused by a genuine checking process or was just created to give that impression. Either way, it didn't matter. He was within his planned target timetable of meeting Anna by February 2021.

As soon as he was approved, he contacted her via the website and was relieved to find that she had used her real name (without a last name, of course), so they were quickly able to begin an email conversation.

She was cautious, and he knew she was no doubt sending him messages she had sent many times before. He explained that with more than a year having passed since the loss of his wife, and with one recent relationship that had ended in disappointment, he was very carefully exploring the chance of dating.

He gave his true age and location (he was going to have to lie about so much; he would keep to the truth when it made no difference). As their dialogue continued, he made it clear that he thought a first date should be at a restaurant, and that since she had admitted that she had already had a few dates, perhaps she knew of a suitable place that was convenient for her. He also told her he had access to a company apartment in central London. It was one of the perks he received in return for occasionally helping his old company on tricky projects. So, he could have a late dinner with her and not have to worry about enjoying a glass of wine or having to depend on the parlous state of late-night trains from London into Kent for his return journey.

He had already made it very clear that he was available any day of the week. He did not know whether Anna was averse to dating married men – a significant proportion of the male customers of this site must surely be married, he correctly assumed – but making it clear that he was available every day of the week indicated that he was less likely to be married. Married men asked for dates on Mondays to Thursdays only.

Progress was slow and was interrupted by Christmas. She let him know that because she was single, she always volunteered for extra shifts over the holiday period so that her colleagues who had families could have more time with them. So, over the holiday period, she had almost no time to even read and write emails, let alone date. For this and other reasons, he grew to like her as they exchanged messages, and so was doubly pleased when she agreed to meet him for dinner. The date was set for Friday, 7th February, and the venue was a restaurant near Whetstone, where he already knew she lived but, of course, could not let her know.

-

Anna was quite looking forward to this date with her new contact. Over the years, she had become choosier in her selections, taking longer before deciding whether to date or not. Some fell by the way because of their over-eagerness to set up the first meeting. Others showed unhealthy personal traits in the email conversations. Neither of these applied to Graham. There was a slight air of mystery about him. She usually could tell if the man was looking for a fling, an affair, or a mistress. She had long since given up any hope that any of them were looking for a life partner, but she was not sure which category Graham fell into.

Currently, her only relationship was with Karl. It had been going on for years and she could not understand quite why. It was financially rewarding because of the terms of engagement that Karl had proposed. He was undemanding, and they had interesting conversations despite there being so many 'red-line areas.' Neither could talk about their job, and Karl was very cagey about his childhood and early adulthood. He had spent some time in Germany – details unspecified - and was a fluent German speaker, so that occasionally they adopted this language when talking about matters back in her home country. But he did have a broad knowledge of world events and often had a different perspective on matters that she found to be both entertaining and thought-provoking.

There was the strange twist that had happened a couple of years ago when he had been posted on an undercover job at a university and had, as a result, spent a year posing as a student of the History of Art. A whole new dimension to their conversations and dates opened up – and he took her on some highly informative visits to some of London's art galleries. However, this long-lasting but sterile relationship was not enough, and she raised her hopes that Graham might add something new to her life.

-

Graham calculated the travel time from his home to the restaurant. Mainline rail into London Victoria station, and then a longish journey on the Underground with one change of line. Allowing for this, he calculated that the six-thirty train from his home station should get him to the restaurant on time – but Graham was a worrier. He decided to catch the six o'clock train instead.

When he arrived at the station and saw the announcement that the train had been cancelled, he was glad of his decision. But when the six-thirty train unexpectedly came to a halt halfway between his home station and London Victoria, and an announcement of a fifteen-minute delay was made, he was not happy.

Anna had not let him know her mobile phone number – even though he had let her know his. A sensible precaution, but he was now less sanguine about the inability to contact her. He emailed from his phone and explained that he was likely to be a quarter of an hour late. He worried for the rest of the journey that she might not get the email and he would arrive to find an empty table at the restaurant. He need not have worried. She was waiting for him and understood his obvious discomfort.

"I returned your email – but I guess you were on the tube by then and didn't get it" she explained.

He apologised and explained that the double jeopardy of a cancelled train followed by a delay had been his undoing.

"So, you did not plan to catch the train that would have had you here on time. You originally planned to catch a train that would have got you here more than half an hour early?"

He nodded a brief confirmation.

"And did you check out the exact route from the local tube station to the restaurant, too?" she asked as the waiter took his drink order. (Anna had already started a glass of white wine.)

"Yes, on Google Maps and Streetview," he answered, forcing a smile as he thought she might be teasing him slightly.

"Well, in that case, I have to say that we may get on very well. I would have done the same. My medical colleagues would never forgive me if I made any reference to OCD in describing my status – but let's just say I have an above-average understanding of those who suffer from it."

Graham smiled and complimented her on how she had made the joke in such a politically correct way.

"But I do have a question to ask," she continued. "Why are you looking at the menu? You've already looked at it online and decided what you're going to order, haven't you?"

This time he smiled openly and congratulated her on her guesswork.

"Not quite. There's always the possibility of a tempting house special or a recommendation from my date, whom I assume has dined here before," he replied.

"Yes, I have – dined here, that is – and I can tell you that everything is good here and that the owner does not believe in house specials."

With their conversation having begun in the middle, as Anna later put it, they chatted effortlessly and enjoyably throughout the meal. Graham enjoyed the evening more than he had expected – Anna was an exceptionally good conversationalist and after gathering his composure somewhat, he realised that she was even better looking than her profile picture on the website.

That photo had been a considerable improvement on the photograph on her hospital HR record, which was all he had to go by until now. In fact, the evening went so well that he had been distracted and completely failed to direct the conversation towards finding out some of the things he wanted to know – and some of the impressions he had planned to make on her. A second date was going to be needed.

At the end of the meal, Anna thanked him – for paying for it and for his excellent company. She told him that she would like to leave the restaurant five minutes before he did – and reassured him that her flat was only five minutes' walk along well-lit streets. But she did want to keep her address secret for the time being. She said that she made a rock-hard commitment to herself to fix a second date only after she had twenty-four hours to think over the first date. He had no choice but to accept her terms, and, after a brief hug, she left.

He ordered a cab to his apartment, where he spent the night for the first time. He went over in his mind what he had learned about her and worried that it was very little. He had to hope against hope that she would agree to a second date.

-

Thankfully, she did, and Graham asked if she would agree to meet at a restaurant close to his London apartment, naturally letting her know that he would pay for her taxi home, and she agreed to meet him on Friday, 28th February. The date proved auspicious for one of his objectives. Knowing that the pandemic was about to sweep the country and that lockdown was now less than a month away – which was hard to imagine when you looked around the crowded restaurant – he wanted to make Anna believe that he knew more about the disease so that she might look to him for his opinion and continue an email conversation during lockdown.

He didn't leap into it as the first subject of conversation. There was a stuttering start to their meeting – maybe because the first date had gone so well. They talked about the recent storms – this woman will think I'm a typical Brit, he thought. I'm sure that Germans believe we talk about nothing but the weather. The ice was broken when she jokingly referred to him as Mister Henderson, and in reply, he called her Frau Mueller.

"You pronounced my last name correctly," she said. So very few English people do. I'm now accustomed to being Miss Mooller, or even sometimes Miss Moo-eller." She parodied a British accent when saying this, and he laughed.

"Did you study German at school?" she asked.

"No, I did a course of intensive German at work to help me communicate with my German customers."

"Well, it seems to have had some effect."

"Oh yes," he continued in mock seriousness, "You must form the lips to make the 'oo' sound but use your mouth to make the 'ee' sound". Just the way the instructor on his course had told the participants to pronounce a German 'u' with an umlaut.

"I have never heard that explanation of how to pronounce it," she said.

"Of course not. You would only hear that if you were an Englishman struggling to pronounce a new sound. Just the same way that we never learn about orange skies and shady clouds over my pillow," he continued.

"What on earth is that?" she asked.

"A friend of mine in Germany told me that was how he learned the order of adjectives in English. I had never realised that this was something that causes foreigners so much trouble."

"And how are orange skies and pillows supposed to help this?"

Graham was beginning to enjoy how she was able to mock his seriousness.

"I don't know. I just remembered the acronym. Something to do with opinion, size, age, shape, and so on. When you learn English growing up you just know that there's an attractive shiny new Italian ceramic vase on that windowsill over there," he said, pointing at the appropriate object. "I don't have to remember the order of those adjectives before the noun."

"That was very clever, the way you did that." Anna imitated, clapping her hands in applause. "But I just learned by listening and repeating. I imagine trying to learn English in the schoolroom would be a nightmare. There's no consistency in it. After twenty years, I still think I learn something every day."

Their conversation then flowed, and a few minutes later, he introduced the subject of Covid, asking if she had heard the news that the first British death had been announced earlier in the day. She admitted she hadn't noticed this – perhaps understandable as she was not British herself.

She had been more concerned with the mass shooting that had happened recently in Germany. He asked if she had any connections with Hanau, and she replied that she was glad not to. In a strange reversal of roles, he let her know that his local town was twinned with Hanau, and both his children had taken part in student exchange visits. But it was so long ago that they could not even remember the names of the children they had swapped with.

He asked if any preparations for Covid were being made at her hospital. She was not aware of any – and didn't expect any since it was an eye hospital. As he had hoped, she asked what his thoughts were. When he told her that he thought the scenes that had just started happening in Wuhan, China, and to a limited extent in Italy – the admitting of a large number of people to hospitals and the commencement of severe restrictions on travel – would soon come to the UK, she thought he was over-reacting. Of course, he told her he hoped she was right (even though he knew she was not).

"We've benefitted in the UK for many hundreds of years from being an international crossroads," was how he put it. "Lots of people passing through, lots of people starting businesses here because it's always good to place your business on a crossroads. Asian and American companies almost always opened their first European office or their European Headquarters in London. And Americans always had the UK as their number one destination on their European vacation. Now I fear we'll suffer for the same reason. We'll get it worse than Italy – and our wonderful relaxed British attitude to making and following rules may be more of a problem than an advantage."

The rest of their conversation was on cheerier topics, and they spent an enjoyable evening together. As Graham called for the bill, Anna agreed they would meet again, and, comparing their diaries, they sadly discovered that they could not fix a mutually convenient date until March 24th. Graham paid the bill and showed her some of the new twenty-pound notes that he obtained that morning from an ATM. Before she got in the taxi, they kissed briefly. Graham was left to make his way back to his apartment for the second time, realising that he would be unlikely to see her or the apartment again for a long time.

When he got back, he poured himself a large Glenmorangie (he drank very little during his meal with Anna for obvious reasons) and mulled over what he had learned during this second date. Methodical as ever, he took out a pen and paper and made some notes. He had steered the conversation as much as he dared and hoped it had appeared as no more than the natural way in which a second date might normally go, with him trying to find out as much as possible to help decide whether to proceed.

His first note was *Family*. Her parents were both dead and her only living relative was her sister, Cornelia, who was married to Reinhard Wobst, an IT teacher who worked in the same school as she did. Cornelia had followed her mother in her career – they even taught in the same school, the very same school that both she and Anna had attended.

Anna was in regular contact with her sister, and despite the duration and distance of their separation, they were obviously still very close. Graham noted these points.

Next, in the order in which they had discussed it over dinner, he wrote *Nationality*. There was no doubt that Anna considered herself German. To her, there was only ever one Germany, and she was a citizen of that country and proud of it. She loved London, enjoyed all that it had brought her, and had a certain fondness for the English people but would never aspire to change nationality.

She was concerned about how Brexit might affect her but remained confident there would be a way for her to remain a UK resident even after the separation. She had never given any thought to how, where, or when she would retire, but Graham thought that he had an important pointer to where she might have disappeared when she chose to do so.

Talks of nationality had led to the next subject heading that Graham wrote on his piece of paper. *Politics*. Anna had been vague about her political leanings. She found it hard – as most foreigners would – to express her politics in terms of British political parties and was completely disinterested in British politics. Considering the current situation, Graham found it easy to agree with her on that score. But as to her deeper political thoughts, she expressed a dislike for the Orwellian view that so many seemed to have - Democracy Good, Socialism Bad – as she put it. They agreed that the world was more nuanced than that.

She gave a couple of examples of how she thought (or remembered) things had been better – especially for the poorer members of society – in the "bad old days" of the East German Democratic Republic compared with how the bright new shining democracy of the United Kingdom treated some of its less fortunate citizens. She was no communist – not even a socialist – but refused to see things in the plain, black-and-white way in which they were so often presented.

Graham had tried to explain that he thought much of the blame for this apparent simplicity of the typical British view came from the one-dimensional way many parts of the mainstream media portrayed matters but was unsure if she entirely believed him.

His last heading on his list was *Job/Work*. There was no disguising the fact that she loved her job and enjoyed her work. It was very important for her. The more that he had dug into the subject over dinner, the more often the name of Professor Karbajanovic cropped up. He wondered if Anna realised how frequently she spoke of him and how fondly. Maybe this was a case where someone was too close to something to know exactly what it was. And in this case, the 'something' was a close relationship that had developed between her and her boss. A very close relationship.

At the end of their date, he had asked about her situation on Select Few. She had made no secret that she had been using the agency for some time and had had many relationships as a result. It had been easy for Graham to be honest and say that he was new to the site and that she was his first date.

He had used this angle to try to discover more about her relationship with the mystery man. He thought of him as a mystery man only because he had learned from the Secret Service, via Tom, that there was a man she had been dating for some time but that they could not (or would not) provide details of.

Graham had an uncanny feeling that this mystery man might somehow be linked to Anna's disappearance. But she never mentioned him, which only made Graham more suspicious. She spoke of some men who went out with her from time to time – company dinners, special events, and so on. She even spoke of some men who tried desperately to tell her they were single when she thought they could not be more obviously married if they had a large M tattooed on their forehead. But she reiterated that there was nobody special in her life. And while she would welcome it if it happened, she was adamant that it was currently nowhere near happening. This only confused Graham further. Was she lying to cover up the relationship with this mystery man – or was it really as meaningless as she had suggested? It only fuelled his suspicions, and he wondered what Tom might make of it when he updated him.

He put the top back on his pen and removed the sheet of paper from the pad. It would go back home with him to add to his original notes about Anna. Then, one final thought struck him. When they had set the date for their next meeting, Anna had remarked, "March twenty-fourth - that's the day before my birthday." It was a throwaway comment, and he had responded automatically by saying something like, "I'll have to get you a present." Then there had been a brief distraction of her asking him for his birthday, which he told her was in October and she had said that she promised to buy him a present if they were still seeing each other at that far distant date. She also said that he didn't need to buy her a present and joked that when a German woman says you don't need to do something, she actually means you do need to do something.

He had thought nothing of her saying her birthday was March 25th but had felt sure that her personnel record had given a birthdate at the end of June. It was always possible that the date on her record was wrong – possible but unlikely. It was also possible that he had misread the record. He decided to make a further note on his paper and check the original date when he returned home. It might be unimportant, but considering the complexity of the task he was pursuing, every discrepancy needed checking. Nobody ever gets their birthday wrong, do they?

As he finished his drink and went to bed, he realised there was one other important aspect of his date to be wary of. He was in danger of falling for her.

She was wonderful company. She was both intelligent and interesting in her conversation and had experiences that led to stimulating exchanges of views. Added to that, she was physically attractive – not just attractive for her age, she was bloody good-looking. And her slight German accent was the icing on the cake. There was something about women with slight accents that was always special to Graham. Not just the obvious ones – even an American accent added to a woman's appeal for Graham.

He had been very tempted to arrange another date that would actually be fulfilled but knew that it was probably not a good idea, and therefore had faked his unavailability until March 24th. He knew that by setting this as the date for their next meeting, it would never happen because lockdown was due to be announced the day before.

He hoped that his caution would be rewarded and that they could conduct an email relationship through the extended period of the various lockdowns that were about to commence. And then hopefully he would be in a good position to either prevent her disappearance or at least know what happened to make her disappear and where she had gone.

18 Lockdown
March 2020

This was Graham's third experience of the 2020-21 UK Covid Lockdown. There was simply no way of avoiding it on any plane of time he had yet experienced. In some ways, this one was going to be better than his previous experiences, but in other ways, it would be worse.

His first lockdown experience was more than a lifetime ago. He had lived a second life since then, so his first experience was over fifty years ago, and his memory of it was as faded as that implied. He recalled vague feelings of unease, excitement, and loneliness while on his own – which was almost all the time. But there had also been a strange sense of camaraderie with strangers once the initial shock had worn off.

At first, people often reacted by stepping out of your way – or even crossing the street – when you passed while out walking. But that soon changed to a kind of 'blitz spirit', and people were more likely to speak to total strangers than normally. And, thanks to the power of basic human emotions and the messages being delivered by politicians, there was always the feeling that the whole lockdown event was a temporary state that we all had to endure together and would be over soon. But it was not an experience he looked forward to reliving.

The second time around, his experience could not have differed more. In his second life, he had believed that what he was experiencing was in some way 'how things are now' and had planned and executed accordingly. He tried to make improvements to the whole experience and mitigate some of the awful conditions front-line medical staff experienced. In cooperation with his nephew, he used the fortune built up during his second life to buy several companies and convert their production lines to the manufacture of Personal Protective Equipment for use by the UK medical profession. His understanding was that by his actions in that plane of time, many lives had been saved.

It meant that he had bypassed the lockdown experience. He had been exceptionally busy running the companies, drastically increasing their output, meeting government officials, etc. Far from being isolated or idle, he was probably busier than at any time in either of his lives.

This would be his third time around and he was back to being a normal citizen facing the full impact, dull as that impact was. Even worse, he was aware that this was not going to be a short-term fix, which so many people expected it to be. It was going to be a series of on/off events lasting almost eighteen months before everything reverted to normal – or as close to normality as the post-Covid world came.

He knew how boring it could be. And it was no help to him to have the feeling that 'all of this is not real' which coloured every day of this second comeback of his. Provided that he didn't do anything stupid – like catch Covid in the early days of the pandemic or walk in front of a bus - his life would not be changed.

There was the added frustration of knowing that he had a job to do; to find out what had happened to Anna, and to let the professor know. And he had to put all his actions working towards this goal on hold. The large sum of money sitting in his bank account was useless too. For the next eighteen months, the chances to spend it were going to be severely limited. Even when travel and entertainment were possible it was going to be inconvenient as well as risky (in terms of contracting the virus).

Elizabeth's unexpected and sudden decision to end their relationship just added to his frustration (in more ways than one).

He had to think positively. He remembered that at some points of the lockdown, it was easy to overcome boredom as the whole day could be spent completing a couple of tasks that normally would occupy only an hour or two.

A trip to the supermarket for the week's groceries and a visit to the local DIY store each involved standing in a queue that wound itself all the way around a car park. And there were the resulting impromptu conversations with the total strangers in front of and behind you in the queue that broadened your experience and whiled away the hours. There was also the feeling that you must go out for an hour's exercise every day when it was all you were legally permitted. He remembered discovering many of the public footpaths around his neighbourhood that had previously been unknown to him. It was now time for him to re-discover them.

He also knew it was useful to have a hobby (or, even better, an obsession) to tide you through. The first time around, he remembered his unsuccessful attempt to learn to play a musical instrument. He would not be repeating that. But he had thought of two ways to help him through this time – one involving indoor activity and one involving outdoor activity.

Indoors, he was going to learn German. In his first life, he had attended an intensive course in the language and had used it a little in his business dealings. But he had learned very little, and it was a very long time ago. He needed to start again almost from scratch. But he had the advantage of the latest software and online tools, plus the whole of the internet and almost limitless amounts of time. He could watch videos on YouTube and even tune his TV into German channels. And it was the perfect excuse to maintain a dialogue via email with Anna.

His proposed outdoor obsession was based on his memory of the excellent weather that had lasted through much of the first lockdown period.

He had never been interested in gardening. While his wife was alive, he had followed her directions to undertake any heavy lifting or messy tasks involved in the upkeep of the plants in their garden. That, and maintaining the lawn, were the limits of his horticultural activity. For him, a garden was to be sat in and enjoyed, not worked on.

Since his wife's death, he had fought a losing battle to keep the flowers and shrubs in good order. His outdoor obsession for the period of the lockdown would be to grow a perfect lawn. In March, he bought a new lawnmower with a heavy roller, and a large supply of seeds, feeds, and stuff to kill weeds.

-

In May 2020 – just over a month after the traumatic announcement of the lockdown was made by Prime Minister Boris Johnson, Graham had all his lockdown plans underway. He had worked hard on his basic German and was already beginning to show progress. He was now watching and understanding children's programs on German daytime TV. One of the advantages of living alone was that there was nobody there to laugh at the ridiculous sight of a nearly seventy-year-old man carefully following programs aimed at seven-year-old German children.

His lawn was looking better – not yet up to his Wembley-like aspirations, but an improvement on its previous state. He was also sporting a tan – his skin weathered from the time spent in the early-year sunshine watering and mowing his lawn and the hour a day spent walking the local footpaths.

One of the walks he followed once a week took him past the front door of Elizabeth's house, and one morning, on the spur of the moment, he decided to walk down her path and knock on her front door. They had parted amicably (just), and he felt it was right to check on her well-being.

It proved to be a good decision. She cautiously invited him in for a cup of coffee, checking not only that he was willing to resume social contact but also that he was neither one of the fanatics who were rejecting all human interaction because of fear of contamination nor a zealot who was closely following all government rules and recommendations.

It was quickly apparent to Graham that Elizabeth was not faring well. Previously, she had always looked at her best, whether behind the counter of the charity shop, out to dinner, or even just relaxing at home. But now she was wearing no makeup, and her hair needed brushing. The house was untidy, where it had previously been spotlessly clean, with nothing ever out of place unless it was in current use. She extended her offering of a cup of coffee to ask him if he would prefer a glass of wine.

"I make it a rule not to drink until evening," he said, hoping not to sound too parsimonious.

He had imposed this rule on himself as he knew how easy it would be to open a bottle of wine at lunchtime and how often this might lead to another bottle being opened before the end of the day. Proof of the damage that this could cause was staring him in the face.

They chatted over a cup of coffee – and then a second cup accompanied by a plate of biscuits. Elizabeth talked a lot, and he listened. Her inability to go into the charity shop had metaphorically pulled the rug from under her. The shop was the keystone of her social life and provided most of her reason for living. Her family lived a long way away (and were not that close in any other sense of the word, he remembered). She was also a natural born worrier, and the unfamiliar circumstances they were all experiencing were feeding her worst fears.

He very cautiously explored the possibility of the two of them meeting on a regular basis – introducing it with joking references of not telling Boris in case it was against the law. Before he knew it, he was engulfed in her embrace and was being showered with thanks for wanting to get back together.

Graham began to explain that his reasons for previously keeping information to himself were that his job had involved some work of a secret nature, and he apologised for not making it clearer.

He knew that this was stretching the truth a long way to explain his absences, and hopefully, she might accept this as a justification for his apparent distance that she had complained about when they split. In turn, she apologised for the way she had overreacted, and they moved on to have lunch together – Graham suggesting that as this was now a special occasion, they could open a bottle of wine to celebrate their getting back together.

Later that afternoon, in bed, he told her that if she was going to come round to his house in the near future, she must not laugh at him watching German children's TV and would have to be very careful when walking on his lawn.

-

By this time, he was in regular email contact with Anna. They had exchanged messages as soon as the lockdown was announced, and their date therefore summarily cancelled. He had said that he would very much like to either speak with her or email her, and she suggested email. Her main reason was that as soon as she realised the parlous state that the front line of the health service was in, she volunteered to do extra shifts at the London Hospital to help share the burden. Taking her usual light touch on a potentially serious issue, she said that if he called her, she might be at work, and if not, she might well be too knackered to speak to him. He particularly liked the way she had picked up precisely the right English word, 'knackered'.

-

With his memories of the TV coverage of the early days of the pandemic and the risks that medical staff were forced to take, he was intent on helping Anna in any way he could. He racked his memory for the contact details of people he had known when heavily involved in the PPE business during his second life. Tony Smith was the name that he eventually dragged up. 'How can I forget such an unusual name?' he joked to himself.

Tony had managed a company in Leicester that had made Type IIR and FFP3 face masks. During Graham's second life, this was one of several companies that he had bought, and, with the help of his nephew, he had transformed its manufacturing plant from a 40-hour working week to a 168-hour working week.

Tony had been really good, staying on after the sale of the company to help the transition. Graham remembered several interesting chats with him about his passion for Leicester City Football Club and the boys' team that Tony sponsored and helped to run.

'One of the many unfortunate aspects of time travel is that even though I know all about him, Tony will not know me from a hole in the wall. I'll have to rely on the man's better nature', Graham thought. He looked up the address of Tony's company and sent him a letter asking for a thousand of both types of masks that his company manufactured to be sent to Anna Mueller, giving her work address at Moorfield Hospital.

He dug deep into his memory for the price at which each of the two types of masks was sold to the NHS under the contracts he had worked on, He calculated that the sale price of the two thousand masks would be about £2,500 in total, so he enclosed a cheque for £5,000 made payable to Tony and asked him to forward any excess profit on the transaction to the Leicester Foxcubs boys football team.

He was delighted to hear from Anna on a subsequent call that this mysterious package had arrived at her office. She had been too busy and too tired to worry about why it had arrived.

A few weeks and several emails later, he asked if she could help him in his quest to learn to speak German. Would she write to him in German so that he could test his ability? And would it be OK for him to answer in the same language? He appreciated that she didn't have time to mark his homework, so to speak, but forcing himself to write real emails in German would help his learning process. She was happy to oblige, telling him that when she was tired, she found it easier to email in her native language anyway.

By now, he had graduated from children's programmes on German TV to full adult shows. He found it absolutely fascinating to see the difference between the way their media and Government handled the whole topic of Covid compared with their opposite numbers back in the UK. Many racial stereotypes were close to the surface, as the German response seemed so much more serious, efficient, and effective compared with that of the UK, he thought.

But many German TV shows, particularly crime dramas, which were a favourite of Graham's, were a disappointment. The level of plot development, attention to detail, and the realism of what was depicted were years behind equivalent UK shows, he thought.

But these shows were excellent in teaching him German slang. He watched with subtitles whenever possible and used the internet to research unfamiliar terms. But he had to seek an explanation from Anna on some occasions. He was flummoxed by a character remarking, "Es regnet Schusterjungen.". His translation software told him that this meant "It's raining cobbler boys," which he understood might mean "It's raining shoemaker's apprentices," but this did not lead him to any greater understanding.

Anna's greater knowledge enabled her to let him know that Schusterjungen was the name of a type of bread roll available in Berlin. So, the sentence translated as 'it's raining bread rolls' or 'The raindrops are as big as bread rolls.' Which Graham thought made as much sense as a British person saying it's raining cats and dogs.

Likewise, "Räubergeschichte" was translated as 'a story about robbers.' She told him this was an indirect, colloquial way of saying it was a lie. He once again reciprocated the learning experience by letting her know that the best English equivalent was probably 'a cock and bull story'.

Their dialogue was peppered with time delays – hers because of work and sleep pressures, his because he could not let Elizabeth see him taking time answering emails. He would never be able to explain why he was emailing another woman in German. Amidst it all, he learned that Anna had found a way to have a social life in the middle of London during an enforced lockdown.

He had to read between the lines of her emails as the information she gave him was incomplete. The best he could put together was that she had been introduced to a group of people who held regular secret social gatherings at a venue in the West End of London (probably in Mayfair from Anna's imprecise description).

If this was not cause enough for worry, it was also almost certain that the person who had introduced her to this illicit social gathering, and her regular companion for her visits, was none other than the long-term dating partner that she had been so coy about when he had first asked. But he had to keep his concerns to himself and make sure he did not ask too many questions about the mystery man.

Instead, he was pleased to note that Anna asked him about how he thought the lockdown would progress, how he thought things were being handled, and crucially, how long he thought it would last.

He conveyed the wisdom that was already gaining ground. The UK had been late in locking down. Neither the large horse-racing event at Cheltenham nor the European Cup football game between Liverpool and Madrid should have been allowed to happen. He gave his opinion of the difficulties that these decisions posed for the Prime Minister, who was libertarian in his views and forced into making restrictive decisions that went against every fibre in his being.

He told her to be prepared for the long haul. Those same instincts that Boris possessed would lead to immense pressure to lift the restrictions too early, and if the government succumbed to this, it might even cause a second lockdown to be needed. He told her to think in terms of months, not weeks.

She asked him about what she thought was the strange way that the mainland UK handled the lockdown in three separate areas – England, Scotland, and Wales. He had to explain that the reasons for this lay in the long-term historical separation of the three countries, reinvigorated by the recent devolving of powers. He reminded her of the separate decisions being made by different states within Germany – a fact he had only become aware of since exercising his newfound mastery of the German language and consequent watching of German newscasts.

He gave his opinion that Nicola Sturgeon was better suited to the task of managing a lockdown in Scotland than Boris was in England. He explained that he thought she had the perfect school-mistress demeanour and capability to show attention to detail, whereas Boris was much more a 'bigger picture' kind of guy who would prefer to be seen as a 'man of the people'. He did his best to uplift her in what he knew was a challenging time – and to not fall into the trap of becoming a doom-monger. For all his knowledge of how difficult the times would be, he had the unique advantage of knowing with one hundred percent certainty that we would come through it. Eventually.

19 False Dawns
July 2020

When the initial lockdown was lifted at the end of July, Anna contacted Graham and raised the possibility of another date. He was both flattered and concerned. Flattered because he knew that she had her regular companion who had been accompanying her to the illicit entertainment venue that she had told him about. And no doubt she would have several other potential suitors from her contact list at the agency. Concerned because he had to balance his wish to see her again with the difficulty of keeping it secret from Elizabeth.

There was a national sense of relief that the lockdown was over. Some members of the public may have been wary – and he was sure that certain members of the medical community who knew the real state of the risk of the disease would also be very cagey about resuming normal social life. But almost everyone else was hell-bent on catching up on lost time and using the newly available government incentives to get extra value from 'eating out to help out'.

He carried the burden of knowing that relief would be temporary. He was also keen to use the opportunities of these incentives and the fabulous warm weather to eat out with Elizabeth in Kent pub gardens rather than in enclosed London restaurants with the inherent risks of catching the disease.

There was also the difficulty of timing visits to London in such a way that Elizabeth did not find out or that necessitated a good excuse to be thought up. The more he told her about undertaking secret work for mysterious government bodies, the more he would stretch her credulity and the higher the pressure on him to expand on the flimsy details he had given her so far.

However, he felt it was essential to maintain a good level of contact with Anna as, figuratively speaking, the clock was now ticking. Her mysterious disappearance was little more than a year away, and something told him that the countdown to whatever the event was, would soon start. If it had not already done so.

He asked if she knew of any open-air venues for their meeting, reminding her of the risks of disease transmission that still existed. She told him of one reasonably near where she lived, and he agreed to meet there.

When they met, she hugged him close for several seconds. But it was the hug given to a friend, not a lover. He was pleased to settle for the role of close friend. Anything closer than that would bring major complications. And besides, the role of a close friend was more likely to be longer lasting.

Even though they had emailed each other frequently and lengthily for the previous four months, they still had plenty to talk about and they easily passed lunch, and much of the afternoon. He was reminded of her magnetism and had to remember that his date had a purpose.

She was getting real release by telling him about some of the events she had witnessed while helping with Covid patients at London Hospital. The stories were bad enough, and he was sure that even these were censored. The stories, documentaries, and dramatisations he had seen before his travel back in time had let him know how bad it had been.

But he pried some information from her about how she had been entertained during the lockdown. She was a little coy, making him promise not to tell tales about what she had been doing, and confessing that everyone there knew they were breaking the rules and that this sense of danger merely added to the fun.

"Everybody called it the Tube Station. It must have been like this to go to a speakeasy during prohibition in America," she said. She admitted that she didn't know anyone, but they all seemed to be very important. About fifty or sixty were there at any one time. Lords and Ladies, government people and foreign ambassadors, that sort of thing. And his suspicions were confirmed. Her long-time dating companion had taken her, and he was more than just her escort for these events. Anna let it slip that he was involved in running the events and many of the people seemed to know him. Several staff consulted him on many issues. Graham knew that he would have to find out more about this.

'Bad enough her going to a speakeasy,' he thought. 'Much worse if she was accompanied by bloody Al Capone.'

He carefully asked her about this long-term dating companion whom she had never spoken of before. She was quick to say that their relationship was based entirely on mutual convenience and that no affection was shared between them. Graham trod carefully, not wanting to show too much interest in the man. The only other information he gathered was that his name was Karl, that he had a confidential government job, and that he had once worked undercover at a university for a year.

When he asked her about her regular job and the prof, she had little to say. They continued treating patients, the professor continued to be very frustrated at the lack of progress in developing his ideas, and the government used the excuse of the pandemic to withdraw what little support they had been providing. It was almost at a standstill.

Eventually, he had to return home. This being Saturday, Elizabeth would have spent the day at her newly reopened charity shop. Judging by her remarks earlier in the week, she was liable to be there until long after closing time, but he still didn't want to be too late back.

They agreed on another date in late August. He would use the time in between to find out more about the mysterious fellow Anna had been dating and to feed back to Tom about the illicit activity during lockdown.

-

Graham had maintained occasional contact with Tom throughout the pandemic. He wanted to keep his issue in the front of Tom's mind – even though he was not going to do much about it for a while yet. So, when he informed Tom about how the pandemic and the lockdown were going to progress, he was both helping a friend and constantly reminding him of the problem he would soon be helping to solve.

The relationship between the two of them was, of necessity, a strange one. Graham had known Tom for over fifty years and, during his second life, had worked with him for several years. However, because of the time travel issue, Tom had only known Graham for a couple of years, and they had only met a few times and held a few phone conversations during that time.

Tom owed his more comfortable recent lifestyle to Graham. Every lottery winner may have a slight feeling of guilt and a tiny worry that this huge fortune could be snatched away every bit as easily as it was delivered. For Tom, these feelings were stronger because of the strange circumstances surrounding his win. He would always worry that it had been an ill-gotten gain and therefore at risk. But he was grateful, nonetheless.

The relationship with Tom was special for Graham too. Tom was the only person with whom he could discuss time travel and the issues it raised. He had often considered telling Elizabeth about his strange past, but every time he thought about it, he concluded that it was best not to divulge his secret. While it might bring them closer and explain some of his periods of absence and some of the strange things he sometimes said, telling her would raise other problems. It would reveal that he had lied to her for the entire time they had been together – which was not a great start. And it might give her a feeling of unease. Was he going to time-travel again? Once she understood that he did not regard this as his 'real' plane of time, it might undermine their whole relationship. And if she asked him if and when he might travel in time again, he could not give an honest answer. Because he didn't know.

It could be said that his relationship with Tom was the only truly honest one he had. So, he made sure to be frank with Tom in every respect. He told him about his dates with Anna. He even admitted to the attraction he felt and how he took steps to minimise the frequency of their dates for fear of getting too close. But now it was time to move a few of the playing pieces on the board of this game of life.

He told Tom what he had learned about Karl including his mysterious undercover job at a British university, which, although very vague, might prove to be useful background material. But the information about the underground gatherings during the pandemic was more important. In particular, the real likelihood that Karl played a key role in organising the events and running the establishment.

"But isn't that somewhat moot now?" asked Tom. "Presumably, the place will shut down now that lockdown has been lifted, won't it?"

"I think you're forgetting what I told you before. This lockdown has finished, but the limitations on public gatherings haven't finished. And there'll be a whole new lockdown in six months."

They discussed the issue at some length. He shared Tom's opinion that the Tube Station was probably an intelligence-gathering operation. It would be only too easy to have cameras and microphones in place. Even if the visitors were as cautious as they should be when visiting (and who could be sure of that?), the very fact that they had taken part in an illegal gathering – and probably taken part on multiple occasions – could be used against them in the future. They agreed that Tom should pass this information on to his old colleagues. Whatever action they decided to take was up to them. But it would do no harm to be seen as helping them. In return, they might even return the favour in some unspecified way at some future date.

"What do you think they'll do?" Graham asked.

"Don't ask me to predict what that bunch will do. I can only say that if it were my decision, I would arrange surveillance of the place and take note of every person who goes in. Then, at a suitable future date, arrange a meeting with each of the attendees and let them know that their lockdown-breaking activities were known, and they should report any person or organisation that sought to ask them for a favour in return for keeping quiet about it."

Tom also added one further comment before ending the call.

"Since we are now moving into the world of secret activities and compromising situations …."

"The world you are more familiar with?" Graham interrupted.

"Exactly," Tom replied. "Since we are now in this world, I suggest, no, I insist, that you invest in a mobile that is not registered in your name. Write its number on a piece of paper and mail it to the Fox Inn, Llangennith."

"You mean a burner phone?"

"Yes. One that you use solely for calling me and not for any other purpose. Memorise the number and do not write it anywhere…"

"OK, OK – I get the message."

"Excellent. I'll call you from my burner phone as soon as you let me know the number."

To reinforce the importance of security, Tom ended the call without saying anything more.

As promised, Graham bought a 'burner' phone, wrote down its number, and sent it to the landlord of The Fox public house in Llangennith. A few days later, he received a call and did not need to ask the caller for his name.

"Hi Tom," he said, pressing the green button to accept the call.

Tom was equally abrupt, but whether it was for security reasons, keeping the call as short as possible, or just natural grumpiness, Graham could not tell.

"It seems our fears were well grounded. It looks like the Tube Station was an intelligence-gathering operation operated by Karl and his friends. Have you had any more dates with your girlfriend?"

"I'm assuming you're referring to Anna, in which case the answer is no. We've spoken a few times on the 'phone but I'm not keen to risk my health by going to meet her unless there's a specific purpose."

"Good. I've had an update from my ex-colleagues. I know it's still a year until she's due to vanish – but it's time we got together and planned our strategy. You're going to have to get the prof involved at some time. We need to know what to do about our Rusky friend, and I want to arrange some protection for you. Could you come down here any time soon?"

"I don't know. Are your lot still repelling boarders at the Severn Bridge?"

Graham knew that the Welsh Government had only been refusing entry to cars from England at the height of the pandemic but couldn't resist the jibe.

"Very funny – you know they're not."

"OK. I'll come down on Tuesday."

-

Tom pointedly offered him a Diet Pepsi when they sat down in his sitting room. Graham noted the improvements that had been made to the house – especially the glass wall of patio doors looking out over Oxwich Bay.

"This is how I remember it," he said with a smile. "Good to see you're well underway on converting the property next door, too. Your sister and her kids will love it."

Tom didn't respond – he knew that Graham was just rubbing his nose in his time-travel experience. Instead, he gave an update on the government's renewed interest in the project at Moorfields Hospital and

Anna's role within it. He spoke of his feeling that things were coming to a head, apologising for his lack of specific detail but quoting his many years of experience in these types of situations.

"There's a feeling that something is planned for next year".

20 Tales of Old London
March 2020

The building where Karl's office was situated had a basement comprising multiple levels – and even the considerable requirements that his organisation had for storing paper-based information were not enough to use even half the available space. This would not have been significant if it had not been for Covid, the lockdown, and the creative thought process of one of Karl's superiors.

The subject of what lies beneath the surface of London's streets is a fascinating one. The areas where subterranean developments are most significant are in the central and west-central areas of London – around and to the immediate west of the old financial district; the area denoted by postal codes W1 and those beginning with the letters EC or WC. It is here that London has been continuously occupied for thousands of years. Most of this area has something man-made below the surface, but with the limited technologies available until relatively recently, any subterranean construction would have been very limited, so the ancient finds are relatively close to the surface.

In the nineteenth century, the first significant work took place below ground in central London, not just in the aforementioned central area but also in many areas to the immediate north and west of the centre.

Karl's office was based in the area between the main thoroughfares of Piccadilly and Oxford Street, and immediately east of Hyde Park. This area, known as Mayfair, is populated by offices, hotels, embassies, expensive car dealerships, and extremely expensive apartments. It is not without reason that the most expensive square on the London edition of Monopoly is Mayfair, although its four-hundred-pound price would not pay the rent on a square foot of space these days.

Here, as in much of the densely populated areas north of the River Thames, the rapid expansion in the population from 1800 onwards created the need for much underground construction. Amongst their many building projects, the Victorians built massive sewers. Many of the old rivers that had crossed the area were encased in underground tunnels. The most famous example probably being the Fleet River, which flowed across north London into the Thames, and whose name lives on in the name of Fleet Street, once the heart of the UK newspaper world. It still runs, but its entire length is within brick tunnels and beneath street level.

The main underground structure is the railway network known as 'The London Underground' or, more usually, 'The Tube'. This was begun in the late nineteenth century when underground railways were constructed using the method known as 'cut and cover'. As described, this entailed digging a large trench into which a railway line was laid with a tunnel built over the top. In other words, it was not too deep below the surface. Later lines were added, and newer technology allowed them to be built deeper and deeper.

Other tunnels were built to carry both pedestrian and vehicular traffic beneath the river Thames, and the underground spider's web was added to by organisations such as the Post Office, which built a series of tunnels to carry mail between its central sorting office and mainline rail stations.

In the twentieth century, the government continued to build underground in preparation for war, both real and anticipated. The Cabinet War Rooms is now a tourist attraction, but during World War II, it housed many critical components of the central government, allowing it to continue to function during the heavy bombardment that London sustained.

Another series of underground works, known as the Kingsway Exchange Tunnels, below Chancery Lane tube station were built to shelter Londoners from the Blitz bombing campaign. That was the last time they were open to the public. Their next role was as the home of Britain's top-secret Special Operations Executive, an offshoot of MI6. They were then expanded to become the Kingsway Telephone Exchange, which served as an internal communications exchange during the Cold War. It even hosted the "hotline" which directly connected the leaders of the USA and the USSR. British Telecom took over the site in the 1980s, creating, amongst other things, the world's deepest licensed bar for use by government staff, with a games room containing snooker tables and a tropical fish tank.

Less well-known are the structures built by the government in the post-war period to protect its people in the event of nuclear war, which was feared and much anticipated at the time.

The population profile of London is unlike that of many other European cities. Relatively few people actually live in the capital, but its daytime population is huge as it continues to be the financial, media, and commercial capital, as well as the centre of government and the official capital of the country. Hence, underground shelters were constructed where people would be located during the daytime. The shelters were (and still are) located in centres of commercial activity and were planned to open up and be available to whoever found themselves there in the unlikely event of the unthinkable happening.

Last of all, in considering what lies beneath, comes the private underground construction that occurred over the years. When the large houses in Mayfair were first built, most were private dwellings. Cellars were only required to house coal, food, wine, and servants, and so were relatively small. However, as private use of these properties was superseded by commercial or ambassadorial use, larger subterranean structures were hollowed out. Offices and hotels needed more storage, and embassies needed truly secure places.

It's all well and good to have the area on which your embassy stands to be granted the legal status of being a piece of your home country, but what privacy is there if your building is within very few feet of a rival? 'Walls have ears', so they say – especially when within touching distance of a building occupied by a rival country. And rooms usually have windows, which enable seeing in, as well as seeing out. But underground areas offer greater protection.

So, unofficially, many of these buildings acquired multi-level cellars over the years. Building works would be conducted ostensibly affecting only the parts of the building above ground, but simultaneous scooping out of an additional cellar would take place. The landlord would be informed when the building changed hands, which it would do only once in a while.

Understanding how this could happen secretly is easier if you understand that the freehold ownership of these buildings has not changed in hundreds of years. Vast swathes of central London are owned by 'the gentry', who were awarded ownership for services rendered to the ruling monarch at some time in the history of England. For example, much of Mayfair is owned by the Duke of Westminster, generally known to be the richest man in England. Other areas are owned by various Dukes and some by the Monarch.

Ownership of this type and amount of highly profitable land nurtures a culture of long-term thinking. Short-term gains made by informing one tenant about the actions of another just would not happen. Long-term thinking for this group of landlords is not measured in years, it is measured in centuries.

An apocryphal example can be found in the history of a large hospital located in the area. As London grew larger and busier, the government, now running the hospital as part of the National Health Service, at a certain point in the second half of the twentieth century, decided it was no longer economically sensible to house a hospital in such a busy area. Problems with staff recruitment, emergency access, and routine materials delivery were just three of the unsolvable headaches. It was decided that relocation would be the best course of action.

Various government department heads figuratively rubbed their hands in glee at the thought of the huge amount of money that would be realised by selling a large piece of real estate in such a prestigious location and how these funds might be spent. The hand rubbing ceased when the government was contacted by representatives of the duke whose family was the previous landowner and had passed the land to the state some hundreds of years earlier.

The letter referred to reports of recent government decisions to close the hospital and sell the land. It reminded readers that the original transfer of the land had included a clause that stipulated that should the land cease to be used as a hospital, it would be sold back to the Dukedom at the same price at which it had originally been purchased—a sum rumoured to be in the order of ten pounds.

Organisations that think in those terms and timescales do not divulge the activities of one tenant to another – no matter how important the tenant might deem himself or herself to be.

It was rumoured – probably inaccurately – that one of the reasons that the United States of America relocated its embassy from the cramped area of Mayfair to the more open area of Nine Elms south of the River Thames was the discovery that its underground facilities were not as secure as they had thought; because the occupiers of a neighbouring building had constructed cellars that were extremely close to theirs. There was not much point in constructing and equipping a secret communications centre below ground if neighbours could listen in to what was happening within it by using a method that was not much more sophisticated than holding an empty wineglass to a party wall.

The story is possibly a myth, but it was noted that in the years immediately following the vacating of the large building in Grosvenor Square, which had housed the US Embassy for decades, several other changes of ownership of nearby buildings took place.

The vacating of the building brought to light two other pieces of information. The building was put up for sale by the appointed Estate Agency and the details made public that the building was comprised of nine stories – *three of which were underground.*

Further proof of the long-term thinking of the landowners in this part of the world also emerged in the reporting of an exchange of correspondence between the US Government and the landlords of the new embassy – the Duchy of Westminster – which took place shortly after the embassy was opened.

Having agreed that the tenant would pay only a peppercorn rent (defined by the dictionary as a very low or nominal rent), the duchy was asked if the tenant could purchase the freehold. In response, the duke's trustee requested that such a discussion could not take place until the return of lands confiscated from his ancestors following the American Revolutionary War. The main parcel of this ceased land now formed the city of Miami

Further rumours were fuelled when, in January 2018, US President Donald Trump scrapped a planned visit to the UK, blaming his predecessor, Barack Obama, for a "bad deal" on the new embassy due to be opened in London, despite the fact it was agreed under the administration of George W. Bush.

If it was true that the underground encroachment was real, the question would arise as to how this might have been found out. Probably in the way that certain embassies find out all sorts of information, employing several people in roles purely for that purpose. It is unlikely that the information would have come from the property owner.

-

The lockdown imposed by the British government in March 2020 to prevent the spread of the SARS-COVID virus was all-encompassing. From the date of the announcement, no pubs, clubs, cinemas, theatres, restaurants, or other places of entertainment could open for business. Compliance with these restrictions by the general public was near total. Fuelled by fear, reinforced by government messaging, the population accepted the necessity.

There were, of course, exceptions. Within the UK population, there is a group of people who feel that rules simply do not apply to them. The same group may also exist in other countries – but that is irrelevant to the story. What is relevant is that this group existed and is (or was) large enough and influential enough to be significant. Some part of this became apparent a few years later when it emerged that parties were taking place regularly throughout the pandemic in government offices in total defiance of the regulations imposed by the same government.

But this was not the total picture. Whilst not being described as 'The tip of the iceberg', government parties were a subset of activities that continued throughout the lockdown. The fact that it never came to light is not terribly surprising when you understand that the participants were some of the most wealthy and influential people in the country. Any official pursuing a righteous crusade to expose this period of rule-breaking might find his future career prospects to be minimal.

One of the venues for this type of activity was the basement of the office where Karl worked. It was a multi-story building in Mayfair, which, according to official records, was the home address of a wealthy individual who did not have British nationality but did have the UK as his country of residence.

One of Karl's bosses anticipated the opportunity that would be presented and obtained approval from his superiors for one level of the basement to be temporarily converted into a place of entertainment. No official permission for a change of use was deemed advisable. Karl was placed in charge of the project and was told that while he could expect full co-operation from the embassy in sourcing all the necessary work and supplies for the enterprise, no transactions must occur through normal channels. Everything was to be dealt with on a cash basis and no records of transactions were to be traceable back to the embassy.

A firm of builders, known for their previous ability to maintain secrecy concerning work done on the premises, carried out the construction in rapid time. Tables and chairs, bar fittings, glasses, and copious quantities of drinks were ordered and delivered securely and rapidly. Plain packaging was used for every item.

A small group of musicians, self-employed and desperate for the only source of work in the foreseeable future, manned the miniature stage, in front of which was a small dance floor.

Karl followed his instructions diligently. Suppliers were told that all transactions would be in cash – and no paperwork was to exist. The only difference between the instructions he had been given and those passed on to the firms he dealt with was that there would be a ten percent discount on all transactions. More than once, he was asked how there could be a discount on a transaction when the original price was not shown anywhere, and his answer was always the same, "If anyone other than me asks you the price, you tell them the higher figure."

Karl submitted the larger figure in his report to the treasury department of the Embassy but paid the supplier the lower figure. He deposited the difference in his account via the local bank branch on one of his permitted daily walks.

The sections of the building that were to be used for this venture were, of course, going to be covered by security devices. It was a vital part of the plan that everyone who attended would have their presence noted. If their conversations could be recorded, that would be a bonus. It was naturally assumed that most would be careful in what they said and that most of the conversation would be social and unrelated to any real topics of interest anyway. But a clear record needed to be made of their presence at an illegal gathering.

The IT company was well-accustomed to the requirements of this type of client and advised Karl on the number and placement of the necessary cameras. Based on the number of hours they would be recording, the company came up with the specifications for the central storage unit. It would record onto multi-terabyte hard disks, which would be removed and stored at the end of every day of operation.

"Will you require a cloud backup of the information?" the technical consultant asked Karl. Sensing his customer's lack of technical experience, he explained that 'cloud backup' was a way of taking an additional copy of the recorded data and storing it on a secure, remote system.

"I can assure you of the security of this information. It will be kept in the same location as the data we store for the embassy, but a separate password will be needed to access it. Whoever accesses this information will set the password and will be able to access the data, but not the main data of the embassy, and the embassy will not be able to access this data."

Karl agreed that this service should be provided and that he would be the sole holder of the password. He had just found another vital asset that could potentially be converted to cash at some future point.

-

He had spent some time pondering that future. He missed the wide-open spaces of the land of his birth. He had never been able to replicate the unique feeling that this gave him, even though the comparison between the rural area where he had been born and the cities in which he had spent his working life was unfair.

The parts of Germany and the UK he had seen were highly urbanised. He knew that both countries had many open spaces – he just had not been able to see them because his work had necessitated him staying in and around built-up areas. But he knew that even the countryside of these countries could never match that wild feeling of the true vastness of the Russian Steppes.

But he also knew that it would be very difficult to achieve the levels of domestic comfort he had come to expect. He had been spoilt by his time in the West. His return to Russia reminded him of this. Even with the additional funds he had squirrelled away – which would be very difficult to access if he did return to Russia – would not make his life as comfortable as he aspired to. Yes, he had grown soft. The only place he could think of that offered the potential of combining material comfort and the type of wide-open space that he was seeking was America. The more he read about it, or saw it on TV, the more he knew that this was what he aspired to. But he also realised how inaccessible that destination was to him.

So, Karl took his second series of steps away from his ordained career path, and his bank account – devoid of any transaction activity since his assignment to guard Christina had finished – began to receive a weekly boost. And his dreams of a passage to the USA lingered in his mind.

-

Invites to the venue were by word of mouth only, and the clientele grew swiftly. About a hundred people knew of its existence, and sixty or seventy showed up most evenings the club operated, arriving any time between seven and nine and leaving between eleven and twelve – the official closing time.

The house was ideally located for the purpose, being situated on a narrow street in the heart of Mayfair. So narrow was the street that not even single-file traffic was permitted and all guests either had to walk from their nearby residences or ask the taxi driver to drop them in one of the cross-streets.

The venue soon became known as The Tube Station when someone compared its architectural merit to the nearby Marble Arch underground station. Events were held on random days – the next day of opening passed on by word of mouth. Sensible precautions against Covid were taken. The room was air-conditioned to the highest standard, and all visitors were required to take a Covid test before entering (and refused admission if the test was positive). Apart from the musicians, there were no other outsiders employed. Karl and his colleagues all had to take shifts doing bar work, testing, or security. Since they were paid a small additional allowance, in cash - funded from the profits of the enterprise, and there were so few alternative means of entertainment available, they accepted willingly.

The whole undertaking was easily justified. The original proposer had described it as an extension of the organisation's core function of information gathering. All the guests who attended would be recorded on hidden cameras. If – or more likely when – at some future date they might be able to help the organisation in any way, the request might be couched in terms of "I trust you enjoyed our hospitality during the lockdown. Could you possibly help us by …."

For anyone receiving such a request, there was a distinction between possible public knowledge that lockdown-breaking parties happened, and photographic evidence that they had attended one (or more) of them. So, the request would be complied with.

Visitors drank and chatted. Cameras clicked and stored.

-

On the third night of the operation, Karl's boss spoke to him across the bar. "Pretty good, isn't it?" he asked, sweeping his arm to indicate the visitors enjoying themselves."

"It's OK," Karl replied. "But if my girlfriend was here, people would be dancing."

His boss smiled and nodded in response. "You must bring her tomorrow," he said.

From the next night onwards, dancing was a regular activity at The Tube Station, and Karl's girlfriend was a regular and welcome attendee.

21 Reinvigoration
August 2021

Very few people had ever seen the Colonel in this state. And those who saw him during the meeting never wanted to see him in this mood again. His presentation to the meeting did not rely heavily on visual props. He had a list on display for them all to see and went through each item on the list quickly and painfully.

"Let's have a look at the last few months, ladies and gentlemen," he began. His gentle introduction did not warn of the storm to come.

"May. A member of our Royal Family is accused by a TV company of using his royal status to sell secrets to President Putin's regime. He denied it, but we know what Miss Rice Davis said, don't we? Of course, he bloody would!" The temperature was beginning to rise, and he paused for effect.

"What did we do about this? Nothing! We didn't even know about it!"

Gaining steam, he clicked his presentation device and revealed a new topic.

"May. A jury ruled that failings by MI5 and the police contributed to the deaths of Saskia Jones and Jack Merritt in the 2019 London Bridge stabbing. Nothing we can do about that now – but not the best publicity, is it?"

A third topic appeared on the screen alongside him.

"June. A public inquiry into the 2017 suicide bombing at Manchester Arena identifies **serious shortcomings** by those in charge of security. Getting to be a bit of a trend, isn't it?"

The fourth topic appeared below the others on his screen.

"June. Classified Ministry of Defence documents are found at a bus stop in Kent. OK, so there's not much we can do about civil servants who would forget their bloody heads if they weren't screwed on – but we get the bad publicity. Especially when it's the fourth time in two months that the press and the public can have a pop at us."

He sat down and placed his clicker on the table in front of him. The other attendees at the meeting took some consolation that the list seemed to have ended.

"Ladies and gentlemen, I spent yesterday getting my arse kicked by the Home Secretary. I can tell you that was not a pleasant experience. Her language was strong enough to peel the paint off a barrack room wall!" He gazed around the room to confirm that the various section heads were getting the message. Their silence was a good indicator that they were.

"If that wasn't enough, we're supposed to prepare for a rise in terrorist activity now that we have finally given up the ghost in Afghanistan. We can expect an influx of immigrants from there in the coming months, and it's a safe bet that there'll be some terrorists amongst 'em. My message to you is twofold. Firstly, I will not put up with any more of this shit," He pointed to the screen behind him in case anyone was unclear what he was referring to. Clarity abounded through the room.

"Secondly, we need to strike back. I want an action plan from each of you. A suggestion of one action that your section could take in the coming months. Either something we can put in the papers or something we can't. I don't care. We need to show that now we've all finished with lockdowns, working from home and all the other b/s that's stood in our way for the last few months, we're back on our game. Is that clear?"

The attendees all indicated that they had received the message, and after a few brief questions, each section head was glad to depart and work with their team to provide a suggestion.

-

Sometimes using a cliché is unavoidable when describing actions and consequences. The Colonel threw a mighty big stone into the pool at his staff meeting in August 2021, and within a couple of months, one of the resulting ripples reached the professor and Anna in Moorfields Hospital.

They had both been very frustrated at the lack of progress on what they thought was their project. Even if the prof was the actual brains behind it, the support he found in Anna was such that he admitted that it probably would not have lasted until now without her. But, the past two years had seen no progress, and the only reason for this was that the government support had withered almost to a state of non-existence. But it now seemed that a new, post-pandemic phase of investment from the government was about to commence.

In their quarterly progress meeting (or lack-of-progress meetings, as they had come to refer to them), the government representative announced that a proposal had been made for new investment, and they were ready to implement it with the cooperation of the medical team.

They acknowledged that part of the reason for earlier delays in the project was that there were two distinct phases where progress was wanted. And the two parties to the project – the government and the scientists – each prioritised a different phase. The government was keen to see progress in the ability to transmit signals from one site to another. But this would never be one of the priorities of the medics. They did not need to transmit the signal more than a few inches. Their priorities were to make improvements to the data capture aspect – the viewer or camera as it was usually referred to. The medical need was for enhancements to the unit that captured the data, compressed, and transmitted it. This unit needed to have more power and to be substantially miniaturised.

So, the proposal that accompanied the investment was for the government technicians to take a lead role in the data transmission aspect, possibly even taking it over completely, while the medics, with some support from government technicians, worked on the camera unit.

The medics were happy with this division – especially since those who had been there long enough knew that the danger inherent in the project – the aspect that had caused the unfortunate incident years previously and the resulting pause in the project – was all contained within the data transfer part of the project. They would be blameless if any further incidents were to happen in that area.

As the project proceeded, it became obvious that the work done so far had been poorly documented. Anna was given the task of documenting the project and, even though she had never tackled such a task before, proved to be singly adept at it. It may have been because, excellent though her command of the language was, English was still her second language. It had the effect that she would keep the information clear and uncomplicated, using the simplest terms to convey the message. Many complimented her on her work, the separation of the two phases progressed apace, and there seemed to be a real chance at last of significant progress.

-

David Allinson was the government man who brought the good news to them about Project Petra as it was now known. He also informed them that he would be the lead man from the government side and the person to whom they should direct any communication beyond the day-to-day events. What he did not tell them was the key stage he was aiming for in the communication phase of the project. As a direct result of the meeting at which the Colonel had fired up his team, the project had a new aim. It would start again in early 2022.

As David had explained to the Colonel, his idea had three main benefits. Firstly, it met the stated objective of being a set of actions to demonstrate that his section was still capable of positive action. The nature of the action would mean that it would not be possible to publicise it in any way, but it was certain to have an impact on those who did find out about it.

Secondly, it solved the problem of what to do with the two double agents they had discovered within their ranks. They had been keeping a close watch on them in the weeks since their activities became known, and they had been fed nothing but disinformation to pass back to their paymasters in that period. However, this could not go on forever – the falsehoods would become obvious sooner or later. And then what? An arrest and a trial, producing nothing but negative publicity – even with the copious restrictions placed on the media's capability to report. Worse still, there was the danger of their flight to Russia and the concomitant triumphal announcement of another intelligence victory over the West.

Lastly, David's plan would let the Russians know that the UK had a weapon capable of striking an opponent through an office window without leaving a trace – the victim appearing to die of natural causes several hours later. That should make them think carefully about some of their actions.

There would, unfortunately, be a delay before the action could take place. The project had to progress to the point where there was a working receiver. This had not progressed as far as it needed to because so far, all the receiving had been done by humans. To persuade the medical team that the test was real, they needed to have a working electronic unit, which would take a few months. In the meantime, the two agents would be kept under close surveillance and told to expect to be soon moved to a key involvement in this secret project. That should be enough to whet the appetite of the other side and to keep them in place for the necessary few months.

The project would also not need a huge budget. They would need to assign three scientists to it – they could be sourced from GCHQ. From his understanding of what was involved, the project also had the benefit that most of the actual technology involved was relatively low-tech, and hence not too expensive.

The next test, with a target date of 2022, was to replicate the test of 10 years ago. However, this time, two people would be posted to the remote office to receive the data and confirm that they could see what was being transmitted from the main hospital building.

They would be briefed that it was necessary to check whether the information transmitted to them would work when transferred in a foreign script and character set. Much time was spent on a complex pseudo-science brief to convince the two participants (both fluent Russian speakers) that this formed a vital part of the test.

-

Anna had been very pleased to take on the responsibility of documenting the reinvigorated project and was unaware that this new role removed her from the new work being done on the communication aspect of the project.

Following the discovery of the additional information about her father, the project supervisors had been told that Anna was only ever to see information relating to the medical aspects. The government was not concerned if information about this were to leak, but the communication protocols and the possible use of the project as a weapon were not things that they wanted any foreign government to know about.

But she was happy to see how the new level of activity had raised the spirits of the prof. She had regretted seeing so little of him for the past eighteen months. They had never shared any social time, but with both of them spending so much time at work, their relationship had always been very close; they spoke at length about themselves and their lives during coffee and lunch breaks.

With the shiftwork she had been doing at London Hospital during the pandemic's peak, she had not had the time to keep up this relationship and had noticed that the prof had seemed shrunken. But now, he was more like himself, and they were able to pick up where they had left off.

The extra hours at work dovetailed with the recent downturn in her social life. She had received few new contacts from the agency and Karl was calling upon her less often. She had hoped for a step up in the relationship she had with Graham, but it had mostly involved only email for the last eighteen months and she had become close friends with him as a result. But their relationship was still only a friendship.

She had hoped that with the lifting of the lockdown restrictions, their relationship would grow and involve more face-to-face meetings. There was certainly something different about him, and she had looked forward to seeing him more often. But it seemed that her feelings were not reciprocated, and he was happy to keep things just as they were. She was going along with his wishes and hoping for improvement. It certainly left more time available for work.

She was unable to put her finger on the exact moment when she became suspicious of what was going on. She worked diligently on the task of documenting the project – and, with the lull in her social life, was able to do this extra work while assisting the prof in his day-to-day tasks.

Her unique position of needing access to every part of the project and to interact with everyone involved in it – to make sure she had all the details to create the documentation and to verify that what she produced was both accurate and understandable – probably gave her a more complete overview of the whole undertaking than anyone else. Her personality, and, with all the government scientists being male, her good looks also helped her maintain a remarkably full dialogue with everyone involved.

The more she thought about what was going on, the more she realised that the goals of the government scientists were not totally in line with those of the medical team. Progress was being made on miniaturising the camera and transmitting device – it was now the size of a small suitcase. There remained some way to go to achieve the prof's aim of it being no bigger than a smartphone – and hopefully one day capable of being built into a pair of glasses, but it was progressing. She always knew that this area of the project was less interesting to their government backers than the data transmission side of things. The tragic outcome of the first test all those years ago had certainly not been forgotten. Anna gradually realised that this capability of the transmission beam was not being designed out. It was included in the documentation. She began to see past the fact that it was always noted with severe warnings, but it was there, nonetheless.

If what she suspected was true, and she was sure it was, her biggest problem was what to do with this information. Her first thought was to bring it to the attention of the prof. She knew he would treat her suspicions seriously – but did she want to load this concern on top of his existing burdens? She remembered how devastated he had been when the accident had occurred. The thought that he was ultimately responsible for the deaths of several innocent people had almost finished him. How much worse would he feel if he were to discover that he had been working, albeit unknowingly, on a piece of equipment that was being designed with that very purpose included in its capabilities?

Anna could think of only one person with whom she could discuss this. One person whom she could trust to keep her secrets. Luckily it was also a person whose advice she would trust.

She booked a few days off work and bought a return flight to Dresden, intending to talk it over with her sister.

-

Meanwhile, Graham continued his relationship with Elizabeth, appreciating that with the clock ticking inevitably towards the date of Anna's disappearance, this period represented the calm before the storm. The only matter that disturbed his equilibrium was not something that happened, instead it was something that didn't happen.

He suddenly realised that he was missing a grandchild. On his original plane of time, his fourth grandchild, a girl named Rosie, had been born to his daughter in early 2021. He could not put an exact date on it – but was certain she had been born in the early months of 2021. But not on this plane of time. And he did not know what to do about it. There was nobody he could talk to about it, least of all his daughter. He could only dismiss it to himself by realising that changing one thing in a person's life would have consequences that might not be immediately obvious.

'I suppose I gave them a bunch of money, and maybe they didn't need to cuddle up so close to each other to keep warm' he joked to himself.

The only person to whom he could potentially ever mention it was Tom, the only one who knew about Graham's time travelling, and there seemed no point in telling him.

Just one of those unforeseen consequences of his time travel, and a rather sad one at that.

22 The City with the Highest Rim of the Plate
September 2021

The smell of Sauerbraten mit Klöße greeted Anna as she walked along the corridor to the apartment where her sister Cornelia lived, and a sudden unusual wave of homesickness hit her. She had been away too long and yearned for her old home-town to envelope her once again.

Dresden was known in Germany as 'Die Stadt mit dem höchsten Tellerrand der Platte' – a reference to its inhabitants' reputation for not caring too much about what happened outside their city walls. She felt she could do with a large dose of that, right now.

Cornelia hugged her warmly after opening the door and took her bag. A less intense but equally warm hug was then bestowed by her brother-in-law, Reinhard. They chatted over family and friends, old times and new times, and everything in between whilst eating the perfectly cooked pork and dumplings and sharing the bottle of wine Anna had brought with her. They relaxed in the sitting room, rounding off their celebrations with a glass of schnapps. No mention was made of the problems that Anna was facing. The problems that her sister knew only too well must exist because she had never before arranged to visit them at such short notice.

Those problems were left for Saturday morning, over a kitchen table still carrying the remnants of breakfast – with added cups of strong coffee.

"I know you're wondering why I came at such short notice," Anna said when the conversation had halted and a suitable opening presented itself for discussion to take place.

"Thank you for making me so welcome," she continued, and her sister made a dismissive gesture but said nothing. She knew Anna was working herself up to say something serious.

"There are some problems with the project I'm working on in London, and I needed a few days completely away from it and a chance to think about what I'm going to do."

"Do you want to tell us about it?" Cornelia asked. "I'm not sure if we can help if it's something technical – but you know what they say – a problem shared is a problem halved and all that."

"It's not anything technical – but I'm worried about what I suspect is going on, and I'm not sure what to do about it – or even if I can do anything about it," Anna continued, knowing that she was being repetitive but not sure if there was any other way of telling her sister what she was worried about – without telling her everything.

"Have you talked it over with the professor?" Her sister had heard Anna talk of him often and knew they were very close. She had noticed that up until now, everything had been spoken in the first-person singular. It was not a problem about what 'we' suspect is going on but one that 'I' suspect. This did not bode well.

"I don't want to bother him with it," Anna said.

"Well, you'd better bother us then," Cornelia replied, trying to lighten the mood.

"You remember we had that problem years ago," Anna continued. She had decided to tell all.

"Yes," her sister replied cagily. "Weren't some people injured?"

"Worse than that. They were killed when we operated the beam at full strength. We were only using it that way because the government wanted to test it for transmitting over distance. Anyway, it stopped everything for years, but now the government has given us some more manpower and resources, and they're insisting we do some testing of the same thing again."

Anna paused for a few seconds, and Reinhard thought he would come into the discussion.

"Are they testing to see what the limit is?" he asked, qualifying it by adding, "There presumably must be a level where it's OK to use and a level where it's dangerous."

"Yes, you're right. But it's the way they are doing what they are doing. They aren't putting any emphasis on finding where that limit is. I'm convinced they want to use it anyway. They plan to use it as a weapon."

"But they can't expect you and the professor to get involved in that, surely. You're medical people. You're sworn to do no harm, aren't you?" Cornelia said. Her sense of shock and outrage were not faked.

"Oh, they've worked their way around that. They've ensured that we've trained everyone and documented how it all works, so they don't need us to be there. They can use it without us," Anna replied.

They kicked the subject around for several minutes, asking how she had reached this conclusion and understanding that while she had no absolute proof, her suspicions seemed very well founded.

Having departed the table briefly to brew another pot of coffee, Cornelia returned and sent the conversation in a slightly different direction. "Your problem reminds me of a book I once read. It was a short story I read a few years ago when I was catching up on some of the stuff we couldn't get hold of back in the old days. It concerned a bunch of scientists having a problem with government regulations. The lead character is a Doctor of History. He knows the government has some secret device that enables them to look back in time. It was probably called a chronograph or something similar, and it worked by tracing some secret particles that had been discovered, and by determining their path, you could see images of the past on a kind of TV set. Anyway, the government owns the only one of these chronographs in existence, and the Doctor of History keeps being refused permission to use it. So, he talks to his friend in the physics department and asks how difficult it would be to build one. His friend tells him that the government has long since banned all research into chronographs – or anything that could lead to the discovery of how to build one.

"The two university doctors have a long discussion and agree that this is a really bad situation, so they decide to gather some like-minded individuals and resolve to build one in secret. When it's nearly completed, there is a falling out between the members of the group, and when they get together, some of them are missing from their meeting. Then the government agents burst into their meeting and tell them they are all under arrest for breaking the law, working on a chronograph.

"At this point, one group member argues that it is wrong for a government to suppress the freedom of scientists to research what they want, which was why they had built the chronograph. And, if the government thought they could stop it, they were wrong because the members of the group who were not present had published their findings, and by now, scientists all over the world will now be able to find out how to build the device.

"The reaction of the government agent is to ridicule their ignorance. He tells them that they have been so focussed on using the chronograph for historical research that they have not thought through the consequences. He ends with a speech that goes something like, 'Where does the past begin? A year ago? A day ago? A minute ago? How do you think we traced you? We used a chronograph, of course. Throughout history, mankind has been able to conduct his life in secret. You have destroyed this. The secrecy of the bathroom or the bedroom has been wiped out. Welcome to the goldfish bowl that mankind will live in forever more!'"

Anna and Reinhard had listened to Cornelia's story, and both were silent, thinking for a moment about the story and its relevance to Anna's situation. "So, the moral of the story is that government is good and is always looking out for the benefit of its citizens?" Anna asked rhetorically. "I can't see why it was banned. I would have thought that story would have gone down very well in the old DDR!"

"That is one possible conclusion," Cornelia replied. "Alternatively, you could say that the government felt it was perfectly acceptable for them to see everything that everyone was doing while denying this right to its citizens, which would not have been such a popular summary. Anyway, it does relate to your problem in a way."

"I'm not sure it does help much," Anna said, giving the matter some thought. "The cause of my unhappiness is not that the government is being secretive. I'm just not happy about what it is doing. If it is making a weapon out of this, I'm unhappy that the work that the professor and I have done has been so badly misused, But I'm also unhappy that it is a particularly vile weapon. This isn't a weapon to kill soldiers on a battlefield, bad as that is. It's a weapon that can kill innocent people going about their daily tasks. This can be used to kill a scientist, a politician, or a dissenter. Who knows what they might use it for."

"Well, there's only one way that you might be able to stop it being used," said Reinhard. He had spoken so little all morning that his interruption surprised and briefly silenced both the women.

"How is that?" Anna asked.

"It's not foolproof, but the best way to stop a weapon being used is for both sides in a conflict to know about the weapon's existence and to fear its use. A lot of people believe that the only reason that there has never been any use of nuclear weapons after the first time they were used is that both sides possess the weapon and know that if they used it, so would the other side. If only one side had nuclear capability, it might have been used in the last eighty years."

"So, you're saying I should inform the Russians about this?"

"Well, think about it. Who would worry more? Putin? He wouldn't care. He doesn't have to be seen in public - and rarely is, anyway. They say that when he poses for a photo opportunity with a bunch of cheerful factory workers or loyal wives of military heroes, the people around him are all stooges. They've done facial recognition on the photos to prove it. No, he doesn't need to go out and be seen. But Western politicians do. Anyway, if Putin wanted to use this weapon domestically it makes little difference. It would merely save him the bother of pushing someone out of a window, smearing them with polonium, or sabotaging their helicopter. But if Western politicians were aware that if they used this on an opponent, then they could never again go out and meet the public. Their chances of re-election would disappear overnight."

The discussion petered out soon after Reinhard's suggestion, leaving Anna with some food for thought. She could feel a decision brewing.

She spent the next day alone – turning down her sister's kind invitation to accompany her and Reinhard on a day out. She wanted time to think, and took the S-Bahn into the city centre and wandered the streets for several hours. Not completely aimlessly. She was familiarising herself with the sights, sounds, and smells of her childhood and adolescence, and preparing herself for what she knew would be a new chapter in her life. She stopped for lunch in one of the many cafes, enjoying sitting in the warm sunshine, eating a plate of Quarkkeulchen.

By the time she finished the cheese curd cakes, the warmth disappeared from the sun, and she knew what she must do. She had possibly known it all along. Her priorities were clear, and her possible range of actions was limited. She needed to do all she could to prevent the use of this awful weapon that she had been instrumental in creating. But at the same time, the professor's valuable work must continue. Her inconvenience and possible infringement of other lesser principles were of minor importance. She would return to her sister's apartment, let her know her intentions, and begin planning a course of action.

Cornelia and Reinhard did not get back from their day out until quite late, so it was Sunday morning before there was a chance to talk. Reinhard had marking to do, and the sisters had no problem in excusing him. He would work in the kitchen while they talked in the sitting room.

"Your husband was right," Anna began. "The only thing I can do is let more people know about the terrible potential of this device. I know the government is going to use it. And I know that other parties know of its existence. The only way they'll be able to replicate it is by getting the results of our work. Starting from scratch, it would take them years to get to where we are. I can cut that time to weeks or even days."

"But what will this mean for you?" Cornelia asked – her concern for her sister's welfare heavily outweighed any thoughts of global politics.

"I'll have to disappear, at least for a while," Anna replied. She knew that the phrase 'at least for a while' was probably an understatement. If she was able to resurface, it would not be until a long time in the future. She suspected that her sister knew this too – but nothing was said.

"But how will you do it? How will you get the information to the right people? And how will you be able to disappear, as you put it?"

"I know who and how to pass the information to – and I've got some plans that will make me very difficult to find." Anna hoped that her calm reassurance would work. She was confident that the two statements she had just made were accurate but equally did not underestimate the difficulty and danger she might be facing.

"And how will I know if you're alright?" Cornelia persisted.

"If you receive any mail at this address for a Frau Dreier, you'll know I'm OK. Open the mail and keep it. It may not make any sense, but please keep hold of it."

Anna had spent the previous day putting her thoughts straight in her mind and was now bringing them together to form a complete plan. One small element was missing; she would address that in a short conversation with Reinhard before she flew back on Monday morning.

23 Preparations
October 2021

Anthony Bairstow dug through his old records to find the details of the flat he had sold to Anna Mueller all those years ago. He remembered it vaguely – the epitome of an old lady's home that had been kept clean and tidy all its life but had not seen a paintbrush in decades. The sale of the flat had been a very profitable deal for him – a quick sale, no complications, and a willing buyer who was only too pleased to snap up a bargain and not quibble about the run-down state.

If he remembered correctly, she had even been willing to keep the furniture that remained in the property, which saved him the task and expense of getting it dumped. Reading the file refreshed his memory of the exact location and the price it had sold at. 'It'll be many times that price now', he thought.

He remembered his brief fling with Anna, too. A beautiful woman, he recalled. One of those few times in life when business and pleasure mixed very well together. 'But this time around it'll unfortunately have to be business only,' he assumed.

Anna's words had been music to his ears. Nothing sweeter than a seller wanting to sell quickly and willing to pay the price for doing so. When Anna showed him around the apartment – the viewing had to take place before dinner, he insisted, to enable him to see the property in daylight – he was even more pleased. She had obviously had it professionally redecorated and had kept it clean. She had furnished it tastefully, and it was presented in a neat and tidy state.

Over dinner, she told him about the sad deterioration of her parents' health and the likelihood of them needing her, their only surviving child, to return home to look after them. She was not happy to do so, she confided. She loved her job and her life in London – but family comes first. Anthony expressed his sympathy and agreement.

"When these things happen, I know from many of my colleagues that no matter how much you think you are prepared, it often happens suddenly," she said. "So, I thought I'd be as prepared as possible and see what you might be able to do if I was put in that position. It's probably going to happen in the next year or so."

"Have you thought of keeping the property and renting it out?" he asked. It was good to know at the outset if there was any chance of her taking this path. If she had not considered this option, he did not want her to think of it later and then make him change his plans. So even if this turned out to be a 'beans up the nose remark' he was still going to bring it up.

"No," she replied. "I'd like to avoid complications – there's probably half a dozen things that could go wrong since I'll be leaving the country – these things have got worse since Brexit – so I'd rather make it a clean sale."

"No problem there," Anthony replied with a rare dash of honesty. "But you know that if you want a quick sale, you might not be able to get as much as you could do with a bit more patience."

She made it clear to him that she understood, and asked him if the correct English phrase was "time is of the essence" and he confirmed it was. "I thought so – it was in a TV show about lawyers, so I remembered it," she answered in a charming, self-deprecating way.

"What about the furniture?" he asked after a pause, realising that removals could be complicated if she intended to return to Germany.

"I'll be taking a few small pieces – but could you take care of the rest?"

With this added piece of information, Anthony began to think differently about the property. One major change in the property market of recent years was the total upheaval in the furnished letting business – largely thanks to Airbnb.

Years ago, furnished lettings was a down-market sector with the main customers being students and the itinerate population. It was a risky sector for all but the very top of the market. But Airbnb changed all that. You now had multiple markets into which a furnished property could be targeted. There was the weekend visitor – especially a family with one or two small children – who did not want the restrictions of a family room in a hotel nor the expense of renting two rooms. There was also a business market for the traveller staying for two or three nights in the middle of the week – a salesman, an auditor, or a similar professional. And lastly, the jackpot of the longer stay – a business move, a young footballer getting his first professional role, or even the marital separation of a wealthy couple. With all these different targets and a property within fifteen minutes' walk of a tube station (fifteen minutes when walking briskly downhill to the station). Anthony started to calculate the potential rental return as being five or six hundred pounds a week after costs.

He looked forward to helping Anna in her hour of need and made a mental note to make sure he could raise the three hundred thousand pounds that this property would fetch – allowing for its price reduction for a quick sale, of course. He did not begrudge paying for dinner for two after all – even if it was for business without pleasure.

But Anthony had to wait a few months while Anna kept in touch every once in a while, letting him know she had not forgotten their conversation but telling him she was not quite ready yet and would call him as soon as she was.

Then one July afternoon he was sitting in his office, doing that very English thing – cursing the weather – when the call came from Anna. It was an unnaturally hot day, as so many had been recently, and the Estate Agency offices were typically English and not air-conditioned. The noise of the traffic on Whetstone High Road, only a few yards from his office, meant that the windows had to be kept closed to be able to hear Anna on the telephone. But the discomfort was worth it – she was ready to sell.

They dined together again a few nights later and the price was agreed. They set a timetable to complete the purchase by late September and Anna asked if the date he took possession could be a little flexible as she had to make some arrangements. He was happy to comply, and she was happy to let him have a spare set of keys.

He arranged visits for the company surveyor to check the property over, and the company photographer to take photos for his website. He had a page set up on Airbnb by early July, and had started to take bookings within days. Even before he had bought it.

-

It had been an odd six months in so many ways for Anna. She had experienced some unusually strong feelings that confirmed to her that she was still a foreigner despite the many years she had lived in the UK. She just could not raise the same level of joy within herself, when yet another jubilee of Queen Elizabeth's reign was celebrated. She understood the significance of fifty-year and hundred-year anniversaries – but the amount of pageantry celebrating seventy years – which seemed such an arbitrary number – seemed excessive.

Like most of the rest of Europe, she had been deeply shocked by the Russian invasion of Ukraine. She was glad that she was not in regular contact with Karl as she was now certain that he was Russian, and she would have had to confront him.

She was also sad that she was unable to take in a Ukrainian refugee like so many people were doing. She had the space and would have done it if her own immediate future was not so deeply in doubt. And then, in June, just as she was starting to make plans to return to Germany, came the news that someone had driven a car into a group of pedestrians in Berlin and injured seventeen people, one of them terminally. She even recognised the reported location on the corner of Kurfuerstendamm and Rankestrasse across from the Kaiser Wilhelm Memorial Church in Charlottenburg, as somewhere she had often taken coffee and cake on sunny summer days in her Berlin days.

She had thought of having a German newspaper delivered so that she could be up to speed with events in Germany, where she was now sure she would be shortly making her home. It could be easily arranged at one of the newsagents near her office, but she thought that such behaviour might be noticed and offer a lead to anyone who tried to follow her when she fled. She had to glean what information she could from the international pages of The Times.

She was ultimately convinced that she was still German and had not become English when the final of the Women's Euro Football Championship, took place at Wembley, just five miles from where she lived. It pitted the hosts, England, against the team from her homeland, and there was no doubt she supported Germany and shared their bitter disappointment when they lost.

She was working her way through a checklist of things she wanted to do before her departure – which was looming large in her thoughts and expected to take place in the autumn. After much thought, one evening she sent an unusual email.

-

Massimo, the proprietor of Anna's favourite restaurant, also had a key role in her plans. He had known Anna for more years than he cared to remember. The unusual request she had made of him all those years ago, the small introduction fee she suggested that he paid her whenever she brought business to his restaurant, had proved to be a wise investment. Over the years, she had eaten there many times, always in the company of a gentleman who was pleased to have nothing but the best, to pay well and tip heavily as he sought to impress his date. And Anna had become not just a customer, but a friend.

So, when she dined alone at his restaurant and asked if they could speak together, he knew that there would be a good reason.

"Massimo, I need you to help me," she began. "I have a little problem with a man, and I need to get away from him."

"How can I help?" was the answer she had hoped for, and they were indeed Massimo's first words.

"He is watching me all the time. He has not done anything yet, but I fear he might. So, I'm going to try to get away for a little while and hope that it is enough to make him stop."

"If you think that will work, I would be pleased to help. What would you have me do?"

"I plan to slip away one evening and hope he doesn't notice. I will go and stay with my sister for a time. But I don't want him to see me carrying bags from my house or getting into a taxi."

Anna went on to describe how she needed Massimo to help—starting with an Amazon delivery of a large new suitcase to his restaurant. She would bring a bag of clothes with her on each of her next few visits. Then, if everything went to plan, she would need further help on the evening she intended to leave—which would be in about six weeks' time. Massimo was pleased to offer his assistance.

"I hope you do not have to stay away too long," he replied.

Anna added to the lies she had told him by saying that she hoped to be back soon. But she was pretty sure that she would never be enjoying Massimo's cooking again.

She completed her packing on the fourth trip to the restaurant. Massimo had been very polite in leaving her alone as she transferred the contents of her shopping bag to the big suitcase on each visit. There was no particular need for privacy, as all she was transferring were clothes, cosmetics, toiletries, and items she would need in her new life. But he would have been surprised if he had seen the last consignment, as some of the clothes looked fit only for wearing when gardening or cleaning the house. But they were there for a purpose.

The other local business to profit from Anna's departure was the local shop that acted as a collection point for a major courier. Many parcels containing the nicest of the possessions which she was forsaking were sent to Anna's sister in Dresden.

-

Graham was also making plans for the second half of the year. He had the date of October 8th circled on his calendar, and as July began, it was time for an update call with Tom.

Tom agreed they should put their heads together and prepare activities in more detail. He had received no significant updates from his ex-colleagues, but realised that with three months to go, they needed to have a serious plan.

"When do you want to contact the prof?" he asked.

"I've been thinking about that," Graham replied. "I don't think we should speak to him before the start of October. We should wait until we know for sure what she's done. But we need to get in front of him immediately after she goes."

"You're probably right. But I'm not keen on having too long a conversation with you – even on burner phones. I think we should get together. And I also want to talk to you about your safety. Can we meet at your place in London – that should be safe."

They agreed on the date and time for the meeting – chosen by Graham to avoid needing to say anything to Elizabeth.

"OK. I can also update you with what I hear from Anna when we meet next week."

"You're meeting her again?" Tom betrayed his concern at this news.

"Yes. I received an email from her – we've kept in touch by email ever since we met – but this last one was unusual. She asked me for a date. And she never normally does that."

"What do you plan to do?"

"Eat pasta and talk to her."

"Very funny – I mean do you plan to steer the conversation in any particular direction?"

"Of course. I'll have to be careful – but I'll be as normal as possible. Ask her about how things are going at work. Any plans for a holiday? That sort of thing."

"Just be careful, that's all. Just let me know where and when you're meeting her, just to be on the safe side, OK?"

"Yes, Dad," Graham replied and ended the call. But he did send Tom the name of the restaurant and the date and time of his planned meeting with Anna.

24 Third Time Lucky
September 2022

When Graham let Tom into his apartment, he was surprised to see him carrying a holdall.

"Planning to stay the night?" he asked, indicating the bulky bag.

"No, just routine precautions," Tom replied and removed a piece of electronic equipment from the bag. Despite his years in the computer industry, Graham did not immediately recognise what it was. But when Tom attached a device resembling an electronic wand and began waving it around the room, he knew that the room was being swept for electronic bugs. He kept silent until the process was complete a few minutes later.

"Can't be too careful," Tom said, returning his toy to its bag.

Their meeting began once the obligatory Diet Pepsi cans were on the table – this had become a standing joke ever since their first meeting back in Tom's cottage in Wales.

"How did your date with Anna go?" Tom asked. He wasted no time in small talk.

"Mmmm, well enough," Graham replied. "It was odd. She was very cagey."

"Did she say why she wanted to see you?"

"Well, as I said, we stayed in touch throughout the lockdown and exchanged a lot of emails at a time when I guess she was feeling very vulnerable. She was working double shifts – including some in a Covid ward at a very difficult time – and almost all her social contact had been removed."

"Except for our mutual friend, Karl," Tom said pointedly. "Did she mention him at all?"

"Only to say that he seemed to have gone off the boil recently."

"Probably feels he's got all the info he's going to get," was Tom's cynical reply.

"So why the meeting with you?" Tom asked, obviously feeling that his previous posing of this question had not been answered.

"As I said," Graham began and realised he was repeating himself and had not properly thought through exactly why she had asked to meet him or what exactly he had learned from the meeting.

"She's said it to me multiple times, but she does think I'm different to her other dates. I can only believe it's because I really am not like them. I didn't join this website for the same reason those other guys did. That's all I can put it down to."

"But did she actually tell you anything?" Tom's frustration was beginning to show.

"Not directly, but I did get a very strong feeling that this was a goodbye. She'd told me before that she never asked a man for a date, and here she was doing exactly that. It was a powerful vibe – that's all I can say. Otherwise, it was just a perfectly normal meeting of two friends who had not seen each other for a while."

"Well, at least it's good news in one way. It looks like she is planning a departure. And since we know that she is going to disappear, that much is good news. If she gets to execute her plan, that is. There's still the possibility that someone takes her before she makes her own way, but we've got to make sure we keep a close eye on her from the date when we know she was last seen at the hospital." Tom continued and then, noticing the smile on Graham's face, asked, "What are you smiling at?"

"I love the way you've got in line with my thinking. The way you say 'when she was last seen' even though you're referring to something that hasn't happened yet and isn't going to happen for another couple of months. This time travel lark is fun, isn't it?"

"Yeah, great." Tom's sense of humour did not stretch far enough for him to join in.

"I'm still concerned, though. If I remember what you said, when she disappeared, nobody was able to find her."

"Yes." Graham did some quick mental arithmetic. "It was mid-November by the time I did the jump back, so she had been missing for six weeks by then."

"Do you think that she has the ability to do that? And the resources? To manage to get away, stay away, and not be found?"

Graham thought for a few seconds. "She is a very resourceful lady. She's got plenty of influential contacts, and she's highly intelligent, multi-lingual, confident, and very, very determined. If anyone can do it, I guess she can."

"Well, let's just hope she had the opportunity to put those gifts to the test. But before we talk about that, I'd like to know how and when we're going to approach the prof?" Tom asked, and Graham explained how he had previously made contact at the start of this leg of his adventure.

"I think it should work again. A personally addressed note, dropped into the hospital mail system. We should time it so that it lands on his desk immediately after Anna goes missing."

"You don't think we should contact him before she disappears?"

"No, I've thought about it and I'm worried that if we tell him before she goes, he'll either do or say something that will affect her plans. We're going to give him a lot to think about. We'll probably have to talk about time travel and all that stuff. A lot for him to take on board. If we wait until after she's gone, he will have a reason to see us, and, hopefully, we'll be in a position where we know where she is so that we can bring him some good news."

"And what do you plan to put in the note?" Tom asked.

"A request for a meeting. I think the note should come from you since he knows who you are – it'll be signed by Martin Knight, of course – and it should request a meeting at his club. We'll need plenty of time to tell him all about time travel. I'm confident he'll believe me – after all, I have already told him all about it – twice. On two different planes of time. Unfortunately, he won't remember either of them, and I'll have to do it all over again."

Graham fished a printed note from his desk drawer.

"Here's a first draft. What do you think of it?"

Tom looked at the note Graham had handed him.

> *Professor*
>
> *As you know I was responsible for the security of your Optic Nerve Research Project, before I took early retirement after the sad consequences of the experiment that took place on Friday, October 7th, 2012.*
>
> *I know that a repeat of this experiment took place last week and that since this date your assistant, Anna Mueller, has gone missing.*
>
> *I understand that you are concerned about Anna – and that your concern goes beyond the professional. I possess information you will want to hear, and I would welcome the opportunity to pass this on to you as soon as possible.*
>
> *There is plenty of information to convey, and I fully understand the importance of secrecy. Might I suggest that we meet at your club in Tavistock Square at the earliest convenient time?*
>
> *I know that your communications are carefully monitored, which is why I have sent this invitation to you in the way I have.*
>
> *To keep our meeting confidential, might I suggest that you invite my colleague, Graham Henderson for a routine appointment? His contact information can be found on his NHS record, NHS number 567 322 2715.*

> *At the date/time you specify for the appointment, we will meet you at your club.*
>
> *Graham will also attend the meeting. He will explain how we obtained this information and how we know that you keep a photograph of a woman in a blue evening gown between the pages of your family bible.*
>
> *I look forward to meeting you again.*

"Looks good," Tom said, "I presume the bit about the woman in blue is something he told you?"

"That's right. Before I made the jump back in time, I told him I'd need a piece of information that nobody knew – something so private that he would be intrigued enough to agree to a meeting, and that's what he told me."

"And who is the lady in the blue dress?"

"None other than the lovely Ms. Mueller, I believe."

"So, not just a professional relationship, then?"

"Let's just say I believe the prof would like it to be more than just a professional relationship. And maybe, in an ideal world, I believe Anna would too."

Having finalised how they were going to deal with the prof, they then moved on to discuss what they thought Anna's plans might be.

"She didn't give you any hint as to what she planned?" Tom probed once more, hoping for some guidance.

"No. I got the impression she was going to do something and then go – but I've no idea what."

"We'll need to keep a close eye on her from the day of the experiment onwards. And that's something I'd like to speak more about over lunch. I don't know about you, but I'm starving. It was an early start this morning, and British Rail breakfasts aren't what they used to be."

"What do you fancy for lunch?" Graham asked.

"I hope you don't mind, but I've taken the liberty of booking a table for lunch," Tom replied, glancing at his watch. "There's a fish restaurant just round the corner from here with excellent reviews on Trip Advisor. We've got ten minutes to spare."

"Fine by me," Graham replied.

On the way to the restaurant, Tom casually advised Graham that they would be joined at lunch by an ex-colleague of his.

"You're going to need some assistance at keeping an eye on Anna, and this guy is one of the very best."

"And he can be trusted? If he's one of your ex-colleagues, how can we know he won't pass them any information on her, if they should ask?"

"One thing you can be very sure about Richard is that he owes absolutely no loyalty to our mutual ex-employers," Tom replied ruefully. "As I'm sure he'll tell you, he always makes sure to show complete loyalty to whoever signs his pay cheque."

They talked a little more about their lunch guest as they walked to the restaurant. By the time they were seated, Tom had done enough to convince Graham that he had found the ideal man for the job they had in mind. Graham decided to trust him totally.

-

Richard Barton, Private Detective, joined them fifteen minutes after they were at their table. After a few minutes of introductory small talk, Graham observed, "What a coincidence, Richard. You were eating at the same Italian restaurant as me one evening last week, weren't you?"

"Indeed," replied Richard. "Did you happen to notice the young lady who I was with?"

"A small, rather good-looking woman with a dark complexion?"

"Then you have met my partner, Sandra."

"Is that 'partner' as in 'business' or as in 'personal'?"

"Both."

Graham echoed Richard's question and asked him, "Did you happen to notice the woman I ate with? That's the lady we want you to keep an eye on."

Richard and Tom exchanged a glance, and Tom broke the silence.

"Looks like we're all going to get on just fine. Our expert P.D. does his homework, and the complete amateur that we two professionals are trying to protect is not too bad at observation skills either."

The ice was broken, glasses were raised, and a new set of relationships began. Having heard from Tom that he had only given a very brief overview of the situation to Richard, over lunch, Graham outlined the situation and the task that needed performing.

"We are pretty certain that at some point on Friday, October seventh, or over the weekend of the eighth or ninth, she is going to leave her home and go into hiding. We believe that she will be doing this of her own accord – but there is also the possibility that she will be taken either willingly or unwillingly by person or persons unknown. We would like to know the circumstances of her getaway and her destination," was the final part of the briefing.

Terms and conditions were agreed – and they exchanged contact details.

25 Old Maid

September 2022

Some of Richard Barton's fondest memories of his childhood included the time he spent playing with his grandfather. He taught the young Richard so many games: draughts, dominoes, including Richard's favourite version – known as 5's and 3's – where you scored points by adding up the total number of spots at both ends of the chain and scoring one point for each time the total could be divided by 5 or 3. Having a double six at one end and a three at the other end was the best situation because then you had an exposed total of fifteen and scored eight points – three for the number of times it was divisible by five and five for the number of times it was divisible by three. It's quite possible that his grandfather was not only responsible for his lifelong love of games but also for some part of his precocity in mathematics.

Card games began with child-specific ones like Happy Families, but soon moved on to rummy, whist, and the one he enjoyed most, cribbage.

Richard often wondered whether grandparents still taught these games to their children. It was doubtful that the Happy Families game he remembered could still exist in modern society. In the version he remembered, every family in the pack of cards comprised two parents, one male and one female, who were married to each other and shared the same last name. And, of course, they had two perfectly formed children, one male and one female. The father was the only adult to have a trade or profession, and the mother of the children was happy to be known only as 'The baker's wife' or whatever. Not a sign of any disabilities, and every face was white. If the game wasn't actually banned, its modern version would be severely altered from the one he remembered, no doubt.

He had played with a deck of cards where you would make a set by collecting Mister Bunn the baker, Mrs. Bunn the baker's wife, and their children, Johnny Bunn and Jenny Bunn. Nowadays, you would have to complete a set by matching Mister Bunn the baker with Miss Thompson, the Social Worker, who is married to Mister Bunn but uses her maiden name for professional purposes. Or by matching Mister Data the computer programmer with Mister Ellis the interior decorator, who is the civil partner of Mister Data, and Johnny Embufaguo, who is the adopted son of Mister Data and Mister Ellis.

It would make for a much more complicated game. At least in that way, it would accurately reflect modern life.

He loved cribbage as proficiency in the game relied so much on mathematical skill, and every hand was different. And then there was the tactile element, as scores were recorded by moving pegs along a board drilled with tiny holes. Of course, all the pegs had been lost ages ago and were substituted by matchsticks. Back then, matchsticks were ubiquitous. Even if his grandfather had not been a heavy smoker, matches would have been needed to light the gas cooker or the coal fires in the two downstairs rooms that, apart from the two-bar electric fire that was only required in icy weather, constituted the only heating in his grandparents' house. Undoubtedly, today's cribbage players needed to take more care not to lose their pegs.

Of all the many games that he learned from his grandfather, and the ones later added to his repertoire, like Gin Rummy, Canasta, Solo, Bridge, and Brag, there were only two that he could honestly say he disliked.

The first was Flounders – one of the first games he had ever learned. Players roll dice and collect a body part of a fish (the Flounder) according to the number rolled – 1 for the head, 2 for the upper fin, 3 for the upper body, and so on. The winner is the one who builds the most fish. Apart from the lack of satisfaction inherent in building a fish, Richard rapidly came to dislike the game as it was so obviously based solely on chance, with absolutely no opportunity for the player to show skill or develop tactics.

The other one he disliked was Old Maid. Another example of a game that would face severe difficulties in the modern, Politically Correct world. Richard's memory of it was not precise. Players received a number of character cards, which they had to pair off by taking cards in some non-remembered way from other players. Every card in the deck had a pair except the Old Maid card. Whoever was left with this card at the end was the loser.

It offered some reward for skill – possibly in duping another player to take the Old Maid card from you, but what irked Richard was that there was no winner. Just a loser. He did not like that as a child and still believed that it was not a good game for children to be introduced to.

-

Looking back, he felt that in so many ways, his whole life could be mapped in terms of the games he had played. From the Happy Families and Rummy of his early childhood through 9-card Brag in the common room at school, via countless hands of Bridge at university to the eventual late-night games of Blackjack or Poker played in smoke-filled casinos and depressingly poorly furnished flats and safe houses.

His grandfather died before Richard was eighteen, so he never got to see his progress nor to receive his share of praise for his grandson's continued excellence in Maths, which took him all the way from Catholic Primary School via ancient but respected Grammar School to a first-class honours degree at Cambridge University. Richard would have enjoyed the chance to thank him for the contribution made by those early games of cards and dominoes.

It was during his university years that he received the proverbial 'tap on the shoulder' and an invitation to meet some people in the civil service who might be able to offer him some interesting employment.

It came at the perfect time for him, because in the way that things were back then, he had not the faintest idea of what he was going to do with the rest of his life. Until the last year of university, his life had been focussed on getting the best results in whatever the next set of examinations the educational system's conveyor belt served up for him: O Levels, A Levels, Degree, or whatever.

So, after a couple of interviews (and the necessary security vetting of his blameless family and friends), Richard was offered and accepted a job with the security services. To him, it offered a reasonable income, attractive prospects, and the chance of being presented with some interesting challenges to overcome.

What the service thought of him was that he seemed to combine a high IQ, a decent work ethic, and excellent problem-solving skills. All achieved whilst maintaining enough of a personality that enabled him to get on well and easily with everyone he came in contact with. He had not had the 'personality by-pass operation' that so many high-achieving students seemed to have experienced.

Apart from the normal hurdles that challenged a new entrant to the service, he had one more barrier to overcome — his name. Having the name Richard Barton in the nineteen seventies was entirely unremarkable for a child or adolescent. But entering the world of work where so many of the bosses still had memories of (and some would say one foot still in) the nineteen fifties was a different matter.

Dick Barton is the name of a fictional detective that was the hero of a radio programme in the UK in the late nineteen forties and early nineteen fifties. It was almost compulsory for all children to listen to the highly addictive weekly adventures of this larger-than-life hero.

On entering the service, Richard – his first name shortened to Dick as was almost always the case - had to tolerate numerous 'funny' remarks about his crime-solving pedigree. Until the jokes wore off or age thinned out the number of people who understood such jibes as "Where are Snowy and Jock, then?" (The nicknames of Dick Barton's two assistants.)

But he overcame all obstacles. A career of almost twenty years of steady progress through various jobs in various locations, a failed marriage, and the mental and physical scars acquired in this unusual occupation and life probably erased the memory of the Old Maid card game from Richard's mind. Which was a pity, because he was figuratively left holding the card after a particularly difficult round of the game in real life.

He committed the grave error – equally grave in gameplay and real life – of believing he was playing one game when everyone else was playing something completely different. In a situation where the other players were playing poker, he found himself playing Old Maid.

Even the longest-serving members of the Secret Service refer to it as a game. Often, 'Our Game'. That is not to make light of its danger or difficulty. Perhaps it is an acknowledgement that its practices are often so far removed from everyday life – and often played to a set of rules that can be diametrically opposed to the rules of normal civilisation. But it is referred to as a game. And each phase of the game, each round, can produce winners and losers.

Playing this game on the bleeding edge of danger and difficulty, all players acknowledge that they cannot win every round. Life progresses in the hope and expectation that the next win will offset the size of the most recent defeat. But once in a while, there is such a heavy defeat – or which is worse, a defeat that is easily visible – that someone has to take the blame. There are no winners, only losers. And on one such occasion, at the end of a bad loss, Richard was left holding the Old Maid card. For the safety of the remaining players, it was deemed necessary for him to leave the game.

Being 'Old Maid' at the start of your career is bad. It is unusual for it to happen when near the start, but it occurs sometimes, and the player concerned must console himself with the fact that he still has his whole life in front of him and he probably wasn't cut out for this line of work anyway. And he leaves the game with no serious damage done, a redundancy package above the minimum statutory requirement, and a perfect set of references. Not the worst that can happen.

Likewise, being left holding this card towards the end of your career is not the worst that can happen either. An official leaving 'do' gives you one last chance to drink copious quantities of alcohol on the government's tab; there's a leaving present, an indexed-linked pension, and the opportunity to start your retirement in full health.

Probably the worst time to have it happen is the time when it happened to Richard. Mid-career. Mid-forties. A genuine catalyst for a mid-life crisis. But he survived and even prospered from it when it happened to him. He briefly considered the 'non-job' he was offered as the next step in his career. Despite its fancy title of 'Strategic Situation Management' or some such management-speak, he recognised it as a label for the role of cleaning up everyone else's mess, thereby robbing you of the chance of creating your own. He took the alternative of early retirement, or 'outplacement' as the despicable person from HR labelled it.

His high IQ, his ability to get on with people from all walks of life, his undented self-confidence, and his sheer bloody-mindedness all came to the fore. He saw a gap in the market. It was a time when everything was being outsourced or privatised. Every chance that the government had to disown responsibility for failure was being taken. And even in the security services – jobs were being offloaded to private contractors.

Richard took his severance money and set up an investigations company. He offered his services on the open market, where he was confident that the contacts that he had made in the last twenty years would recommend clients to him and maybe even use his services themselves. And he knew one sure tactic to gain government business. His services were only available at exorbitant rates. Only then could the percentages added on for introductions and referrals be really worthwhile. After all, in the world in which he was dealing, nobody was going to introduce business to him unless there was something in it for them, were they?

And his partner would be his Partner. Shortly after Richard departed the service, Sandra quit her job, too. They had managed to keep their relationship secret for the last two years, even in this most trying of circumstances. And she had all the training she needed – at the taxpayer's expense as well.

26 A New Chapter
September - October 2022

"Karl, you've been very patient. Thank you. I have something important to say and I do appreciate you waiting until I was ready to say what I want to say - because what I want to say is not easy." Anna's repetition betrayed the nervousness she was feeling.

Karl nodded and waited politely for her to continue.

"Please let me finish what I have to say, and then I promise I'll answer any questions. But if you interrupt me, I may lose my nerve."

"Carry on," he said quietly.

"I believe I know who you are and what you are. You've kept it secret, and I'm sure that while you may work for a government," she began, stressing the 'a', "I do not believe it is the British Government. You speak fluent German – but your accent and some of the words you use tell me clearly that there is only one place you could have learned your German. And that's on the streets of Berlin.

"You're not English or American – your language skills are far too good for you to be from either of those monolingual countries. And you're not German. You told me you spent some time in Germany in the nineteen eighties, and there's only one non-German nationality that spent some time in East Berlin at that time, and that's Russian. But that's not a problem for me. And it's not a problem that you've spent time while we've been together trying to find out just a little bit more each time about what I'm doing at Moorfields. Well, now you have a chance to find out all you could ever want to know.

"I need to leave. And I need funds to take me where I want to go. I have a complete set of documentation for the project — every technical detail on the whole thing. And I'm prepared to sell it. I need two hundred thousand pounds. If you can come up with that amount of money, I'll give you the whole thing."

Anna had thought long and hard about the sum she should ask for. She had read somewhere that a retirement fund should have four to five hundred thousand pounds in it. Setting her sights on the higher amount, she deducted the amount she would get from selling her home and thus arrived at the figure of two hundred thousand. She would need a contingency to help keep herself hidden, and she had long realised that her pension from the UK National Health Service was going to remain inaccessible to her.

Having made the offer to Karl, she stopped speaking, and there was silence at the table. Karl was surprised. He had entered the restaurant that evening, aware that there must have been some special reason for her asking him for a date. Something she had never done in all the years they had been dating. They had previously either agreed on a date for their next meeting before they parted – or, if not, it had always been up to him to contact her when he was ready. He had waited patiently throughout the meal, expecting her to say something important. But not this.

"Can I ask why me, and why now?" he asked, somewhat tentatively. Her answers were not that important, but it would buy him a few vital minutes to think about what he really might need to ask her.

"The reasons I need to do it now are very private," she replied and paused before continuing. "And you are the only person I know who might be interested in buying what I have for sale. I'm taking a gamble – but we've known each other a long, long time and there has always been a strange kind of honesty between us. Even when we've been concealing things, we have been as honest as possible with each other. So, all I expect from you now is to answer my question. Do you believe that whoever you work for would be interested in buying what I am offering? Yes or no."

Even with the added time from her lengthy answer, he still needed to know more. But it seemed that Anna had told him just about all she was willing to at this point.

"All I can say is that I'll have to consult my superiors, and then I'll let you know. They'll probably want something on trust. Can you do that?" he asked.

"I'll make this suggestion. If you can give me half what I requested up front, I can give you half the documentation. Then, when you've satisfied yourself that it's genuine, you can give me the other half of the money, and then I'll give you the other half of the documentation. If you want me to meet anyone else from your side, I'd be happy to do so – but I'll want to name the time and place."

Her suggested terms seemed reasonable enough to Karl – but his experience of this type of transaction was non-existent, so he would have to convey her terms to his boss and await his decision. He simply suggested that he would contact her as normal to set a date when he had an answer for her – and would then let her know if her proposition had been accepted or if an alternative offer was on the table. Their meal was conducted with less conversation than usual, and at the end of the evening, Karl rode the tube back into central London, wondering what his boss would say. He would speak with him first thing the following day.

He had never considered himself someone with any form of 'sixth sense'. Generally, he would be sceptical about people who spoke of an 'uncanny sense of foreboding' or some such nonsense in telling their tales. But now he suddenly felt something and had to reconsider his opinions. This situation in which he was placed may well present an opportunity for him to realise some of his life goals. He knew it would be risky, but such chances do not present themselves too frequently, and he knew that when they do appear, they need to be taken swiftly and fearlessly.

-

Karl was surprised by the positive reception of his report. They say that timing is everything, which was certainly the case for the information he had just brought, even though Karl did not know it.

Earlier in the week, his superiors had received reports that a significant test of the project at Moorfields was going to be conducted. The source of the information, which of course was not disclosed, even to Karl's boss, was rated such that there was a very high degree of confidence in its accuracy. Some new information on the project would be most welcome.

With Karl's total belief in the accuracy of the information he had been offered and the final reassurance that it was being offered with the most reliable of capitalist values attached, (for financial gain, not for some misguided ideological reason), the budget for the purchase was agreed.

Karl was told that once he had delivered the money to his contact, she was to deliver the first half of the information physically to the address from which Karl worked. The thinking behind this was that the person would be caught on camera making the delivery – information that might prove valuable at some later date.

-

A week later, the first draft of the money was transferred to Anna's Swiss account, and she delivered the package as requested. It contained a USB memory stick and a note with the following printed on it:

> *The information promised is stored on the enclosed memory stick. There are 2 Word documents. DOC1 contains the index for the whole technical document and the introduction section of the document. DOC2 contains half of the technical document itself – every alternative word (the 1st, 3rd, 5th, usw).*
>
> *Embedded in DOC2 is a macro that was used to split the original document into two documents.*
>
> *When I receive the second half of the money you will receive a second memory stick with DOC3 on it, which will*

contain the other half of the technical document (the 2nd, 4th, 6th words usw). DOC3 will also contain an embedded macro which can be used to reassemble DOC2 and DOC3 into the full technical manual.

If the recipients were disappointed that the document had been split in this way, and their hopes of gaining significant information from the first half of the delivery had been dashed, this was not reported back to Anna. She hoped that one day she would be able to say thank you to her brother-in-law, Reinhard, for his perfect response to the request she had made in their brief conversation during her last visit for a pair of Word macros capable of being used the way she had described them in her note.

Her only surprise was the email she received from Karl after the first delivery. She had expected it to be terse and straightforward, but instead, he asked if they could meet one last time at her favourite restaurant and that she should bring a memory stick containing all three documents.

She was happy to comply and was further surprised at the start of the evening when having taken the package from her, Karl said he knew that they could never meet again and he would like his last memory of her to be untainted with any discussion of the transaction that had just ended their relationship.

He wanted only to speak of Italian food, living in London as a non-British person, the history of art, and all the other topics they had talked about for the many years of their relationship.

At the end of an enjoyable evening, they parted with the closest embrace and the only kiss they had ever shared.

"I shall miss you," Anna said.

"And I will miss you even more than I shall miss the spaghetti con vongole that Massimo cooks," was Karl's parting remark.

-

Karl's return journey normally involved a short walk down the hill to Totteridge and Whetstone tube station, where he would catch the first southbound train on the Northern Line. He would disembark at Tottenham Court Road Station and then transfer onto a westbound Central Line train to Marble Arch, from where a short walk would take him to the small redbrick house that was his home and office.

Occasionally, when there was time to spare, and the weather was good, he would not transfer to the Central Line but instead would exit the underground at Tottenham Court Road Station and walk the length of Oxford Street, enjoying either the bustle of its daytime crowds and traffic or the nighttime quiet of its deserted state.

Tonight, he took neither of these routes. Instead, he continued his original southbound train journey as far as Nine Elms Station, where he exited and took a walk of just less than a mile before presenting himself at the front entrance of the Embassy of the United States of America.

'Anna is not the only person beginning a new chapter of her life', he thought.

27 Moonlighting
October 2022

Karl was not missed until the morning after he changed direction (in so many ways) on his way home.

Certain diplomatic niceties had to be followed, but they were to be put on hold for twenty-four hours so that unofficial enquiries could take place. He would have had only his false English papers – his driving license in the name of Peter Eastwood with an address in Slough – on him. So, inquiries were made to hospitals to see whether anyone of this name had been admitted.

Georgi was frantic. He had allowed Karl to meet Anna face-to-face the previous evening to take hold of the final piece of documentation. This was his most trustworthy employee – and Georgi had granted him this latitude in recognition of the long-term relationship with Anna. Now, he was cursing what could turn out to be a fatal lack of judgement. He assumed the worst, which, in his line of work, was usually the best strategy.

He was able to find Anna's home address and dispatched two employees there immediately. Their instructions were to find out if anyone was currently at the address and call when this was known.

One of them simply knocked on Anna's door with a made-up story of seeking someone with an address written on a piece of paper where the name and road name were clear, but the number had become smudged.

They called the office and let Georgi know that a woman answering Anna's description was indeed at the premises. They also passed on the information that the property was an upper-floor flat and that the front door, the only means of access, had only a simple domestic lock on it.

They were told to keep observing the property and report any developments. When nothing had occurred by late afternoon, they were told to wait until nine p.m. Under cover of darkness and with the level of street traffic low, they were to enter the property, subdue the occupants, and report back. At seven p.m. they reported that Anna had received a takeaway delivery and a young woman (possibly Anna's daughter) had left the property. There was no change in their instructions.

-

Maria, Massimo's daughter, parked her motorbike outside Anna's maisonette, switched off the engine, took the pizza box out of the rear container of the bike, and approached Anna's front door. The door was opened a few seconds after she pressed the bell, and Anna invited her in. She had received the instructions from her father for the unusual nature of this delivery and, upon his request, had repeated them to him one last time before she set out this evening.

Massimo had told her that Anna was escaping an unwanted stalker, but he had reassured her that she had nothing to fear as the man had made no moves at all so far. Anna was pre-empting any problems by escaping under cover. Her father reassured her that she would be safe. He would be keeping watch, and he would never place his daughter in any situation where he thought she might come to harm.

So, Massimo was walking along the road at the time Maria made the delivery and he would walk back fifteen minutes later, which was the time agreed for Maria to leave the house. He saw no sign of Anna's stalker but was not surprised. Such a man would no doubt be hiding somewhere. It was no surprise that he saw nothing of Anna's fictitious stalker. However, he also saw nothing of the three sets of people that were watching Anna's house.

-

The Russians were awaiting nightfall as instructed. The British government agents had been watching every night for the past month. They saw and noted the pizza delivery come and go. The eyes of Richard and Sandra saw much more. They had the advantage that they had only been watching for a few days and had been briefed that something was expected to happen tonight. So, they noticed that the pizza delivery person seemed to have put on a few pounds in weight and grown a couple of inches in height during her brief stay in Anna's place.

Full of admiration for Anna's clever attempt at deception, they got out of the van they'd been sitting in and donned their helmets. The pizza delivery motorcycle and its new driver were followed by a more powerful two-wheeled vehicle as it made the short journey to the Isola Bella restaurant.

Richard called Graham and updated him. "She's at the Italian restaurant near her house. It looks like she'll be getting into a taxi shortly. There's one just pulled up outside the restaurant."

Graham thanked them for the update and said he'd be waiting for their next call when they knew where the taxi was heading.

Forty-five minutes later, Graham took their second call which informed him that Anna had entered Terminal Five at Heathrow. "I'm parking the bike," Richard told him. "Sandra is following Anna into the terminal."

The final call came a few minutes later: "She's booked on the next flight to Dresden. I assume you'll want her followed?"

"Of course."

"I've got a contact in Germany. Do you want me to call him and tell him to meet us at the airport? It would give us belt and braces in case she's got anything else up her sleeve."

"Yes, good idea. I'll meet the cost."

"OK. In that case, I'll stay here just in case she tries anything at this end. Sandra will go to Dresden, and we'll update you when Anna lands."

The last call of the night came about three hours later.

"There was nobody here to meet her, and she's checked into the Ibis Hotel, Wilsdruffer Strasse, in the wrong area of downtown Dresden. We'll give you an update tomorrow."

"Thanks. Can you make sure you find out what name she's travelling under? She can't be using her real name – either that or our border checks are even worse than we thought."

-

When Georgi Golovin heard from his two employees that they had entered Anna's apartment and found it empty, he came as close as humanly possible to exploding with rage. Within seconds he realised that the pizza delivery and the young woman departing must have been some type of switch. It didn't matter how – but she had slipped past the people tasked with watching her. When this information was added to the disturbing but vague reports received earlier in the day of failed communication from other service assets, he knew that solids were sure to hit fans soon. And he was standing right in the receiving line of the wind from those fans.

-

Anna spent the weekend walking the streets of central Dresden. It had changed so much from the little she remembered from her childhood. The opening of the Iron Curtain and all that went with it had transformed central Dresden into a major tourist destination – not just for Germans but for the rest of Europe and even the rest of the world.

The buildings had been recreated faithfully, mimicking how they had looked before the devastation of the Second World War. And now they had all been cleaned up and restored almost like new.

The fine weather and her complete freedom from any form of obligation enabled her to fully experience everything for two whole days. She stopped in cafes - not the global chains, but the genuine local eateries. She enjoyed Bratkartoffeln for the first time in years ('only Germans could make potatoes taste this good', she thought), and a wonderful genuine Schwarzwälder Kirschtorte. (In her first year in the UK she had ordered a

Black Forest gateau in a London restaurant – a mistake she never repeated.)

She knew she would not be able to afford this lifestyle permanently but treated it as a short holiday between two periods in her life—periods that she expected would be very different from each other.

On Monday morning, she dressed in one of the sets of 'gardening clothes' she had brought from London and, having waited until the morning rush period at the hotel was over, she went down the stairs and out of the hotel, trying to make sure that she was seen in her shabby state by as few people as possible. She then walked the short distance to the office of "Blasewitz ist bunt", a charitable organisation that offered support for refugees. She had noticed it the previous day during her walk around the town centre and thought it would ideally suit her plans.

She joined the queue of people waiting to see an advisor – her clothing now provided her with a suitable disguise. When her turn came, she discussed with the advisor her reasons for attending.

"I feel I may be able to offer some help to you, and you might also be able to help me," she started, speaking in German.

"How is that?" the advisor asked with genuine and professional friendliness.

"I can offer medical assistance. I am a qualified doctor where I come from, but unfortunately, I do not have the necessary paperwork to practice properly here in Germany. I also speak English fluently and a little Russian."

"And where is it that you come from?"

"I would prefer to keep that information to myself. My name is Frau Anna Dreier, but for now, it would be safest if I did not reveal my full details."

"And how do you believe we would be able to help you?"

"I have some friends who have kindly provided me with a place to stay, but if I could take my meals here in return for my services, that would be a great help."

-

Anna's plan to use the immigrant centre as a cover for a few weeks was a good one. She remained anonymous and every day provided help with minor medical matters and translation issues for the users, in return for two square meals. She was also in a good position to check that she was not being followed, as anyone observing the centre would stand out. To the best of her knowledge, after a few days, she was confident that there was no threat. She made friends with some of the volunteers in the centre and noted the names of the property owners who rented to the immigrants.

She was confident that soon she would find the right one to make a deal with and establish a permanent home for herself. Until then, she would lie low for a month and hope that no other events would interfere.

But they did.

28 A Great Day for a Walk
October 2022

Graham had a raft of decisions to make over the next few days – but one decision outranked all the others. Which plane of time was he going to settle on?

He now knew where Anna had gone to when she bolted. This was the key piece of information that the prof had asked him to discover. It was his reason for being here, where 'here' referred to a plane of time rather than a geographic location. But what to do next?

He could arrange a trip back to his original plane of time. If he could get the prof to re-run the experiment while he was on the floor above or below the target area with his mind properly focussed, he was confident he could return to the point at which this adventure had started. Once there he could let the prof know where Anna was, and then resume his life. But was that the right decision?

Now that he knew where Anna was, he could not honestly believe that simply passing this information to the prof was the right thing to do. For one thing, he did not yet know why she was there. Nor what her plans were for the short or long term. There had to be a link with Karl, but as yet he did not know what that link was. Whatever it was, it was highly likely that this was some part of the reason for her leaving the country, and it was probably a reason why she might not be able to come back. At least for some time.

If the prof contacted Anna, he would reveal her location to the people watching him, and that surely would not be the best thing for Anna. And if he was not going to contact her, then what purpose could be served by letting him know where she was?

If he went back to that original plane of time, he would not be able to call on the services of Tom Woodward or Richard Barton. Neither of them would know him from a hole in the wall and there was not the golden charm of being able to predict the future as a carrot to offer them.

There was a second course available, and that was to stay in this plane of time and try to resolve the issue. He had several ideas of how his unique knowledge of the whole situation and the key players in it might be used to solve the situation. His ability to foretell the future, which would still be in operation for a few months before it expired, may yet have more use.

Despite the weather being what the Scots so wonderfully described as 'driech', their way of summing up weather that was cold, grey, drizzly, and totally unsuitable for walking, he was putting on his coat and hat and preparing to do just that. There was just no substitute for walking when you needed to make a difficult decision.

And today was, surely, the most appropriate day on which to make the decision. Tomorrow would be his seventieth birthday. Which meant that today was the day on which it all began. The date his first, inadvertent journey back in time had commenced. And when he had lived out that second life, he had completed his loop by travelling from October 8th on that plane of time back to October 8th on the original plane.

His second journey started in December 2022 and took him back to October 2018 on this, the third different plane of time he had experienced. He needed to decide what to do on this plane of time. And the decision had to be made before reaching the date on which this journey had started. He still had two months before that decision had to be made, but now had to consider it seriously.

Setting out down the road, he contemplated his situation. If he stayed in this time plane, for how long would he stay? Of course, the whole question might be moot. He could never be sure that an attempt at time travel would be successful. Just because it had been successful on the three journeys so far, there was no guarantee that it would work, or work in the way he wanted it to, on a fourth trip. So, he might not be able to get back to that original plane of time, even if he wanted to.

He had to stay here a little longer. Going back and just ticking the box that said 'I found her' was helping nobody. But if he solved the problem, or at least made it a little bit less of a mess, on this plane of time, then that would all be undone when he went back. He would, presumably, land back on the same day as he had left and be in the situation he had already thought through. Anna's whereabouts would be known to him, but she would remain unreachable.

So, could he stay in this current plane of time? When he had taken his first ever journey, landing on his eighteenth birthday, he had decided to return eventually to his original plane of time when the date of his original journey came around. The date of his return had been his choice and he had not hesitated to make it, giving up a wealthier situation for a financially much poorer one. He had traded in a life in a large house on the banks of the River Thames with a large, heated swimming pool, his own boat, ownership of several companies, and a more than healthy bank balance. In return he had settled for a much more modest life in suburban Kent, but one in which he had a full family. That had been an easy choice because he missed his family so much. Even a swimming pool and a boat were no substitute, in his mind, for a family of loving children and grandchildren.

But that was not the choice he was now facing. If he went back to his old lifestyle he would, once again, be forsaking substantial wealth. But he would also be forsaking his relationship with Elizabeth. He could try to recreate it but would once again face the barriers caused by his time travel.

He knew where she worked and could probably engineer a meeting, and maybe even start a dating relationship. But there would be the problem that he knew a great deal about her, yet she knew nothing about him. Even if he made a connection with her, how long before he made a slip and she asked, "How the hell do you know that?" And from there, how long until she was breaking up with him because he was "Just too weird" or because "I'm sure you're hiding something from me."

He reached a fork in the path of his walk and had to decide if this was to be a short walk or a longer one. He still hadn't reached a conclusion, and so took the right-hand option – the longer walk.

What was the penalty for staying on this plane of time? His thoughts returned to the plane of time he had left. What would happen if he did not return? For some strange reason, he made a mental connection with a film he'd seen many years ago. Was it called 'The Thirteenth Floor'? He thought so.

He remembered that on one of the planes of time, the participants discovered that their world was not real and that they were characters in some form of virtual reality. The part he remembered was where two characters had driven out of town and discovered that at the edge of the town, there was nothing there. Literally, nothing, as it hadn't been drawn by the illustrators who had created their world.

Would that be the situation in the plane of time he had left? Would he and the rest of the people in his life exist in a badly drawn world? Or would life just go on as it had when he left, presumably with him saying "Sorry, Prof, it looks like the time travel didn't work." He could not get his head around it.

After letting his mind drift for a few yards of his walk he decided that this was not his problem. There was nothing he could do about it. He could not let that be a consideration in his decision process, especially when there were many significant benefits, not just for him and his family, but also for Anna, the prof, Tom, and his family, and (hopefully and immodestly) for Elizabeth if he stayed here and sorted out the mess.

The only thing he could think of that was missing from his current life was one of his grandchildren. That was sad, of course. Rosie had been his youngest grandchild and, because she was his youngest, and probably his last grandchild, she was his favourite. She had been born in early 2021 on that other plane of time, but she had not materialised on this plane. He could not seriously consider giving everything up just for that, surely.

-

What happened next was one of the spookiest timings of an event that he could ever remember. His mobile phone rang. He had meant to switch it off during the walk as he didn't want anything to interrupt his process of reaching an important decision. But now that it had rung, he had to see who it was.

Discovering it was his daughter and knowing how infrequently she called him, he assumed it must be important and took the call. After a brief introductory "How are you?" and listening to a few seconds of his description of the misty grey countryside view, she let him know the purpose of the call.

"I thought you might like to know that you're going to be a grandfather again," she announced.

Graham truly experienced tears of joy at hearing this. He was pleased that there was nobody there to witness him becoming suddenly overcome. Not just with the news of having a new grandchild, lovely as that was, but with the feeling that something that he had thought had been taken away from him, had, in an instant, been returned.

He asked the usual questions. Firstly, the expected arrival date. He was surprised to hear that the due date was only three months away. He wondered whether his daughter may have had some issues which meant that she had delayed the announcement until she was sure – he had heard of such things but understood that she would have given this information to her mum if she had still been alive but would not share it with her father. He didn't ask, instead raising the question that might be answered at this stage in a pregnancy.

"Do you know if it's a boy or a girl?" he asked and was told that they knew. It would be a girl.

He asked how the baby's sister had taken the news and was told she was delighted, and then gave his heartiest congratulations to his daughter and asked her to pass them on to his son-in-law.

After finishing the call, he smiled to himself. 'I even know what the baby's name is going to be', he thought. And, in its way, much more importantly, he had just reached a very important decision in his own life. He was going to stay in this plane of time – hopefully for the rest of his life.

Neither the heavier rain nor the wind blowing towards him as he completed his walk could wipe the smile off his face. Now he had to work out what his plan would be, and how he could get the necessary people to play their parts in its completion.

-

He took his first faltering step of his plan on the following day. Sitting down to Sunday lunch with Elizabeth, he said "There's a few things I need to tell you and to ask you, and now seems as good a time as any."

"I'm all ears," she replied. If she was concerned about what his rather formal introduction would lead to, she did not show it.

"I'm just starting my last project with my ex-employer," he began. A small frown crossed Elizabeth's brow, but he continued anyway. "It will take about a month – I'm afraid it's another of those hush-hush ones, and I may have to spend a day or two away at short notice, so I hope you'll forgive me if I have to break a date or two. But it's definitely the last one."

He paused and waited for feedback, and it came soon enough.

"Forgive my cynicism, but I have experience of you men promising that you've retired and will not be going back to work ever again, so I hope you don't mind me taking that with a grain or two of salt."

"That's fair enough. It's the first time I've made you this promise and it's up to me to keep it, I know. But it leads on to something else. When this month is over, I would like it very much if you and I started living together. We can live here, or at your place, or in a whole new place of our own, but I would like us to live together."

"I suppose that would make it easier for me to see if you do keep your promise about this being your last project."

"Is that a yes?"

"Let's say it's a conditional yes. I'll move in, but I'll keep my options open. If you can't keep your promise, then that will be the end. We need to be completely honest with each other."

"That's perfect. Well, nearly perfect. Because there is one other thing I'd like to ask. I mean I'd be very happy with you living with me as Mrs. Fairbanks, but I would be even happier if you were to live with me as Mrs. Henderson."

"That's not the most romantic proposal a girl's ever received, Graham. I think you need to do a whole lot better than that."

"OK. Let me prove that I can keep my promise – about not working – for a couple of months – and then I'll find a more romantic way of getting you to make a promise to me. How about that?"

"It's a deal," she replied and sealed their bargain with a kiss.

-

On Monday Graham made the journey to London to drop the letter to Professor Karbajanovic into the hospital's internal mail system. Now it was just a case of waiting to hear back from the prof, which Tom and he expected to happen soon.

The following day he was surprised to find he had a couple of visitors. Two policemen, a Detective Inspector and a Detective Sergeant, knocked on his front door and showed their badges, but Graham, in that state of mild panic that affects even the most innocent of citizens when they come face to face with the police, did not take note of their names. He was only too pleased that Elizabeth had not yet moved into his house. Otherwise, this might have taken some explaining.

When he reported the conversation in a call to Tom later, Tom asked if he had noticed which police division they were from. Graham had to say that he had not noticed.

"They're probably Special Branch," Tom stated.

"They told me that it was a missing person inquiry. I'm surprised they've reacted so quickly. She can only have been reported missing today," Graham replied.

"And what did they ask you about?"

"They were particularly interested in what Anna and I had spoken about on our last date – which they seemed to know all about. They presumably wanted to know if she had let me know what her plans were."

"And what did you say to them?"

"What do you think we talked about, I said. The Queen's just died and been buried, the whole British government has fallen apart, and the lionesses are all over the media after beating Germany. Not as if we were short of a topic or two, were we?"

"Okay, okay. But it's perhaps not so surprising they were keen to know all about her when you add in the bit of news that I received in a call yesterday evening from my old colleagues. Anna's Russian friend Karl presented himself to the US Embassy on Friday evening and told them he wanted to defect. The Americans felt they had to let their British cousins know, not just because it's happened on our turf, but also because he was carrying a complete set of documentation for Project Petra."

Graham let rip with a small collection of expletives. "How come they're telling you about it?" he then asked.

"I guess it's partly because I was involved in the project a few years back – and I've been talking to a couple of people about it recently. They were checking to see if I knew where Anna was. So, it's a fair bet they have no idea."

"Obviously, it was the same thing the police were asking me. They said they knew I'd been dating her – I guess they've got a list of her contacts from the agency."

"Yes, one way or another," Tom replied. "Hopefully you didn't let anything slip."

"I don't think I'd still be here if I had given them an inkling that I knew where she was. I guess we just have to wait for the prof to contact us."

"Yep, that'll have to be the plan," Tom ended the call.

29 Repeating Something I've Not Done Before
October 2022

Thursday's mail included the confirmation of Graham's routine appointment with the professor, scheduled for the following day at noon. He called Tom to let him know, and after briefly reiterating what their agreed plan was, they agreed to meet outside the professor's club. Tom declined the offer of overnight accommodation at his apartment.

"Let's not give them the chance to see me visiting your place – just in case," he said.

-

'I'm repeating something I haven't done before. Or else I'm repeating something that I have done before, but when I did it before, it was later this year.' Graham pondered to himself. Such were the crazy thoughts that sometimes went through his brain when he had to walk across different planes of time.

He was on his way to the club in Tavistock Square in central London, to explain his time travel experience to the prof for the third time. But because both the other explanations had occurred on different planes of time, it would be completely new to his one-man audience. On the other occasions, he had succeeded in getting his point across. Hopefully, this would be just as successful as the previous attempts had been, and the prof's thought processes would not be clouded with his concern for Anna's whereabouts.

He arrived in Tavistock Square at a quarter to twelve and took a few minutes to enjoy a leisurely walk around the gardens that filled the centre of the square, enjoying the cool bright autumn sun before joining Tom at the foot of a set of stairs that led to the anonymous front door sandwiched between two houses that had been converted into departments of the University of London.

They pressed the doorbell and were admitted by a smartly dressed receptionist. "We're here to meet Professor Karbajanovic," they informed her, and were shown to a private dining room at the end of a small corridor, whose walls were lined with photographs of famous medical men.

"This is the same room where met in last time," Graham remarked.

"You're not going to keep doing that are you?" Tom asked, "Because that time travel stuff can be boring after a while."

"Except when it produces a lottery jackpot, I suppose," he countered.

The Professor joined them a few minutes later. They conducted five minutes of banal conversation about the room, the club, the weather, and the incredible political turmoil currently unravelling in Westminster until a waiter appeared and took their orders for lunch.

"I asked them not to serve us until one o clock to give us a chance to get the meeting underway. I trust that is acceptable," the professor said as the waiter left. Graham resisted the temptation to say, "Just like you did last time," and merely said "OK."

They sat round the table and after the briefest of introductions from Tom, Graham gave a similar speech to the one he had given a couple of years previously to Tom at his cottage. He covered his personal history, meetings with the professor after returning from his first period of time-travel, and the subsequent request for help with Anna's disappearance. There were few interruptions until he reached the part where Anna entered the story.

"You are saying that I requested your help after she disappeared?"

"Yes. You told me about the picture of the woman in a blue dress that you keep in your family bible - so that I could prove to you that we had met on the other plane of time."

"And have you met her on – how did you put it – on this plane of time?"

"Yes. We met a couple of times, and we have also exchanged many emails. I wanted to be in a position where she knew and trusted me. That way I could hope for a favourable reception when I contact her after her getaway."

"And do you know where she is?"

"Yes. I know where she is, and I can assure you that she is safe. She is in hiding and, at this moment, believes that nobody knows where she is. The only people who know where she is are myself, Tom, and one trusted colleague of ours."

"Are you going to tell me where she is?"

"Not yet, professor. I need to make sure that she wants you to know. And there are certain complications about the circumstances of her departure. She has gone into hiding for good reason because she does not want some people to know where she is. And Tom and I will need to work this out before we can decide what to do."

"What do you require from me?"

"At the moment, we only need your patience. We thought you would want to know she is safe. And I need to know what you will do if and when we let you know where she is."

"That is a good question, Mister Henderson. I obviously hope that she returns to her position as soon as possible, but from what you are saying it seems that might not be possible."

"Yes, that's correct. She could not return to the UK right now," Tom interrupted, making his first contribution since he had introduced Graham. These words had more impact coming from him. It signified to the professor that there was a security involvement in Anna's inability to return.

They were interrupted by the first course being served and only continued when the waiter had left.

"What do you plan to do now?" the professor asked.

"I plan to visit her to find out some of the exact details of why she left," Graham said. "And then Tom and I will put our heads together and see how we work our way out of this mess."

"You need to know that if there is anything I can do to help, you must please ask me," the professor stated with unusual emphasis.

The rest of the lunch conversation added very little to their plans. They could not avoid exchanging their opinions on Boris, Liz Truss, and the generally poor state of British politics. But it did allow for a greater connection to be made between Tom and the professor, which was going to be essential if there was to be a chance of "working their way out of this mess", as Graham had so succinctly put it.

After lunch, they departed with a promise to make contact as soon as there was any development. It was agreed that for security reasons, when he had something to report, Graham would call the professor's office and tell him there was a problem resulting from his treatment, and a consultation would then be arranged as soon as possible.

Graham and Tom adjourned to one of the benches in Tavistock Square Garden. Graham indicated the statue of Mahatma Gandhi in front of them, which had several small candles alight beneath it.

"Why do I think we'll need his level of wisdom to get this sorted out?" he asked, not sure whether he expected an answer or not. All he got in return was another question.

"So, you still plan to go and see her?"

"It's the only way we'll get to hear her side of the story. And I know she'll be honest with me. Then we can see what she wants us to do about the professor."

"But you've got a problem. Now we know that Karl has jumped ship, and you've been visited by Special Branch, you must assume they will be watching you. If you go to her, they'll track you and find her. I could try to get you a false passport, but that will take time."

"I don't think it's a problem," Graham replied. He took Elizabeth's late husband's passport out of his jacket pocket and showed it to Tom. "Do you think I'd get away with this?"

"Bloody hell," replied Tom. "Is this real?"

"Yes. Luckily my girlfriend seems to go for a certain look in her men. It's her ex-husband."

"I won't ask how you got it. But the answer to your question is yes, I think you'll get away with it."

They agreed that Graham would visit Anna to get her side of the story, and then he and Tom would work together to plan a route out of the mess.

"Looks like you'll have the pleasure of staying a couple of nights in our wonderful capital city," Graham said, knowing how much Tom hated London, especially hotels in London.

He reconsidered his decision not to take up Graham's offer of hospitality at his apartment – but knew that security was vital. "At least I can afford something decent," he grumbled.

"Good, because when I get back, we'll have to get our heads together."

There was no reason for further delay. Graham spoke on the phone to Richard Barton who confirmed that Anna was still staying at the Ibis hotel on Wilsdruffer Strasse – and that she seemed to remain in her room all evening. So 'Harry Fairbanks' booked a flight to Dresden, and much later that same evening Graham knocked on Anna's hotel door.

"Guten Abend, Frau Dreier" he began, "Darf ich rein kommen?"

She was unable to hide her shock. "You? How the hell?...Come in." she replied, looking nervously up and down the corridor.

Allowing Anna to sit down, he fetched her a glass of water from the bathroom – she was obviously in a state of shock. He said nothing while she gathered herself.

"How did you find me?" was her first question.

"Quite simple, really. I knew you were going to make a run for it, and so I had you followed."

"And who the hell are you really? And how did you know I was 'going to make a run for it' anyway?"

Her anxiety began to turn into aggression.

"I'll explain as best I can, Anna," he tried to calm her. "First, let me reassure you. You and your secret are safe. The only people who know where you are and what you've done are me and two of my immediate colleagues, and we don't intend to let anyone else know. If you want to stay here for the rest of your life, in fact, whatever your plans are, you will still be able to continue with them.

As to who I am, well, that's more difficult to explain than you might imagine. Let's just say I'm a friend of Professor Karbajanovic. It was out of his concern for you and for your safety and well-being that you were followed, and the only thing we wish to achieve is the best – both for you and for him. If we ever get to the end of this, I promise you will know all you ever need to know about me."

She seemed a little calmer after this little speech, but Graham understood she still would have questions and doubts.

"I'll do my best to answer any questions you have, but I'd like to hope that life holds a better future for you than the Ibis hotel on Wilsdruffer Strasse or an apartment full of cast-offs from Blasewitz ist bunt. But I'll need to know exactly what you've done and what it is you really want to do now. Do you truly wish to never see the professor again?"

And then Anna, faced with what her future might be, for the first time in a very long time began to cry. "Does he know where I am?" she asked.

Graham provided a tissue and a hug, and Anna stopped crying after a few minutes.

"I think it might be easier for us to talk if we had a couple of drinks in front of us, don't you?" he asked, and Anna nodded.

She fixed her makeup, and they adjourned to a nearby bar. Secured at a private booth with two beers in front of them, he told her that the only thing that the professor knew was that she was safe. He added that he had no intention of letting her whereabouts be known to anyone, including the professor, without her permission.

With minimal prompting, Anna gradually told the whole story. How she had felt so awful and so powerless at the events that had unfolded the previous Friday. How she had intended to even things out, believing that if both sides knew about the weapon, it would be less likely that either of them would use it. Graham asked if Karl had told her what he intended to do with the information.

"I assume he will pass it on to his superiors," she replied, "Why?"

"I just need to check everything," he replied. "Just in case he planned to go solo with it,"

"No, he seemed a loyal employee to me," she replied, disappointing Graham who had secretly hoped that she knew of Karl's plans. If she had been an active collaborator, it would be a better fit for a plan that was beginning to form in his head.

—

After a couple of beers and a lot of talk, Graham was confident he knew everything he needed to know. He knew exactly what she had done and had a good idea of why she had done it. He was particularly interested to hear that Karl had asked her to give him all three documents on his second visit, and that, based on the time he left her and the time he had arrived in Nine Elms, he had travelled immediately from their dinner together directly to the US Embassy.

He thought Anna had not completely thought things through – her plans beyond the immediate future were not fully formed, and as soon as she took any steps to establish a more permanent residence, she would run the risk of becoming visible. Several people in the UK, the USA, and Russia were all keen to find out where she was and none of them had her best interests anywhere near the top of their agenda.

He established that she would only want to see the professor when her future was settled, and she did not want him to know where she was – so if they were to meet it would have to be at a neutral venue. Neither she nor Graham were keen on this idea as it risked her becoming visible. He asked only one hypothetical question, "What would you ideally like to do with the rest of your life?" and received a very clear answer, "I'd work with the professor until he achieved his dream of building a device that could help the blind see again."

His last couple of questions puzzled Anna, but despite him refusing to explain, she answered them as honestly as she could.

"Is there something I could say to Karl that would let him know that I had spoken to you?" was the first, and after a moment's thought, she replied, "You could ask him if he has found anywhere that serves good spaghetti con vongole. It doesn't matter what he says – he'll know the question came from me."

"And if I had to ask someone a question that only Karl could answer?" proved more difficult for her to answer, but eventually it came to her.

"You could ask him which course he studied at university in England, and if you get the answer History of Art or something like that, you're getting the answer from him."

Anna agreed to give him her mobile number– she too had purchased a burner phone for emergency use – but on condition that he would only ever call her from a public telephone within Germany, which he reluctantly agreed to. He escorted her safely back to her hotel before taking a cab to his more salubrious lodgings. He was left with the feeling that he had a mightily tangled ball of wool to unravel. But at least he now knew the length of the wool and just how entangled it was.

30 A Rookie as MVP
October 2022

Graham called Tom on Friday afternoon as soon as he arrived home, and they arranged to meet that evening in the bar of Tom's hotel. He detailed his findings from his visit to Dresden, and they agreed that the situation was, to quote Tom's Welsh eloquence, "a right bugger's muddle."

"It seems she was acting from the best of motives," Graham suggested, but he was interrupted by Tom saying, "The road to hell…" before he could continue.

"She knew what was happening that Friday afternoon and was powerless to stop it, so she did what she thought was right, something that would minimise the chance of this weapon being used again."

"And you believe she had no idea what Karl was up to?"

"Yes," Graham answered.

"That's a pity, Tom replied and was asked why.

"Because if she had known that he was going to take it to the US Embassy and was diddling the Russians out of their money, she could make a case that she was playing for our side."

Graham fell silent for a while.

"What if we could convince the powers-that-be that she did know what he was doing? That they were acting together."

"I think that would make it possible for her to at least stay out of jail. I don't know if they'd welcome her back, but one step at a time. But why bother asking? She isn't giving that as a story, nor is Karl."

"Well, I think there's a way that might be achieved," Graham spoke slowly despite his brain racing. "I think I might have a plan. Not a full plan – but the beginnings of one," he explained. "I've had two plane journeys and a night in a chain hotel to think about it. I think we might be able to convince everyone that Anna knew what Karl was planning all along."

"But didn't you say she had no idea what his plans were?"

"Indeed. I see that as a wonderful void that could be filled," Graham answered.

Tom thought a while before continuing his line of reasoning. "I suppose the Americans probably don't care too much either way – it's not their secrets she's told – they'll agree with whatever stance the British take. But right now, the Brits think she's betrayed the secret to the Russians, and so she's a traitor."

"I think we might be able to change that perception. It's a long shot – but before I explain how we might do it, do you have any ideas?"

"That's an easy question to answer. No."

"OK. Do we know where Karl is now?"

"No, but I can probably find out quite easily. Why do you want to know?"

"The way I see it is this – we need to get Karl to say that Anna knew what he was doing all along. And then we need to get Anna to agree. Then maybe, just maybe, we can see about getting her back safely into this country. Do you follow me?"

"I follow you alright, Graham, but there's something I don't like about your idea."

"And what would that be?"

"It contains a lot of things that 'we' are going to do – and I don't know how the hell 'we' are going to do them."

-

It was still early enough in the evening for Tom to try to get an answer about Karl's whereabouts, and he excused himself to go to the quiet of his room and call a contact. He was gone nearly an hour but brought news on his return.

"I've got some good news and some bad news, if you don't mind me using a tired old phrase," he began."

"It's never bothered you before," Graham replied. His mood had not improved by having sat alone for the past hour.

"I can tell you where Karl is."

"And the bad news?"

"By this time tomorrow, he'll be in Virginia."

Undaunted by this potential setback, Graham moved on to the second stage in his plan.

"OK, that's a minor inconvenience. But one we can overcome, I'm sure. I need a second piece of assistance from you, though. I assume you have some contacts over there from your years of working within – what did they call it – oh yes, the special relationship."

"How do you know that?" Tom asked, suddenly cautious about the ground they were figuratively stepping on."

"You need to remember I've passed this way before. And on that occasion, I helped you to provide the cousins with some information about a certain terrorist attack in 2001."

Amidst the banter, Tom searched his mind for suitable contacts.

"What are you looking for, exactly?" he asked.

"Someone who will get us as close as possible to our Russian friend. Preferably someone you can speak to – and ideally someone who is a bit of a sports fan."

"You don't ask for much. Why the need for a sports fan?"

"Well, I don't know the numbers that are going to be drawn in any American lotteries, but I am aware that there is a rather important sports event coming up shortly. One where I might be able to assist a friend to make some profitable bets."

"You mean like the Super Bowl football game?" Tom asked, showing his ignorance of the American sporting calendar.

"Something like that. The baseball equivalent – The World Series."

Tom smiled as a memory came to him. "Oh, if it's baseball, I know just the man. Brad Petersen's the guy you'll need to speak to."

"Any chance he's a betting man?"

"Yes," Tom said, unable to stifle a smile spreading across his face as a memory stirred. "He used to say there were only three great things on this planet, and they all began with the letter B: Beer, Baseball, and Babes. But when he left here at the end of his posting, we had a drink together, and he told me that his stay in England had convinced him that there was a fourth – Betting. 'Hell, I can place bets on my home sports teams easier in the UK than I can back home' he used to say. Now that things are a little easier on the betting front in the USA if you can give him some tips, I'm sure he'll do what he can to help."

"And can he get close to Karl?"

"If there's something in it for him, he'll find a way."

"Then you had better get working on contacting him. I need to speak to him within the next ten days."

"Sounds like a plan," Tom said with less than total conviction. "Or, more accurately, what was it you said? Not a full plan – but the beginnings of one."

-

While Tom reactivated the relays that would enable him to speak to his former sparring partner, Graham did what he could in preparation. 'Harry Fairbanks' applied for a US visa, and Graham sat in a darkened room and wrote down everything he could remember about the 2022 World Series.

It was remarkably fresh in his memory, perhaps because it had been one of the first things he had done after returning from his first time-travel adventure. He had sat up night after night enjoying the way the lead had changed hands during the nine days that the six games had been spread over. For his proposed conversation with Brad, he would need the facts at his fingertips, so he listed them in the notes section of his phone.

A week later, Tom gave him the information he had hoped to receive.

"I've spoken to Brad and told him that you are someone who should be listened to. He'll need some convincing, but here's his number. He's expecting your call."

Graham noted the number and called it immediately.

"Brad, I believe you're expecting a call and I have my reasons to keep the call as short as possible. I need a favour from you – a big one. But I'm prepared to trade with you. And I'll get things going straight away. Tom tells me you're a betting man, so I strongly suggest that you place a bet on the first game of the World Series. The Phillies will win, but they'll need extra innings to do it. If this doesn't happen, you'll never hear from me again. But if it does, I'll call you again and give you an outline of the favour I want and maybe a suggestion of how to bet on the second game. Is that understood?"

"I guess I'm going to listen to you because Tom is such a good guy, but I'm telling you right now, I do not expect to ever hear from you again."

"That's great, Brad. Thanks - and talk to you again soon."

-

The game occurred three days later and as soon as it finished – exactly as Graham had predicted – Graham called Brad again in the early hours of the morning in the UK.

"I don't know how you did that, and I don't want to know," Brad said as soon as he picked up the phone.

"Don't mention it," Graham replied, as he always did to anyone whom he thought should say thank you and who did not.

"What is this favour you want from me?" Brad asked, suspicion still crowding out any gratitude from his response.

"That's far too complicated to say over the phone," Graham replied. "We need to meet face-to-face,"

"Ain't you forgetting that there's a huge ocean between us?"

"No – I hear they have these jet planes now that can get across it. I'm willing to get in one so I can speak to you. And if you can tell me where to go and when, I'll tell you how to bet on tomorrow's second game." Graham wanted to be friendlier, but he had limited time to get his point across, so he kept it short and sharp.

Brad had thought about what he was doing. He could not see how he had broken any laws so far, and he had a couple of hundred dollars in his account that he would not have otherwise had, so he was prepared to take another step.

"It's good news if you're an Astros fan," Graham continued, "They're going to win the second game by two or three runs. Sorry, you're not going to make too much money on that – but in the later games, who knows? Where do we meet?"

"You know the Lincoln Monument in Washington?"

"Sure"

"How soon can you be there?"

Graham checked his notes. It was already the early hours of Saturday morning in the UK and the next game was due to take place on Sunday afternoon, US time.

"I can be there Sunday lunchtime, let's say one p.m.," he replied.

"OK. You sit on one of the benches facing the monument and I'll find you there." The phone call ended.

-

One of the few things that improved after the pandemic was that some official procedures became much less frequently used by the general public, and, as a result, things proceeded more quickly. Harry Fairbanks' visa came through rapidly and Graham was able to book a flight to Washington for Saturday evening. His choice was limited to first class, and he was thankful that he had included lottery funding in his preparations for this adventure. It was becoming more and more needed as time went on.

He sat, well wrapped up against the autumn wind, on a wooden bench looking at the magnificent Lincoln Memorial, checking his watch to confirm he was on time, when another well-wrapped elderly man sat next to him.

"You are looking very well, Mister Fairbanks," was the greeting he received. "Especially for someone who died five years ago. I'm wondering if that's how you know what's going to happen in our little baseball games."

Graham was impressed by the speed with which Brad had gathered his intelligence. A quick check must have been made for someone making a last-minute reservation on a flight from London to Washington, which would have been cross-referenced with recent visa applications and the likely age of the male passenger travelling alone. It probably had not been too difficult. But it confirmed to Graham that he was talking to someone who had access to the type of information he would need if he were to be able to provide the favour Graham was looking for.

"Brad, I'd be more than happy to explain to you how I can predict the future, but it might take so long that you'll be too late to watch the next game."

"Yeah, Tom told me you were smart. I guess you're going to tell me the favor you want from me."

"It's quite simple, really. I'm sure you know that a young Russian by the name of Karl walked into your London Embassy a month ago. I expect he is enjoying some good old-fashioned American hospitality somewhere not far from us right now." Graham waited for a reply, and when he didn't get one, he proceeded anyway. "I would like to talk to him."

Brad responded with the most mirthless laugh Graham had ever heard.

"I don't care if you can predict the number of seconds it will take until the Cubs win their next World Series what you're asking for is something that nobody could get you."

Graham had expected this kind of reply – he had only asked based on the fact that if you don't ask, you don't get. His next (and his real) demand followed.

"Then I'd like to get a message to him. Clearly, accurately, and as privately as possible. And I need to hear his reply."

"Now we're talking about something that might be possible. If there's some way you can maybe oil the wheels, that is. The result of one game isn't going to cut it."

"Well, since you're showing such gratitude for the tips I've given you so far, I'll toss you another one. The Phillies will win this afternoon by a few runs, and it'll be a shutout. If you can get the message to Karl and get me his reply, then I'll let you know who'll win the series and the name of the MVP. How about that?"

He had been tempted to make things more challenging for Brad by using the English terms 'clean sheet' instead of 'shutout' and 'man of the match' instead of 'Most Valuable Player' but decided that clarity of message was more important than teasing his contact.

Brad knew that he could win a sizeable sum of money with all the possibilities Graham had just given him. And the detailed nature of the predictions defied description.

"What's the message?"

"I want him to hear that Anna hopes he has found a restaurant that serves a good spaghetti con vongole and that she is very pleased that the plan they worked out together has been successful. Can you get that exact message to him? And I want to know from him which course he studied at university in England. That way, I'll know he received the message."

"How soon do you need to know the answer?"

"How soon do you need to make your bets?"

Brad thought for a moment. The sooner he could get the answers, the more profitable his bets could be – but he was going to have to pull a huge favour to get access to this guy. And the games were taking place every day.

"Be here Wednesday, same time," he said, got up and walked away.

-

True to his word, Brad returned and sat next to Graham on the same bench three days later.

"You know the guy carving the words on the monument made a mistake?" Graham asked.

"Nope" came the totally disinterested answer.

"You should take a look sometime. They spelled "FUTURE" with an E instead of an F on the north wall. Did you get to see Karl?"

"He studied History of Art at that English University," Brad replied.

Graham repressed a smile. He had needled Brad into answering his question before he had revealed anything about the baseball game.

"I'll take it as read that you delivered the message?" he asked and got an "Aha" in response.

"Well, I guess you should put some money on the Astros to win the series tomorrow and Jeremy Peña to get the MVP award."

If anyone else had told Brad that a rookie, a player in his first professional season, was going to be the MVP in a World Series, he would have contested it heavily. But "Pleasure doing business with you," was all that Brad said. He left Graham sitting on the bench, and the two of them never spoke again. But Graham had the answers he needed and could now plan his next moves with Tom after another long but comfortable flight across the Atlantic. And Brad was able to sizeably increment his 401K retirement pot.

31 The Hunt for a Red in November
November 2022

Once again, Graham called Tom when he returned – this time a little more jetlagged than before.

"How did it go?" Tom asked.

"I doubt whether Brad and I will be sending each other Christmas cards, but I'm confident we got the message delivered to Karl.

"Americans call them holiday cards, and they don't send too many of them anyway. You're not going to ask me to come up to London again, are you?" Tom asked.

"I guess not. If they're still watching me, they know by now that you and I are in cahoots. I'll schlep down to Wales this time," Graham replied.

"Is there anything you need me to do before you get here? Arrange a meeting with the Dalai Lama? Get the combinations to the locks on the Crown Jewels? Anything simple like that?"

"You are getting very cynical. And that is not a good trait." Graham told him. "I'll be there late tomorrow morning."

-

Graham took the first train to Swansea the following day. 'I could get used to this first-class travel habit' he thought to himself.

Tom gave him a quick tour of his cottage to show off the work that the lottery had enabled since his last visit. The back wall was now a set of glass patio doors and floor-to-ceiling windows, which gave a magnificent view of Oxwich Bay. The neighbouring property, little more than a ruin when he had last visited, was now fully developed. Graham was complimentary but couldn't resist saying that it was just how he remembered it, just to wind Tom up a little.

Tom had two cans of Diet Pepsi waiting on the table when Graham arrived. He sat and listened to the report of his successful visit to the USA, which did not take long. Both men knew that reports of success tend to be much shorter than reports of failure – in all walks of life.

"So, what's the next step in 'The Plan' – if it's a fully made plan by now?" Tom asked.

"Well, we are now approaching what I call the 'not quite fully made' part of the plan," Graham replied. "We must make your old friends believe that Anna knew all along that Karl was going to go to the

Americans and that she was helping him to cheat the Russians. They paid for a full set of documentation but only got half."

"But we both know that they'll probably be able to piece together the whole thing, anyway, sooner or later. I did a little test a few days ago. I copied out a couple of pages of a technical manual and then took every other word out of the second page. It was not too difficult to guess what was missing."

"OK, so they only slowed them up. But the important part is that she wasn't all out spying for the other side. She was helping her Russian boyfriend achieve his dreams of getting to America while taking two hundred grand of Soviet money for herself at the same time. Surely you can sell that. And we now know that if they ask Karl, he'll agree with that version of the story."

"I can try. But what are you going to do about our ageing Romeo and Juliet?" Tom asked, referring to the prof and Anna. "We can't leave that pair of star-crossed lovers apart, can we?"

"No – especially as my original reason for getting involved in all this was to reunite them if possible. If you can find out what the official attitude to Anna is, I can move forward. I need to know if she can safely return to the UK or not – it's kind of crucial."

"And if she can, then what? You can't expect them to let her within a mile of anything secret."

"I've been thinking about that. I think I might have an answer, but let's find out first what her options are."

"But then what? You've got to have some plan."

"The aim must be to get the two of them together again. It's so obviously what they both want. And I guess your colleagues …"

"Ex-colleagues," Tom interrupted him, stressing the ex.

"Your ex-colleagues." Graham continued, "Would presumably like to get the project back on the rails. What I think needs to happen is that the whole project gets split into two parts. The prof – and Anna – want it to be a project about helping blind people see. And your ex-colleagues," this time Graham stressed the ex, "want it to be about communicating with satellites and frying the brains of anyone they don't like."

"Harsh, but fair," Tom responded with a smile.

"Wouldn't it be nice if we could achieve that?"

"Just like Motherhood and apple pie."

They adjourned for lunchtime refreshment at the Fox. Some ideas needed kicking around.

"Did Anna give you a contact number she could be reached on?"

"Yes, but she made me swear I would only use it from public phones in Germany. She's very worried about being traced."

"Understandable. So, what do you plan to do?"

"I'll have to arrange to take the prof out there with me. Then leave them two to sort it out between them. Once we know what our options are."

"I'll call my ex-colleagues after lunch – give them a couple of days to let me know what their position is – once I've told them about Anna and Karl's little understanding. But if you take the prof out of the country, they'll know. They're bound to have a trace on his passport. And if it shows up, they'll probably find her. Either by tracing you two or by questioning him once you're back. Can you take that risk?"

"No. I'm not even sure I can use my fake passport anymore. Brad was able to trace me, but I may have no choice but to risk it one more time. And I'd already decided that if I'm taking the prof to meet her, I daren't take him to Dresden. It has to be somewhere else. I don't feel I can trust him with secrets, do you?"

Tom agreed and there was not much more business discussed as they moved on to the second pint, accompanying a fine spread of bread, cheese, and pickle that any ploughman would have been pleased to call his lunch.

-

The day after Graham returned home from Wales, he went through the rigmarole they had agreed to get a message to the prof, telephoning the hospital to request an urgent appointment because of a complication resulting from his (non-existent) treatment. Two days later he renewed his one-way acquaintance with Margaret, Anna's unsuitable replacement, as she escorted him to the professor's office. Once she had closed the door, the professor changed his demeanour from concerned doctor to excitedly asking for news.

"You need to book some time off," Graham said, trying hard not to get swept up in the professor's enthusiasm. He knew this planned reunion still could go wrong in so many ways.

"How much time? How soon?" the prof asked.

"I'd suggest a week if that is possible,"

"Where are we going?"

"I hate to use the old phrase 'need to know', Prof, but it is best if I don't tell you. That way you can't inadvertently let it slip. Walls have ears and all that. But you'll need to bring your passport. Can you do it next week?"

"Probably not. I could do it the week after next, and I'll still need to make an excuse, though. There will be several appointments that will need rescheduling."

"Margaret will not be pleased," Graham tried unsuccessfully to lighten the mood. "You had better invent a family emergency."

"Yes, I'll do that." The professor thought for a moment. "Yes, the week after next. Where and when do I meet you?"

Graham had put a little thought into a journey that would make the professor difficult to follow and any tail placed on him easy to notice.

"Take the first train after 8:30 am from Saint Pancras Station to Ebbsfleet. It's about a thirty-minute journey and I will meet you there when you exit the station." Pack one bag with casual clothes, and don't forget your passport. I'll take care of the rest."

The professor asked a few more questions that Graham either could not or would not answer, and after enough time had passed that Margaret would not be suspicious, the professor showed him out.

"Thanks for your reassurance, professor," Graham said for the benefit of the professor's assistant. "I'll try to stop worrying."

Graham was waiting at Ebbsfleet Station when the prof arrived, and they walked to Graham's car. He had deliberately parked a distance from the station and was thus reasonably sure that nobody was following the prof. They drove along the A2 and the A20 towards the Channel Tunnel, chatting about everything and nothing. They pulled into a service station and Graham broke the first piece of bad news to the prof.

"I'm reasonably sure the authorities will be tracing your passport, and we can't let them track you. You'll need to hide before we go through the tunnel."

He had spent the previous day removing the panel from the floor of the boot of his old car and shaping it into a panel to fit into the boot of his new one. It provided a small compartment between the drop-down back seats and the boot. The false back would not survive a detailed inspection, but there was no reason to expect that the security at the border would even inspect at all. The professor had to suffer the indignity and discomfort of fitting into the enclosed space so that he was not visible as a passenger, and hence there would be no need to show his passport at the border.

Once they were on board the shuttle train under the channel, Graham was able to get into the back of his car, drop the seat-back, and allow the prof to return to his previous position. They were several miles into France before the prof had finished complaining about his discomfort.

"Just concentrate on the fact that you'll be seeing Anna soon," Graham told him repeatedly, and eventually the moaning ceased.

-

Graham drove, with a couple of stops for refreshment, until early evening when they reached their initial destination, a hotel on the outskirts of Karlsruhe in Germany. He had told the prof that their eventual destination would be Munich, the following day. He had chosen this as it was a city where Anna had spent some of her life, and if there was a need to misdirect anyone as to where she had settled, this was one possibility.

He was pleased with the way his plan was coming together and was confident that nobody had followed them. He'd chosen a route through France into Germany – the quicker route via Belgium would have involved more border crossings, and there was always the fear that they might be stopped at any one of them. It was extremely unlikely, but Graham felt a touch of paranoia might be healthy for the next few days.

He kept his word with Anna by calling her from a public phone in the motorway service area where their hotel was located. She confirmed that she could meet them the following afternoon at their hotel in Munich, which would offer a somewhat higher standard of accommodation than any of them were currently enjoying. It would be a venue that befitted such a momentous reunion.

In the meantime, he informed the prof that Anna had agreed to see him the next day. The prof responded with an unexpected and aggressively warm hug, and an order of drinks for the two of them. The first of many rounds of drinks they shared that evening.

32 Star-Crossed Lovers
November 2022

The combination of a large quantity of alcohol and a professorial mind can produce some strange results. Graham remembered many years previously, in his first life, a professor of Mathematics at a faculty dinner who had imbibed a few too many glasses of wine. He was holding forth on the advantages of cycling more than ten miles a day – which he himself did, travelling between his home and the university.

"It is generally good for the body and especially good at building huge thigh muscles," he explained. Taking another gulp from his glass, he continued, "And having large thigh muscles is a major advantage if you intend cycling more than ten miles per day." He failed to understand why laughter rang out from his immediate circle.

Graham expected something similar from the Professor - and was not disappointed.

The bar did not have an official closing time, but when Graham and the prof found themselves to be the only remaining customers and the recipients of an unfriendly stare from the barman, they ordered a final round of doubles and took their glasses to Graham's room – chosen because it was the first they came to.

He restarted the conversation by asking the professor about the picture of the woman in the blue dress, which he had secreted in his family bible and had become a signal of their connection across two different planes of time.

"What is so special about it?" he asked.

The prof took on a contemplative air as he answered.

"It was a faculty dinner. We were invited because our project had been nominated for some award or other. I cannot remember the award, but I can remember the evening. There was just something about her in that dress. The shade of blue matched her eyes so beautifully, and the shape of the dress showed off her figure so well. At that moment, I believed that she was the most beautiful woman on earth." The professor paused, lost in an alcoholically enhanced reverie.

"And yet you have never asked her to move your relationship on from being just a professional one?" Graham chose his words carefully.

"Ah, so you wonder why I do not wish to enter a permanent closer relationship with her. Why I do not wish to take her as my woman."

"I wouldn't quite put it that way...."

"Well, this is the whole problem that mankind has with relationships, with sexual congress, and so forth."

Graham could sense that what he was hearing was coming partly from the professor and partly from the several large cognacs the professor had consumed through the evening.

"Of course, I share man's basic urges," he continued in the same vein. "The desires that evolution has pre-programmed us with. The urge to spread my mitochondrial DNA. As well as the desires that we have imposed on ourselves in our development as civilised beings – the need for company, companionship, and so forth. But perhaps I am not normal. I may lack the desire to impose myself on another human being."

"It need not necessarily be imposing yourself," I interjected as he seemed to have temporarily run out of steam. My words had the effect of spurring him on.

"But of course, it is an imposition. This is the fundamental problem that mankind has with the whole issue. We are apes. And the act of sexual congress requires domination by one partner and submission by the other. Goodness, man, requires the woman to allow the man to insert part of his body into hers. And to deposit some of his bodily fluid inside her. There can be no more straightforward act of domination and submission than this. And so, our modern, civilised, sophisticated world cannot square this act with the wish for equality of the sexes."

Again, he paused briefly, and Graham tried to lighten the mood. "Inserting bodily parts? Depositing bodily fluids? Prof, you are going to have to improve your chat-up lines. She is, after all, a highly attractive woman."

"Absolutely. She has the necessary regularity and symmetry of features. Clear blue eyes, a healthy complexion, and high cheekbones. These combine to make her very attractive."

"And the rest of her is not too bad either," Graham said, trying again to get him to relax and failing once more.

"Ah, if you were being polite, you would say you are referring to her figure. When actually, you are referring to her breasts."

Graham refused to be drawn, and the prof continued. "This is also an area where our modern society imposes so many problems upon itself. The fact that a woman has two protuberances designed by nature to enhance her sexual appeal."

"Surely a woman's breasts have other biological purposes than that?" Graham replied.

"No, this is not true. Let me repeat myself, we are apes. All apes mate in a position that we humans now refer to as 'doggy style'. Then, some tens, possibly hundreds of thousands of years ago, man, for some unknown reason, decided to change this practice and begin mating face to face. As a result, the male of the species was deprived of one of the fundamental sexual stimuli – the female buttocks.

"So, over many generations, the females of our species began to develop more fleshy breasts. It is a fallacy to believe that they are this way to store or deliver milk to offspring. All other apes are flat-chested and manage the process quite adequately. Also, if you speak to midwives or nurses with maternity experience, you will hear that larger-breasted women can have problems when first attempting to feed a young baby because their nipples are at the wrong angle. No, the fleshy breast is there to provide a sexual stimulant to men. And this leads to many problems. First, this provides the male of our species now with a dichotomy. The place where he first found solace and comfort – the breast and the nipple – is a powerful memory. And upon reaching puberty, its purpose changes entirely to become a tool for sexual arousal, which is why it is so powerful.

"But it also presents the woman with many problems. If she shows any part of it to the male, she causes him to be sexually aroused. Even if she does not intend to, she cannot compete with thousands of years of evolution. At some level, he will experience some arousal. In fact, even if she does not show any part of her breast, if she merely causes her breasts to move, she is also sending him a deep-level message."

Graham tried to interrupt, but the professor was on a roll and paused only briefly to take a swig from his glass.

"Of course, the many layers of civilisation prevent this signal from being interpreted literally. But it is still there, and in the case of members of the species who do not have strong control mechanisms, it can have far-reaching consequences."

"But don't apes have the same problem?"

"No – because when the female moves away from him, she may well be agitating her buttocks, but she is departing – so one low-level signal cancels out the other. It is only if she moves her buttocks and does not move away from him that she is sending a sexual message. Compare that with the human female, who sends out this low-level signal at the same time as she walks towards the male. That is the fundamental problem."

"I don't suppose you have a solution to this problem?" Graham asked – hoping that he would either hear something profound or possibly change the direction of the dialogue (or the monologue, to be more accurate).

"No, I can neither compete with the entire history of man's evolution nor the millions of dollars involved in the soft porn industry," he replied, took another swig of his drink, and seemed to have exhausted the subject.

"But can we leave these heady topics and return to the here and now? You do still want to meet Anna, don't you?"

"Of course. That is why I am here."

"And you will think of something to say that might persuade her to return."

"It will not be easy."

"That, at least we can agree on. Even if you persuade her that there is a reason to reunite with you, there are still several hurdles that will have to be overcome. But I need you to think long and hard about what you will say to her."

"I will do my best," he replied. Graham feared that the professor's promise was given somewhat lamely.

-

The next day, they left late in the morning to drive to Munich. The professor, who had either drunk far more than Graham the night before or was less able to handle the results, was nursing a hangover and dozed quietly. Eventually, they reached their hotel. Graham had chosen the Kempinski Hotel as it offered a three-room suite. They placed their bags in the two smaller bedrooms, leaving the largest for Anna.

She arrived late in the afternoon and called Graham from reception. She had not been included in the names attached to the reservation and she was still being careful about her security. He escorted her to the penthouse suite.

"It's a little better than I'm used to," she remarked, indicating the luxurious furnishings of the hotel.

"My excuse is that it's the only one in Munich that has a three-bedroom suite," he replied with a smile. As they ascended in the lift, he reminded her that the prof knew nothing about her real whereabouts, nor why she left at such short notice.

"My advice is that you tell him as little as possible. He may well be questioned when we return to London, and it's obvious that if he doesn't know something, he cannot let the information slip."

"I'll do my best," she answered.

When he showed her into the room, she embraced the prof warmly and he expressed his joy at seeing her safe and well. Graham indicated which room was hers and asked if she wanted time to freshen up.

"What a wonderful English phrase," she laughed. "How I miss your wonderful language. I am fresh enough, thank you."

Graham told them he did not intend to stay with them for the evening.

"If you wish, you can order dinner and drinks to be served in this suite, for additional privacy," he informed them. "I think it's important that you two talk. You can tell me what you've decided at breakfast tomorrow."

They made noises about inviting him to stay with them, but Graham insisted he had other plans and shortly left the room.

-

Despite the Kempinski Hotel being located on the edge of the airport complex in Munich, Graham was still able to enjoy some of his favourite food and drink. Munich's Franz Josef Strauss Airport is one of the few that has a micro-brewery on site. Airbräu serves traditional Bavarian food alongside its brews. Before settling down to some fine pork knuckle, Graham had a couple of calls to make.

He spoke with Elizabeth and let her know that his project was going well and that he was on his own for the evening because the technical people were working together and didn't need him. She asked if he would be visiting any of the places they had visited when they had been in Munich a few months earlier, and he let her know that business meetings took place at airport hotels, not city centre ones. He added that he was confident of being home for the weekend and would call her again tomorrow.

He then called Tom for a mutual update.

"I've left the pair of them together for the evening. Do you have any update? I'd like to let them know what the possibilities are tomorrow when we get together."

"I'm afraid it may take a bit longer than that," Tom replied. "They've asked me to come back into the office for a few days to help with the debrief of Karl."

"Are they that short-handed?" Graham asked.

"Thanks for that," Tom replied to the good-natured jibe. "They say that they think I've got a special insight into this case, and they'd like my input."

"What does that mean when you take the jargon out of it?"

"I think it means that they suspect I have some other source of information, but they don't know what it is, so they want to keep an eye on me."

"How long do you think this will take?"

"I've got a ticket out Monday and back home Friday."

"To Washington?"

"Yup, in the good old US of A."

Graham had a raft of questions he wanted to ask Tom but knew they should keep their airtime to the minimum, just in case.

"Give my regards to Brad," he joked and hung up.

-

He delayed his return to the hotel suite until just after eleven pm. The service in Airbräu had been a little slow, which suited him well. He took a walk around the perimeter of the hotel grounds and lingered over a fine malt whisky in the hotel bar, enjoying the live piano jazz.

He did not know what to expect when he returned to the suite but found a deserted main room. The dinner dishes had been cleared away and only two empty wine glasses were left on the table. All the bedroom doors were closed, and he resisted the temptation of listening at keyholes to see how many of the bedrooms were occupied. He would find out soon enough.

-

When he woke the next morning, both the other bedroom doors were still closed. After a shave and a shower, he went down to the restaurant for breakfast.

His two colleagues joined him half an hour later. Their demeanour had changed. Although they fell short of holding hands, they nonetheless seemed to stand just a little closer to each other, and their conversational tone was much warmer and more intimate than it had been at their reunion the previous evening. He put down his newspaper and invited them to join him at his table.

Once they had ordered breakfast from the waitress, Graham told them that he had no plans for the day and asked what their plans were.

"We were waiting to see what you had to say," the professor began. "Since we seem to be so much in your hands for this entire …. episode," he continued, hesitating to come up with the correct final word to describe events.

Graham told them that he was not yet able to tell them whether Anna would be able to return to the UK and that the answer would not be his to give for at least a couple more weeks.

"I thought you might want a day together so that you can decide what you would like to do – although you'll probably have to make two sets of plans – one where Anna can return and one where she cannot. Until we know which it is to be, we need to keep Anna's location secret. The suite is booked until tomorrow."

"Do you not have any plans?" Anna asked.

"I always enjoyed my visits here during my working life, so I would like to have a brief look at the city. And there's a football match this evening that I would love to attend. It's the local team's last home game before the winter break, so it should be quite an occasion."

Graham had read about Bayern Munich's forthcoming game in the paper a few minutes earlier. He had no idea what the score in the game would be as he had not followed German football in the same detail as English football. His self-imposed ban on watching major games until he caught up with 'real-time' on this plane of time therefore did not apply. He also thought it would be a great excuse to allow his two companions to spend another 'evening' together.

More than that it triggered another chain of thought. He was rapidly approaching the date when he could once again start enjoying British football. The date when he would no longer know the result before the game kicked off. The date of his most recent jump back in time. He would have to give some thought to how to handle that date, now he had decided to stay and not try to engineer a return.

He did not want to dwell on the thought that he only knew one occasion when someone had stayed on a plane of time after a jump. That was Carol, his partner during his first time-travel adventure. On that journey back in time, he had managed to jump back to his starting point when the date came around to the date of his original jump. For many reasons, she had stayed on the same plane but had not survived. She had died during the night that marked the date when she had originally made her jump.

Graham knew all too well that he would be facing the same situation in the near future. But that was a few weeks away. For now, he had to deal with the current situation.

"Maybe we could all go into the city together," Anna said.

"That's a good idea," Graham replied. "I suppose you have not had much chance to look around since you returned?"

Anna recognised the heavy hint. She had momentarily forgotten that they were trying to make the prof believe that her place of residence was here, not in a different city, five hundred kilometres away.

"That's very true," she replied.

-

The rest of their stay in Munich passed without incident. The three of them rode the S-Bahn together into the centre of Munich and spent a pleasant couple of hours wandering around the Englischer Garten. Anna took the opportunity to send a card to her sister. It would reassure her that she was safe and well – and the Munich postmark would prove to be a distraction both to her sister and to anyone trying to find her.

They enjoyed a late, light lunch in one of the many cafes in the Garten before Graham departed to head to the Allianz Arena. He called Elizabeth and confirmed he would arrive home very late the following day and that they would have a house guest for one night. He told her he was again alone for the evening but was going to a football match. He did not tell her how much he would be paying to buy a ticket from a ticket tout, though.

At breakfast the next day, Anna and the prof asked how he had enjoyed his evening, and he was pleased to report that the last Bayern home game before the winter break had been a great night – helped by a thumping win for the home team. They told him that they had decided they would like to get back together again, but they understood that until Anna's situation was decided, no plans could be made. They would wait to hear from him before deciding.

Some sixth sense told Graham that Anna had given the prof some way of communicating with her. 'What a powerful force true love is,' he cynically thought. 'She's risking her liberty to be able to exchange messages with him.'

When the prof was out of earshot, he told Anna to call him once a week from now on – at irregular times using public phones and calling his burner phone. He would tell her when a decision was made, one way or the other.

By mid-morning, they were ready to depart – Graham and the prof for a very long drive, and Anna ostensibly going into the airport terminal to catch an S-Bahn to her home. Graham hoped that only he knew that she was catching the next flight to Dresden and that this remained outside the professor's knowledge.

-

The car journey was lengthy, punctuated by several rest stops, and they did not reach the terminal for Le Shuttle until very late at night. When they saw the first signs for the channel tunnel, the professor began moaning about having to squeeze into the narrow space again.

"Don't worry," Graham told him. "They'll only be watching for you leaving the country, not entering it." He proved to be right, and their channel crossing passed without incident. There were no trains for the prof to take into London, so he spent the night in one of Graham's spare bedrooms. His presence added credence to the tales that Graham had told Elizabeth about working with strange secretive people. Elizabeth found him fascinating.

33 Loose Ends
November 2022

Graham had thought about calling Tom for an update about what had happened during his trip to the USA but remained patient. He recognised that Tom had only just returned and may need a couple of days to get over the jet lag. He would also need time to receive clear feedback from his ex-colleagues on the results of the trip and what their stand would be on a possible return to the UK for Anna.

On Tuesday morning he received a call on his everyday mobile phone. 'Surely Tom has not forgotten that we agreed to use burner phones for security' he thought and was about to make a remark to Tom along these lines when he was pre-empted.

"I thought I'd call you on your normal cell to let you know that we've got the all-clear," he began.

"Graham recognised that Tom must have been spending some time with Americans recently as he had adopted their use of the word 'cell' to describe a mobile phone. He decided not to remark on it as he was much more interested to find out what was meant by 'we've got the all-clear'.

"They're delighted with the results they got from their trip," Tom continued. "Running around like dogs with two tails, the lot of them."

He went on to explain that the Americans had already obtained everything they thought they would ever get from Karl and had given the Brits several days of unrestricted access to him. Filled with the optimism that his simple request was about to be fulfilled – a small home in rural America and a job working in the open air – Karl had been most forthcoming with information.

"He gave them way more than they expected about everyday matters in London, and to top it all he gave them the password to access all the files they gathered during their 'Tube Station' operation. Apparently, he was the only one who knew this, so now the Brits have more info than the Russians who collected it all. They believe they can get the files transferred so the Russians'll never even see them."

"Did they have to promise him the earth in return for all this?" Graham asked. He did not need to know but was becoming fascinated by his involvement in this very secluded world.

"No. The Yanks had already promised him a home and a job – he wanted to be somewhere really remote, and the States has plenty of places with that spec. All that the Brits had to do was to promise him he could have the money he had squirrelled away in a UK bank account. It seems he's been preparing for this type of opportunity and has about fifty grand in an ISA!

And he kept his promise of telling them that Anna was in on his plan all along – which they've totally accepted. He's told them that his former bosses only ever got half the information as he was on his way to deliver the second half of the info when he took his detour to Nine Elms. And you and I are in the clear too," Tom continued, "Which means I can speak to you by phone as much or as little as I want to."

"I'm sure you're delighted about that. And you don't have to make any more trips to the evil English capital?" Graham joked. "But we have a loose end to tie up. If Anna is to return to the UK, we need to keep her safe. I'm assuming the Russians might not be members of her fan club."

"Luckily, I thought of that," Tom replied. Graham could picture exactly the self-satisfied look he knew Tom would be wearing.

"While my ex-colleagues were all patting themselves on the back for how well they had handled the situation, I managed to extract a promise from them. They'll use the 'normal channels' to let the Russians know that if she so much as catches a heavy cold, they'll publicise Karl's defection and all the information obtained about their illicit activities during the lockdown. So long as she remains safe, nobody will be any the wiser."

Excellent work, Mister Woodward. Now we can give a full update to the happy couple and let them know what they can and can't get up to."

"But she can't go within a mile of the project, although I've got some ideas on how that might be resolved."

Tom reinforced his statement about talking as much as he liked on the telephone by giving Graham a lengthy explanation of how he interpreted the government's plans for the project and how this might work out to the satisfaction of all parties, including both the Professor and Anna.

"Seems like a good plan," Graham agreed. "I guess it's down to me to organise a meeting as soon as I can get everyone together."

"Let me know, and I'll be there," Tom replied.

Two weeks later, Graham was able to schedule the meeting that he and Tom had spoken about. He met Anna at the airport, and they took a taxi to the professor's club.

It was the same dining room – for the third time, Graham thought – but there was less tension involved than there had been for any of the previous meetings. Polite chatter filled the time between placing their orders for lunch and its arrival. Once the meal was served and the staff had left the room, Tom began his resume of the situation.

"The government is very interested in continuing some aspects of the project," he began, "But not others."

He explained that they wanted to push forward with the development of the communication aspects of the project. The part that had originally piqued their interest as it offered a super-secure method of collecting data from satellites. The use of the transmission beam as a weapon was to be placed on the back burner. Now that all parties were aware of its existence, its main purpose had been served. Further use was unlikely since protecting against its employment would necessitate all politicians and major figures becoming almost invisible to the public. It was agreed that this would be more harmful to the way of life of both Britain and the USA than it would ever be to Russia.

The government was also coming clean that they had very little interest in the original aim of the project – restoring sight to people who had suffered damage to their optical nerves. Whilst they applauded the aim, its cost-benefit analysis – in these times of belt-tightening within the NHS – did not encourage them to invest in this aspect.

At this point, Tom had to restrain the professor's wish to make rude comments about the Ministry of Health and politicians in general.

"Don't worry, prof," he reassured him, "There's a way that your research can continue – I'll get to that in a minute."

He resumed his planned discourse, explaining that the government wanted only consultative input from the prof, and would make some financial contribution to his experiments in return, and before the prof could react again, made the telling statement that they were quite happy to hand the project over to the private sector.

"Which is where I was able to contribute my idea," Tom continued, unable to prevent himself from showing his pride in what he thought, and Graham agreed, was a brilliant idea.

He reiterated that the government had no interest in the original aspects of the project and was willing to turn it over to a third party. They would like to maintain a share in any venture. However, the government was mostly concerned that the work would continue in a way that would be approved by the professor. Their thinking is that he will then be available to input to their communication project.

"If I understand it correctly," Tom continued, in a tone of voice only ever used by someone who does understand it correctly and knows that they do, "There is only one development hurdle that needs to be overcome. You need to make the device which captures and transmits the image much smaller than it is now, is that correct?"

The professor confirmed that it was. There had been two hurdles, but they had made good progress in overcoming one of them. The quality of the images being good enough to allow moving images to be collected and transferred, had been much improved in recent months. Tom asked how significant the remaining hurdle might be.

"I've talked with some of the government technicians, and they say it would take some work, but it should be achievable if you had a competent project manager and a million pounds of development capital. Then you'd need to hire the right people and buy the right equipment."

"Which is where I believe you might come into the picture," Tom continued, indicating Anna – who had neither featured in nor contributed to the discussion so far.

"Me?" she replied. "I don't think I could come up with a million pounds."

"No, but you would be a more than capable project manager," Graham interrupted.

"All well and good," the professor interjected. "But where do we find the money?"

"You can leave that to us," Tom said. "We have identified a couple of partners who would be willing to invest the funds, provided that you agree to take charge of the project and that you provide technical consultancy," indicating Anna and the professor in turn.

Strangely, neither Anna nor the professor queried the identity of the two partners who would provide the funding. They did not realise that they were sharing lunch with them. They were far more concerned with the details of a situation that seemed too good to be true but, for once, was not.

The rest of the lunch was punctuated by many conversations about how Anna would go about starting the company – which Tom agreed to help her with – where to locate it, how to source the necessary equipment, and where to find the skilled technicians. Anna, at one point, went in search of a notepad and pen and took copious notes of everyone's input.

It was only much later, as the meal was winding to a close, that she asked where the funding was going to come from.

"You've just had lunch with the two moneymen who'll be sitting on your board of directors," Graham said. "When Tom helps you draw up the company's Articles, he'll agree with you on how the shares are to be split, and we'll be available to advise at any time. But if you don't want us involved, that's good too. We won't be greedy, but we are both hoping for a healthy return on our investment."

Both Tom and Graham received kisses of thanks from Anna and a strong and lengthy handshake from the prof.

Shortly after this, having set up a provisional schedule for the steps involved in setting up the company that Anna would be heading, Tom and Graham parted company from Anna and the professor.

"It's too cold today to sit outside with Mahatma," Graham said, "But there's some stuff you need to tell me about what happened in Washington."

"Starbucks, it is then," said Tom, "I believe that in the modern London you are never more than thirty feet away from one," pointing to the branch on the other side of the square.

"Yes, we can say thank you to Mahatma when we pass by. It seems this is ending a whole lot better than I feared."

As they passed the statue, Graham had to recite one of his favourite corny jokes. "Did you know he had a brother who was a cloakroom attendant?" he asked, pointing at the statue. "His name was Mahatma Coat." Tom gave an obligatory groan.

Once seated with their coffees, Graham prompted Tom, "I understand why your colleagues are happy with the way things worked out, but the reason the Americans appear so happy escapes me."

"I was puzzled too," Tom replied, so I took Brad out for a couple of drinks to see if I could loosen his tongue a little."

"And did you succeed?"

His smile could have been answer enough, but he gave more detail. "Us Welshmen are good at three things, see: singing, playing rugby, and drinking. And I employed the last of those three talents to good effect. There is no good drinking beer in America; a man would explode before getting drunk. We switched to some of the fine liquor that comes out of Kentucky, and eventually, he let me know. He was quite proud of it, actually. It's all to do with the detail of the project they got from the documentation."

"But surely our lot had already told them everything about the project, hadn't they?" Graham queried.

"It seems that they had told them everything about the signal output from the prof's device. But they had never told them anything about the input. And that's what has got them excited."

"Why are they so interested in that?"

"You should have seen Brad once he got started. Those Americans can be quite something when they think they've got one over you."

He paused to take a drink from his mug. Graham sensed that a lengthy speech was about to be delivered.

"Their plan, as he put it to me, involves using Artificial Intelligence to input to the unit. Then they secrete the unit in the bedroom of the target and set the unit to play. Imagine a visiting head of state being a guest at the White House. If they want to influence his thinking on a subject, they'll play a set of images to him while he sleeps. Now, if he had seen those images on a TV or computer screen, then he might think, 'Those images have been doctored.' But if they are directly transmitted into his brain while he sleeps, he truly believes he has seen them with his own eyes.

"Apparently, they tried an experiment with a couple of White House staff who were sleeping overnight in staff accommodation. They played them a set of faked images of President Biden passionately embracing Jennifer Anniston. They chose her because she is the most recognisable woman in America. She's also a Democrat supporter, but I don't believe she's quite as keen on Biden as their faked images implied."

With a smile, Tom paused for another gulp of coffee.

"Anyway, they did a separate soft debrief of the people to whom they'd played the images. Both were embarrassed to reveal that they had inadvertently witnessed their President in a compromising position with America's best-loved actress. Totally convinced they'd actually seen it.

"So, our American counterparts now believe they can influence any world leader to believe anything they want. And if they can't get them to stay overnight in the White House, they only need to plant their playing device in the room above or below their target's hotel room to get the same result."

"Wow!" was all Graham said for a few seconds as he took in the immediate implications of what he had heard. "I assume you passed this information on to your ex-colleagues?"

"Not yet. I fully intend to – but I thought I'd just make sure that everything else went as they promised before I let them in on this."

"You mean the 'happy ever after' for Anna and the professor?"

"And for me and you, don't forget. We don't want any comebacks – and I'm sure we want our new joint investment to prosper, don't we?"

"Sure do," was Graham's final word on the subject for the time being.

The number of decisions that were taken and actions put in place in the following three weeks was only possible with the combined energy of a new business set-up and a couple of people moving in to live together after waiting for years.

A set of offices was found on the edge of London, a company was formed, equipment was ordered, and a specialist employment agency was briefed on the technical requirements of the employees they were ready to hire.

Conferring by email and Zoom conference calls achieved most things satisfactorily, although the haste with which it was needed produced an uninspiring company name, which they resolved to change as soon as they could come up with something better. For now, the name was the answer to a discussion point suggested by a paper on How to Create Winning Company Names. The question was: "What does your company aim to do for people?" And so, the new company was named Blindsee Limited.

34 Changing Planes
December 2022

The day finally arrived. Friday, December 1st, 2022. Graham was, as anticipated, filled with dread. He was so distracted during the day that he had to tell Elizabeth that he was feeling unwell to explain his changed demeanour.

This was the day on which he had made his most recent jump back in time. He had made the decision several months ago to remain on this plane of time but did not truly know if this was possible.

During his second life, he had been with Carol, his fellow time traveller, on the day on which her jump had occurred. She was in no fit state to decide whether or not to jump back to her original plane. Graham was confident that if she had been able to make the choice, she would have decided to stay where she had arrived, so he decided for her.

She had died in her sleep at the end of that day. Facing the same situation as she had on that day was reason enough for Graham to feel distracted as the day wore on.

At bedtime, he told Elizabeth that he was still feeling unwell and would delay going to bed. She left him in the lounge, watching TV and he sat and waited. When the light in the room began to dim and the sound level from the television seemed to drop, he looked at the clock. Midnight.

It was as if a large screen had appeared in front of him, and a series of images were being projected onto it. At first, they were images of things he had witnessed during the day. The images began to appear at the rate of several per second – faster and faster. Not reaching a blur but visible as separate images. Just.

Then he was moving. Even though he wasn't. Many of the day's images were all visible at the same time below and in front of him. He felt he must surely be in an aeroplane to see them in this fashion. But he wasn't. It wasn't possible – he was sitting on a bench seat, not an aircraft seat. On the top deck of a bus. Did they have long seats like this on the top deck of buses? Yes, they used to have them on some of the buses – he remembered from when he used to take a bus home from school every day. From here he could see clearly.

Now he was moving upstairs, not on the bus, but in his house. Even though he had not left his seat. The door to his bedroom opened - only it wasn't his bedroom. There was a large table in the middle of the room with a group of people around it, playing cards. A pile of chips and money was in the middle of the table.

And there was his old boss – standing at the side of the table and welcoming him back to work – thanking him for coming back when he was needed. Looking down, he was far too casually dressed for work and apologised to his boss. He also didn't have any files with him, and no laptop either. His boss told him not to worry, everything he needed would be waiting for him in his office through the door in front of him.

The door was, unusually for a bedroom, painted black. It was tempting. He had enjoyed his time at work; he'd been well respected and well-liked and had worked with a decent group of people. Yes, he'd been very happy, and returning to work was an appealing thought. 'But they always say never go back, don't they?' he thought. So, even though the prospect of going back into his office was very attractive, he decided against it.

And anyway, as he approached the door, he realised something was wrong – the door was not a proper door – it was more like the wooden gate at the side of his house, separating the front and rear gardens. And the paintwork was all peeling. It was not a door he wanted to go through.

Now he was in his front garden, walking away from his house. He could not remember leaving the bedroom, descending the stairs, or leaving the house, but some time had elapsed, and he was now outside. In daylight.

He saw and heard three women standing by the wall that marked the border of his front garden and the pavement. They were talking to each other.

But the three women were Mary, his wife of forty years who had died five years ago, Carol, his partner from his second life, also now dead, and his current girlfriend, Elizabeth. Something was wrong because those three women belonged to three different lives, three different planes of time. They had never met each other – and Carol never knew anything about this house – he didn't live here on the plane of time where he knew her. How could they all be together in one place?

He looked at the road outside his house. It was much wider than he remembered, and it was covered with a mass of potholes, some obviously deep and potentially dangerous. Many of them had crumbling edges and the journey across the road looked to be difficult. And was it worthwhile? The other side of the road seemed to contain far fewer houses than his recollection. At several points along the road, between the houses, there were signposts indicating the start of public footpaths. Footpaths that would, no doubt, lead to interesting views of rear gardens, peoples' secrets, and hidden surprises.

He could hear, or rather sense, the women saying "He's bound to cross the road now it's in front of him. I wonder if he'll realise that the only safe ones to step on are the ones that have been resurfaced."

Looking down, he saw that several of the holes appeared to have been recently repaired. They were covered with flat, shiny black tarmac. He did not want to step on them and decided not to cross the road at all.

Now he was back in the bedroom, sitting at the table, playing a game of cards, and realising he had lost a lot of money. He was invited to leave the table and go somewhere – a place that anyone would much prefer to be.

The door was a door you would want to go through. It was richly padded and spoke of privileged entry to an exclusive club. A large man with an ill-fitting suit invited him to open the door, but when he saw that the padding on the door was all black, he decided not to open it.

Instead, he left the bedroom, closed the door behind him, and walked along the landing. But it wasn't his landing, it was a corridor. In an office building or a hotel. Definitely a hotel – the corridor was windowless with featureless doors regularly spaced along the walls on each side of him.

A few feet in front of him was a much more inviting door, its paint all shiny. It had a uniformed hotel doorman standing in front of it. He recognised the door from a film. What was the film called? It was the one with Richard Gere and Julia Roberts in it – where she played the part of a hooker.

If he went through the door, the lifestyle of Richard Gere's character in that film would await him. Wealth, luxury and all the trappings. If only he could remember the title of the film. There would be a huge bath, full of warm bubbly water in that room, ready for him to jump into. And Julia Roberts, or an equally beautiful woman would be there to join him. It seemed too good to be true. But hadn't life told him that when things seemed too good to be true, they turned out to be just that? Too good to be true. He decided he would not go through the door.

But the hotel doorman was not a hotel doorman – he was a famous politician that Graham recognised but could not name. And the door was the door to number ten Downing Street, complete with the lion's head knocker and the two digits, one and zero, mounted on it. This door exerted the vaguest, and yet the strongest pull on him. It spoke to him of power. Of how a man with his talents for time-travel should be able to use his skill to amass real power. The power that few dreamed of and even fewer achieved could be his so easily. But the door did not appear to have any handle or other means of being opened. The door to ultimate power. Surely that was a door worth going through, wasn't it? But how to open it?

"Don't worry", the politician told him, "The secret is that you just push it, and it will open."

Pretty Woman – it came to him in a flash. That was the name of the film. He remembered the poster, with Julia Roberts standing upright on it. Hadn't there been some controversy about whether it was her body or not? He could see the poster clearly in front of him. She appeared to be leaning against the letters that formed the title of the film. But the woman was moving. And he could hear scratching and clicking noises.

This was the first thing he had truly heard since the lights in the room had dimmed. Minutes ago. Or, more likely, hours ago – he had lost all sense of time. The other things that he had heard – like his ex-boss, his wives, and the politician speaking to him, came into his head clearly enough, but he couldn't say he had actually heard them. But he heard these noises. Scratching and clicking. And the room was looking brighter than it had for some time, and the woman was speaking to him. Holding his hand and asking, "Are you alright?" She was apologising for waking him. It was Elizabeth, and the scratching and clicking sounds were explained. She had just opened the curtains.

"I didn't know whether to wake you. You were asleep, but you looked so bad, I thought I'd better wake you."

As he looked around and realised he had returned from a dream, if that was what it was. Suddenly, a piercing headache struck him, and he winced. It had been no ordinary dream; he was certain of that.

"I must have had a migraine," he said. "I've got a splitting headache."

"I didn't know you suffered from migraines," Elizabeth said sympathetically.

"I don't think I have before now. I think I need to lie down for a while."

This time he really did walk up the stairs to his bedroom. The dream – if that is what it was – was still running around in his mind. It was more than a dream, though. The choices he had been offered in the last few hours had been all too real. The clarity with which he could remember it, the continued offering of a choice for him to go through an opening, his constant refusal to do so. This had been no ordinary dream.

He was also certain that it would have had a completely different ending if he had accepted any of the offers to pass through doorways or step on the black tarmac. He didn't know what that ending would have been if he had accepted any of the invitations but was sure that he would not now be standing by his bed having just left his girlfriend downstairs.

He got into bed, wondering whether he should now refer to her as his fiancée. 'Perhaps not, at least not until I propose properly and she accepts,' he thought.

And he understood that Carol, his partner in his second life, must have experienced something similar to this 'dream', all those years ago. Like him, she had travelled back in time. She had suffered some mental strain when she had landed in the new time zone – on the day of her wedding to a man she knew would abuse her. Refusing to go through with the wedding, coupled with what appeared to be severe short-term memory problems, and probably making incoherent statements caused her parents to send her to some form of rehabilitation centre. She had made a full recovery before spending several happy years with Graham, but a further major setback triggered by her close identification with Princess Diana caused her to relapse later in life. When time moved forward to the original date that she had made her jump back in time, she was once again in an institution. Graham had ordered additional medical surveillance for her on the night in question, but she had died in her sleep, nonetheless.

He guessed that she had probably had an experience like the one that he had just passed through. However, in her weakened state, she would have accepted the invitation to go through one of the doors. He was confident that was what she had done, and why she did not wake the following morning on the same plane of time in which she had gone to sleep. But thankfully he had not accepted any of the offers. The last two offers stayed in his mind. They were clear and they were appealing. In fact, they were very tempting. But he was glad that he had not accepted either of them.

He felt more comfortable now going to sleep. Confident that he would wake up, and that he would wake up on the same plane of time in which he had gone to sleep. His confidence was well placed because he did, and he did.

And in his sleep, which was not really sleep, he had a dream that was not really a dream. It was a plan to propose to Elizabeth. He had to find a way to propose, just as he had promised her. He had not proposed to anyone for nearly fifty years, so he was a little rusty. He would have to come up with a good idea. It was so much more pleasant to drift off thinking of this rather than the dream he had just been through, and he woke with a plan. A plan that used much of the knowledge he had accumulated during his three lives and was sure to result in her accepting his proposal.

"I know how I'm going to do it," he said to himself. He splashed water on his face and brushed his hair before going back downstairs to reassure Elizabeth that all was well and his 'migraine' had completely passed. She had been too worried to go to her charity shop, and it took all his persuasive abilities to get her to go in for the afternoon. He had a complicated proposal to plan, and there was no time to waste.

He remembered that one of his friends had a son who was involved in making promotional videos. A quick call to his friend confirmed this and he got the necessary contact details.

The following call to Dylan, the video producer, to explain what he had in mind took a little longer, but he eventually got his message across. He made it clear that the budget should not restrict the project – but that it was time sensitive – it had to be finished before the year end. He intended that he and Elizabeth should announce their plans to his children at their now traditional Christmas farmhouse gathering.

Once he felt sure he had fully explained his ideas about the video he wanted to be made, he agreed on a date when he and Dylan should meet so that Dylan could outline his proposal.

His next call was to Anna. Again, he described his plan and how she could help him. She explained that although she had taken possession of a set of offices, her new company was still in the process of moving in, and the decorative state of the building left something to be desired. He reassured her that this was not a problem. His idea would combine the two objectives of bringing Elizabeth into the inner circle of people involved with Anna's new company and allow him to make his proposal a special event.

And so, on December 23rd, he was able to take Elizabeth to the new offices of Blindsee Limited.

"I'm going to finally show you what I've been working on for my last project," he had told her.

He had explained that the company was newly formed, and she would have to accept that not everything was perfect. "The company is working on something that will have a huge impact. It will help blind people see. Now, so you can understand it, I need you to put these on," he said as he sat her in the guest chair in the presentation room and placed a specially prepared pair of blackout goggles over her eyes.

"Just relax and enjoy the show."

The video that Dylan had prepared – with Graham's assistance – began showing on the large TV screen in the room. Elizabeth, of course could not see this. But she began to receive the images as the prof's camera, pointed at the same screen, began to transmit. To her, they seemed real.

Elizabeth let out a yelp of surprise as she 'saw' Graham and heard him speak to her.

"You told me that the proposal I made to you was not up to much," he began, "So I'm hoping that this will make a better job of it. I know I'm proposing because it is so convenient for both of us, living together already. But I wanted you to know that if I had to climb the highest mountain…"

At this point, the video changed so that Graham, suddenly clad in the appropriate clothing, appeared to be on top of a large mountain. Elizabeth chuckled in amusement and surprise.

" … or sail the widest ocean …" the video version of Graham continued, the image changing to a version of him on the deck of a yacht, clad in sou'wester and appropriate wet weather gear. This time, Elizabeth's chuckle was entirely due to amusement.

The video continued through half a dozen such ridiculous scenarios. Graham had decided the length of the video by balancing the importance of making his point against the risk of boredom setting in. He ended with a scene that Dylan was particularly proud of, involving Graham elbowing past the two members of the Proclaimers while they sang, "I would walk five hundred miles".

"I would do it all just to ask you to marry me," Graham said on the video, returning once again to the appearance of being in the room with her, on one knee, proffering a ring. Anna, who had been standing next to Elizabeth during the five-minute performance, followed the instructions she had been given and, on cue, removed Elizabeth's goggles and allowed her to readjust her version. Graham was indeed on his knee in front of her, with the boxed ring in his outstretched hand.

When Elizabeth finally overcame her surprise and amusement, she accepted his proposal, and Anna opened a bottle of champagne that had been waiting in the nearby refrigerator.

THE END

List of Characters

Graham Henderson	
Mary Henderson	Graham's wife in his first life (died 2017)
Carol Watkins	Graham's partner during his 'Second Life' (1992 – 2012)
Professor Karbajanovic (aka 'Prof')	Optic Nerve Research Project Director, Moorfields Hospital
Anna Mueller	Professor Karbajanovic's assistant
Doctor Greenwood	Colleague of Professor Karbajanovic
Stefan Schicker	Anna's first boyfriend
Margaret Walters	Temporary replacement for Anna at Moorfields
Paul (aka 'Del Boy', & 'Swiss Tony')	Dating Companion of Anna Mueller
Louise Hillier	HR employee at Moorfields Hospital and friend of Anna Mueller
Cornelia Wobst (nee Mueller)	Anna's sister
Reinhard Wobst	Cornelia's husband
Elizabeth Fairbanks	Manager of Charity Shop
Harry Fairbanks	Elizabeth's late husband
John Bishop	Member of British Secret Service
Martin Knight	Alias of John Bishop
Tom Woodward	Alias (or possibly the real name) of John Bishop

Karl Kominsky	Russian Secret Service Agent
Peter Eastwood	Alias of Karl Kominsky
Ruslan Silyanov	Karl's young colleague
Georgi Golovin	Karl's Boss
Fergus Kelly ('The Irishman')	Senior Member of the British Secret Service
Timothy Williams ('The Colonel')	Senior Member of the British Secret Service
June Davis	Secretary to The Colonel
David Allinson	Junior Member of the British Secret Service
Maksim Komlichenko	Russian Oligarch
Christina Komlichenko	Daughter of Maksim
Cyrille Dupont	Fellow Student of Christina's
Anthony Bairstow	Estate Agent
Brad Petersen	Senior Member of the US Secret Service
Massimo Sereni	Proprietor of the Isola Bella Restaurant
Maria Sereni	Massimo's daughter
Tony Smith	PPE Supplier
Anna Dreier	Alias of Anna Mueller
Richard Barton	Private Eye, ex-member of the British Secret Service
Sandra Kinsella	Richard Barton's Partner and partner

Acknowledgements

My thanks go to the following people who assisted in the contents of this book. The 'real' Reinhard Wobst who is not an IT teacher at Erweiterte Oberschulen Pestalozzi but in real life holds a PhD from the Technical University of Dresden and is the author of Cryptology Unlocked. He provided much useful background information about Dresden and East Germany. Likewise, my thanks go to Ales Mahler who helped with information about Munich and Berlin.

Thanks also to my proofreaders and editors, Barbara Primrose, Mikael Westlund, Susan Folkard, and Cliff Antill.

The acronym that Graham quotes in Chapter 17, Important Dates, is "Orange Skies And Shady Clouds Over My Pillow" and is used to determine the word order for adjectives in English usage. It stands for Opinion Size Age Shape Colour Origin Material Purpose.

The story that Anna's sister tells in Chapter 22, Back Home, is "The Dead Past", a science fiction short story by Isaac Asimov, first published in April 1956.

The film that Graham half remembers in Chapter 28, A Great Day for A Walk, is "The Thirteenth Floor", a 1999 science fiction neo-noir film written and directed by Josef Rusnak and loosely based upon Simulacron-3 (1964), a novel by Daniel F. Galouye,

The extent to which Anna remembers the book, and Graham remembers the film both match my own recollections before I began research for this book.

My thanks, as ever, go to my wife for leaving me alone to write this book while listening to music she abhors.

And lastly, above all, my thanks go to you, the reader, for buying and reading the book. I hope that you enjoyed it, and if you did, that you will post a review on the Amazon website.

Other Books by Ian Cummins:

An Accidental Salesman: Stories from 40 Years in International IT Sales

There was the time my car ran into a river in rural Suffolk; the time I had the FA Cup in my possession for a whole day; or when I was billeted to stay with a dead woman in Germany; and, of course, the incident with the flight attendant, the elderly hippy, and the gallon of olive oil on the flight from Athens. There are also my thoughts on how Brits can best deal with Americans, and how to sell successfully to customers who don't have English as a first language.

But it's mostly about the stories.

The Wrong Briefcase

What would you do if you suddenly found a large amount of money?

Mark Reynolds is facing the uncomfortable changes of middle age when he mistakenly picks up a briefcase containing a very large amount of cash. Unable to trace its owner, and having received no contact, he decides to keep the vast sum, and discretely invest it - a decision which leads him into an unfamiliar world populated by interesting people.

My Time Again – A Time Travel Novel

How often have you said, "If I had my time again, I would ...."

On the eve of his 70th birthday, Graham Henderson gets the chance to re-live his adult life when he is transported back to his 18-year-old self in 1970 - with all his memories intact.

Must he live the same life the second time around? Will he be able to find a partner to share the re-run of his life? What about changing things for the better in the wider world - is it possible? Surely, he can do something!

Eventually, he discovers he is not the only person to have this experience, and this helps him to find the cause of his jump in time. But it does not solve everything .....

Social Murderer

A deadly puzzle, random victims, a deranged killer ....But who is it?

It was only supposed to be a novel. A hobby for a top-notch computer programmer forced into early retirement by an accident.

The story of a deranged killer choosing victims at random from social media – their names linked together to create a puzzle, to be solved for a huge reward.

But now the killings are real. And the clues all point one way. Is the author guilty? Or the victim of a clever frame-up?

DI Linda Evans is tasked to solve a 'routine murder' and finds it is anything but routine.

Copyright © Ian Cummins 2024

All Rights Reserved

Printed in Great Britain
by Amazon